Eyeless in Cooley

David M. Kiely

PARSIFAL PRESS

Published by the Parsifal Press, Newry, 2015

A CIP record for this title is available from The British Library

ISBN: 978-0-9933960-3-8

Cover photograph by Jason Varley, Carlingford
Cover art and design by the author
Set in 11 on 17 Sabon by the author

For McKenna, as always

* * *

By the same author:

Fiction

A Night in the Catacombs

The Angel Tapes

The Epic of Mesopotamia

The Ghost of '98

Usher's Island

The Faustian Gambit

Baron Livingstone and the King of Manhattan

Non-fiction

John Millington Synge: A Biography

The Dark Sacrament (IRL)

The Dark Sacrament (USA)

Bloody Women

Deadlier than the Male

More Bloody Women

One

Had it not been for Tippy then she wouldn't have been there in the first place. And definitely not this early. Five a.m. It was hardly daylight yet.

But Tippy was old, heading for nineteen, a ripe age for a cocker spaniel. His bladder was weak. He'd woken Sara with a whimpering and a wet tongue across her face, and she couldn't refuse him—not his customary hike to the old mill and back.

The mill lay a short distance from Sara's home: a caravan, dilapidated but with a half acre of land attached. She could grow vegetables and flowers when Tippy allowed her to.

The original mill belonged to the friars of Carlingford many centuries ago. The friars diverted the course of the river, built a milldam and a millrace to drive the wheel. The friars are long gone. The present building—a ruin, no more than a shell—dates from the nineteenth century. It is reached by a dirt track in the shadow of the old Dominican abbey.

"Tippy!" she called out, and thought to see a bush move. The dog had already vented his bladder and was now engaged in the things dogs do in early morning, no matter what their ages. "*Ti-i-ppy!*"

Sara heard a whine, long drawn out and mournful. She grew anxious. Anything could happen to a dog that age, in that poor state of health. He was all Sara had now.

The cocker spaniel lay still on the grass, forepaws stretched out in front of him, haunches raised, floppy ears tucked behind his head. He continued to whine.

The first thing Sara saw was a pair of boots; the rest of the body was hidden among the nettles and long grass. She thought at first that the man must be sleeping. It was Saturday and it was not unknown for a Friday-night reveller to lie down in a ditch to rest for a while before resuming his march home. The nights were balmy in Carlingford, though the summer had passed its peak. You could still sleep outside without a coat.

But the man wasn't sleeping—not with his hands bound behind him. Not with his mouth taped shut and half his head missing. The red grass beside the head was alive with flies and crawling insects.

Sara screeched. Tippy wailed on hearing his mistress's distress.

She knew the dead man, just as everybody knew him in the little town of Carlingford, County Louth. She recognized the clothing: the cheap, blue anorak he always wore, winter and summer. She'd known him for a quarter of her life, for almost twenty years.

Sara, calmer, approached the corpse. Blood did not bother her overmuch; throughout her long years of nursing she'd seen enough of it. She'd thought that the blood from the shattered head had run down the face and into the man's eyes. On closer inspection, however, she saw she'd been mistaken.

There were no eyes.

Sara should have seen the words earlier; they were prominent enough. But she'd been so shocked by the dead and mutilated body that all else in the vicinity was rendered invisible and insignificant. She saw the words at last. They'd been spray-painted from an aerosol can on the wall of the old mill, just above the lintel. Sara had seen the slogan countless times. But always on the other side of Carlingford Lough, on the Northern Ireland side. Never here in the South. It was the battle cry of the Unionists, the Loyalists, the bitter foes of the IRA and all Republicans. The words read:

NO SURRENDER!

Two

"Watch this, Sweetman," Blade Macken said. "I was saving these in case I chickened out."

He took from a drawer a slim, yellow packet. Hamlet, the Mild Cigar. He opened the packet to reveal the fact that only one of its five cigars had been smoked. Then he dropped it in the wastepaper basket with a flourish.

"Janey, Blade, I never thought I'd see the day," said his assistant. "Doctor's orders, is it?"

Macken sucked in his slight paunch and beat a proud, two-handed tattoo on his ribcage.

"Not at all," he told her. "I haven't gone near a doctor in yonks. Don't need to. No, Sweetman, I woke up yesterday with a mouth that tasted like a sow had given birth in it, and I had this funny sensation in my windpipe. So it's *adieu* to the smokes. From now on you're going to see a forty-five-year-old detective superintendent with the health and stamina of a man half his age. If Duffy can do it, then by Christ so can I."

He took off his jacket, tossed it onto a filing cabinet and went to the coffee percolator.

"Oh, thanks for reminding me," Detective Sergeant Orla

Sweetman said. "He wanted to see you as soon as you got in."

"Who, Duffy?" Blade said as he plopped three sugar cubes into his beaker. "I *told* him I'd have that report filed before twelve." He cleared a space on the desk and sat down. "There you are, Sweetman: that's what comes of giving up the fags. Duffy's being a right pain in the arse. If I become like that you'll tell me, won't you?"

Sweetman crossed her slim legs and smoothed her skirt. She reached for her own coffee.

"No, it's not the Gallagher thing," she said. "It's something new."

"Oh? Did he say what?" Macken knew that the assistant commissioner tended to be tight-lipped.

"He didn't say much about it. He just asked whether we could be missed for a few days. I told him we'd nothing else on."

"Jesus, Sweetman, how many times do I have to say it? Never say that to Duffy. Tell him any old shite. Tell him you're updating your files, tell him you're putting in some in-service training. Knowing Duffy, he'd have you cleaning the bloody toilets, just as long as he knew you weren't idle."

Blade got up and crossed to the window. His office had one of the best views in Harcourt Square, headquarters of the Dublin Metropolitan Area gardaí; it afforded a glimpse of the mountains to the south. Blade cursed as bright sunlight flooded the room. He'd looked forward to spending time in those very mountains.

"Doesn't he know I'm taking a fortnight's holidays on Monday?"

"He does. He said it'll be a good opportunity to combine business with pleasure. He said we should pack a toothbrush."

"A toothbrush?" Blade gave her a quizzical look, returned to his desk and reached into a drawer for his portable shaver. He sipped his coffee while removing the strong growth of black stubble; it would return before the afternoon was out. The shave completed, he retrieved his jacket.

"A toothbrush?" he said again. "He didn't say anything about passports, I suppose? So that rules out the Algarve—or special duty in Mustique for that matter. Well, we'd better get it over and done with." He glanced into the waste-paper basket at the little, yellow packet—and kicked the basket.

Duffy received them in shirt-sleeves; the jacket of his uniform hung neatly on a coat hanger. The tidiness of the office was in stark contrast to Macken's.

Duffy was known for his composure, a man not quick to anger. But something had upset his demeanour. His face was florid.

"Guns, Blade, guns!" he fumed. "Bloody, goddamned guns. They're everywhere. Time was when I could send a couple of Guards out on the job armed only with batons. Now your average thug doesn't feel properly dressed unless he's carrying at least a sawn-off shotgun."

"I know, sir. It's bloody awful."

Duffy stabbed a report in front of him. "We had a shoot-out this morning in Pearse Street, would you believe. Somebody was using an assault rifle. My God, this town is getting to be more like America every day. And where are all these weapons coming from? That's what I'd like to know."

He relaxed then somewhat and indicated two chairs.

"So how goes it with Gallagher?"

"Nearly there, sir. Everything's covered. He thought he could beat the forty-eight-hour deadline and be out today, but he didn't reckon on that new evidence. We *have* the bastard."

"Good, good. Well done. Now: I want you to have a look at these."

He passed a small pile of black-and-white photographs across the desk. Macken looked at them without emotion. He heard Sweetman's breath catch.

"That's what's left", said the assistant commissioner, "of one Martin O'Neill, retired schoolteacher."

"Shocking mess," Blade said. "Where was this?"

"Carlingford, County Louth."

"That's near the Border, isn't it?" They could forget the passports and suntan oil.

Duffy nodded. "It is and it isn't, Blade. Geographically speaking it's right next door but, as far as Northern Ireland is concerned, Carlingford could be in Outer Mongolia. They've never had anything like this before."

"When did it happen?"

"Probably very late last night. The body was found early this morning, and they're doing a post-mortem even as we speak."

Blade raised an eyebrow. He'd listened to the nine o'clock news. Duffy read his thoughts.

"We won't be releasing it until this evening—not until we know what's involved." He saw Blade pause at a picture; it showed old masonry. And a slogan. "That's the reason."

Blade grunted.

"If that means what I think it does," Duffy continued, "it'll stir up a hornet's nest. Dundalk have requested our support so I recommended you."

Blade grunted again. "Why didn't they approach Drogheda? Isn't Carlingford their district?"

"It is. But Ed Farley, the chief super in Dundalk, is a friend of mine. He's a good man, Blade; you'll get on well with him. Farley contacted me first; he'll be alerting Drogheda later today. So I want you and Sweetman up there as soon as possible. My guess is that it's much more straightforward than it appears; and Farley agrees. All being well, ye'll have it cleared up in a couple of days."

"I hope so, sir," Blade said. "I'm off as from Monday."

"I know, and this couldn't have come at a worse time. Toner's off sick, Kinnear is still tied up with that Downey business, so that only leaves you and Stafford. And frankly, Blade, I'd rather it was you."

"What about Kelly?"

Duffy shook his head. "He's been in court all week and he thinks they'll be calling on him again. No, Blade, I'm sorry. What holiday plans did you make anyway?"

"Fishing. With Peter."

"Your boy."

"Yeah."

"Maybe you still can. Look, if it's any consolation, I'm making extra funds available. You and Sweetman can book yourselves into a nice hotel. Carlingford's lovely."

"So I'm told," Blade said. "An uncle of mine lives quite close by."

Duffy brightened. "There you are then. Look him up." He glanced at the clock on the wall. "How soon can ye leave?"

"What about Gallagher, sir?"

"Don't worry about it. I'll have somebody bring me the file. Right, I'll give Ed Farley a ring now and say you're on your way."

"Blade . . . " Sweetman said later as she tidied her desk.

"Yes? What is it?"

"You asked me to tell you . . . "

"What?"

"If you were becoming a pain in the arse. You've been cursing and swearing to yourself for the past ten minutes."

"Thanks, Sweetman."

"When," Macken asked wearily, "are they going to build a bloody bypass?"

"Er, this *is* the bypass, Blade," Sweetman told him. "You should have seen the place before they built this road. Chaos altogether."

"Oh, I remember only too well," Macken said. "You'd have some farmer driving his tractor through the main street at two miles an hour, and holding up ten miles of traffic on its way to Belfast."

He looked at the snarl of cars and heavy lorries coughing out exhaust fumes on the road that skirted the river Boyne, once the main artery of the town of Drogheda.

The Boyne. Here on its banks, in 1690, James II of England had faced William of Orange. Two kings on a chequered field. Who was black and who was white depended on your standpoint and religious persuasion—even now, more than three centuries on. Northern Ireland was too complex to be defined in black-and-white terms. There was never checkmate, only an uneasy stalemate.

The traffic finally moved. Blade swore mightily when he saw what was causing the hold-up: cars from two directions had blocked the busy junction; in the meantime the lights had changed several times without any noticeable progress of traffic. A uniformed policeman was sorting out the mess. He paused when he spotted Sweetman at the wheel.

"Orla!" he exclaimed with a grin. "Jayziz, long time no see. How's she cutting?"

"Sergeant Sweetman to you, Mick. And I'm grand; how's yourself?"

The police officer ignored the frustrated and furious faces of the drivers behind Sweetman's car and leaned against her door frame.

"Sergeant! Be the holy. Well, all I can say is it couldn't have happened to a nicer person." He glanced quickly at Blade Macken, then returned his attention to Sweetman. "Listen, I'm free on Wednesday evening. What say we—"

"Sorry, Mick," Sweetman said, putting the car into gear. "Maybe another time. Look, can you get us through in a hurry? We're due in Dundalk in a quarter of an hour, and we'll be late as it is."

The Guard was paying more attention to Sweetman's passenger.

"You wouldn't be Superintendent Macken, would you, sir?" he asked. "I seen your picture in the *Garda Review*. When ye had that 'Angel' business."

Blade grunted. There came the sounds of angry horns.

"Well, now," continued the Guard, unperturbed, "it's a great honour to meet you, sir, so it is. I'm just after hearing you were going up to Dundalk for the Carlingford thing. God, it's all excitement up there today. It's like—"

"Mick, *please*. We're in a hurry."

"Sorry, Orla . . . ehh, sarge. Jayziz, that takes a bit of getting used to." He turned, signalled to the traffic on their right and Sweetman drove on. "Remember what I said about Wednesday!" he shouted after her. "It's—"

She waved.

"My God," Blade breathed, "who in the name of—"

"Mick Strong. We were in training together in Templemore," Sweetman said, taking a bend with a squeal of tyres. Macken had long given up commenting on her driving style. "Mick'd talk the hindlegs off a donkey."

"He seems to know more than is good for him too," Blade said gruffly. "I thought Duffy said they were keeping quiet about it for the moment."

"Are you joking me, Blade?" she said with a smile. "You can't keep things quiet in a place like Drogheda. We're not in Harcourt Square now. You know yourself what provincial stations are like."

Blade grunted and sat back in his seat. They had reached the periphery of Drogheda, County Louth's southernmost town. Dundalk still lay some twenty miles distant. Sweetman floored the accelerator.

"You're very quiet," Macken said after a time. "What's eating you?"

She nodded in the direction they travelled. "Ah, John."

"The fiancé?"

"Who else? We had a row when I was collecting my things. He wants to come up to Carlingford."

"I hope you said no."

"I did. But it wouldn't surprise me if he showed up on the doorstep anyway. He said he's due a holiday as much as I am."

"Holiday!" Blade snorted. "What the fuck does he think you'll be doing up there? Drinking sangria on the beach? Didn't you tell him it's work?"

"You don't know John. . . . "

"Nor do I think I want to. I hope you didn't give him the name of the hotel."

"Of course I did. He *is* my fiancé."

"Lucky him. Take it from your Uncle Blade, Sweetman: ditch the guy. There's nothing worse than having a clinging vine for a husband. He'll make your life a misery."

She looked pained. "With respect, sir, I don't think it's any of your business."

She floored the accelerator again and Macken knew he'd gone too far.

"Ah, don't mind me, Sweetman," he said. "I'm being a pain in the arse again. Let's drop it, shall we?"

Sweetman was silent and Macken regretted his remarks. And who was he to talk? His own marriage had ended in disaster, largely because of his drinking. Joan had been left to bring up three children single-handed. His youngest daughter Sandra, now nineteen, loathed her father; Anne, the eldest, married with kids of her own in London, he seldom saw. Only twenty-year-old Peter maintained ties. So who was he to offer advice? He changed the subject.

"What do you make of this 'no surrender' bit, Sweetman?"

She had to brake sharply when, on rounding a bend, she found herself behind a line of slow-moving cars. She indicated and sped past three of them, tucking her car neatly into the tight space afforded between the leading vehicles.

"Loyalists, Blade," she said. "They're the ones that're keeping it going."

She eased the car into the hard shoulder, overtook on the inside and returned to the roadway. Blade whistled.

"I take it you're a Catholic, Sweetman?" he said. "Not that it matters to *me*."

"Catholic and proud of it."

"Religion is an accident of birth, Sweetman. If you'd been born in Iran you'd be nutting your prayer mat five times a day and calling for Salman Rushdie's head."

She had to laugh at that. "So what are *you*, Blade?" she said after a few moments. "I always meant to ask."

"Me?" He chuckled. "Did you ever hear of the Vicar of Bray?"

"I can't say I have, no."

Macken reached for a roll of peppermints on the dashboard. He was getting through six rolls a day now.

"The Vicar of Bray," he said, "was a man who changed with the times. Whenever a Catholic king came to power he'd become a Catholic, and if it was a Protestant king he'd convert again. Similar thing with the Mackens. My dad and my grandfather were Church of Ireland, but Great-grandfather was Catholic—and *his* father was Presbyterian. It all depended on who they married you see; they were going for the money and the estate. So it didn't matter a damn what religion the other family were, the Mackens would convert to it, just to get their hands on the dosh and the land."

Sweetman shook her head in bemusement. "Amazing. So what does that make you?"

"Me? I'm nothing."

"An agnostic?"

"An atheist."

She turned to stare.

"You don't even believe in *God?*"

"God . . . God. That's the trouble with this whole bloody country. Look at the North, for chrissake. It's totally fucked up by religion."

"And by the British. They shouldn't be there in the first place."

"I agree with you. But it all comes down to religion in the end, Sweetman. If they'd all been the one in sixteen ninety then there wouldn't be the shite they have up there today."

"I don't know about that. Isn't it all about supremacy . . . power?"

"Of course it is. But we'll always have that: the one clodhopper thinking he's better than somebody else just because his old man owned an acre or two more of bogland. And of course it helps when his neighbour goes to a different church of a Sunday. Gives him an excuse to put a bullet in the man's brain. No, don't talk to me about religion, Sweetman. Thank God I'm an atheist is what I say."

"Very funny, Blade—I don't think."

She reached for the roll of mints, extracted one and popped it into her mouth while, at the same time, overtaking a lorry pulling two long trailers. Angry headlights flashed from an oncoming Mercedes; Blade saw the driver turn pale.

"But it's good to see you smile for a change," Sweetman went on as though nothing untoward had happened. "You've been like I-don't-know-what since you gave up the cigars. How long has it been now?"

Macken consulted his watch. "Thirty-six hours and ten minutes. A record. And I wasn't smiling just then. I was gritting my teeth."

"If you don't mind me asking, Blade: how long have you been a smoker?"

Macken looked at his pretty, auburn-haired assistant. What age, he thought, would she be? Twenty-six, twenty-seven?

"Let's just say since before you were born, Sweetman."

Chief Superintendent Farley of the Garda Síochána's Louth Division ushered them into the conference room. It was cool to the point of chilliness; the warm sun didn't penetrate the thick, granite walls of the Dundalk police station. The furnishings were depressing too: the drab earth colours and formica of the sixties. But the chairs were comfortable.

Duffy had not been mistaken: Blade liked Ed Farley from the first. Farley spoke softly, almost deferentially, yet had the bearing of a man who didn't suffer fools gladly. Blade felt at ease with him.

"How was your journey?" Farley enquired politely, while assembling his papers.

"Fast," Blade said, with a glance at Sweetman. She studied the nails on her left hand.

"Good. You come highly commended by Mr Duffy, you

know. I asked for someone who'd be able to look over what we have in Carlingford and give us his thoughts. Quite frankly, we don't know what we have here; none of it makes much sense. But it could be simpler than it looks. My guess is that somebody close to O'Neill put a contract out on him. It was a professional hit—these boys knew what they were doing."

He reached into a file and took out a set of photographs; they matched those Duffy had shown them.

"Martin O'Neill was a nobody," Farley went on. "By that I mean he'd no apparent connection with paramilitaries. He was innocence itself: no garda record, not even a parking fine. No known enemies either; he was well-liked in the town. He kept to himself a lot but, from all reports, you couldn't have met a nicer man."

"It could be," Blade said, "that these professionals of yours made a mistake. Could be they hit the wrong man. It's happened before."

"We thought of that," Farley said. "But we ruled it out. Do you know Carlingford at all?"

"Slightly."

"It's a very close-knit little place: everybody knows everybody else. And the lads at the station know everybody as well. They know the people, even the ones who've moved in recently. There's a lot of that; people with money like to retire there. I'll tell you this: if there was a potential target for terrorists living there then the local Guards would know about him. But there isn't. Nobody even *mentions* Ulster politics in Carlingford. They simply don't want to know. And the same holds for professional hitmen. If O'Neill had been somehow mixed up in major crime then you can be sure the neighbours would have known."

Blade was thoughtful. "You say O'Neill was well liked. What about family ties? You know as well as I do that family troubles account for most murders."

"That's true. But O'Neill hadn't much of a family. He was a widower. There's a son who lives in County Down and that's about the extent of it."

"No one else? That's odd, isn't it? What about relatives?"

Farley shook his head. "If he had any then we haven't been able to locate them. Maybe you and Sweetman will have better luck."

Blade took the hint and rose. "We'll start, sir, in Carlingford. If you can point us in the general direction."

Farley got up and held the door. "One last thing," he said. "I told Mr Duffy we were holding off with a press statement until I spoke to you. I can't stall any longer. What's your advice?"

Blade had been expecting the question and replied without hesitation.

"Tell them the gardaí aren't ruling out foul play."

"That's all? What about the eyes?"

"Eyes?" said Blade. "I didn't see any eyes, did you?"

Three

Blade Macken pulled up the plastic tape and held it so that Sweetman could duck under it; he followed, and went to the spot where two men in garda uniforms crouched. Gary O'Donnell looked up at their approach; he pushed up the peak of his cap.

"Good afternoon, detective superintendent . . . DS," he greeted them. "Nice enough afternoon too."

"This is where the body was found?" Blade said.

"Yes. The feet were right where you're standing now."

Blade studied the crumbling walls of the old mill. His eyes were drawn inexorably to the tarpaulin that covered part of the wall above the door. He went to it and raised it slightly, read the spray-painted message it concealed:

NO SURRENDER!

O'Donnell was on his feet. "That's about all we have to go on at the moment," he told them. "We've been over every square inch of the place. Not a thing. No spent bullet cases. Nothing."

"What about footprints?" Sweetman asked.

"Oh, there's plenty of them, sarge. We'd a bit of rain last night—not much, but enough to soften the ground. Size nine and ten. At least two men—apart from old Martin.”

“Were you able to get casts?” Blade said. He looked at the place where the grass was gore-blackened. Small vermin still feasted there.

The Guard shook his head. “Nothing that’s of any use I’m afraid, sir. There weren’t any profiles on the soles of the shoes. It’s my guess that the bastards wrapped thick plastic around their shoes. Aye, these fellas knew what they were doing right enough.”

“Professionals would you say?”

“Looks like it.” O’Donnell thumbed his chin. “One thing puzzles me though. If it was a paramilitary execution then it’s nothing I’ve ever seen or heard of before. I’m talking about the missing eyes.”

“We wondered about that too,” Blade said.

“With respect, sir, you may not know this—you not being from this part of the world—but paramilitary executions tend to follow a pattern—a standard procedure, you might say.”

“Go on.”

“See, our man was shot in the back of the head at very close range, and with a heavy-calibre gun. Normally what they do is wind gaffer tape around the head—that’s the stuff photographers and—”

“I know what it is,” Blade said.

“Yes. Well, they do that to stop the head bursting apart when the bullet goes in. If you don’t do that, the eyes will be blown out through the front. Not only that, but the guy who pulls the trigger will be covered from head to toe with blood and brains. Er, I hope I’m not being too graphic, sarge?”

"It's okay," Sweetman assured him. "I've been at scenes of shootings before."

"Of course. Sorry." He turned to Blade again. "But you see what I'm getting at, sir? There was little enough left of poor oul' Martin's head when we found him, so his executioner must have been in a right mess as well. And what about the eyes? We found no trace of them."

Despite the warmth of the afternoon sun, Sweetman's face had gone cold.

"What I'm saying, sir," O'Donnell went on, "is that they must have gouged out his eyes before they shot him."

"My Christ," Blade said.

"It's horrible, isn't it? Now why do you suppose anybody would want to do a thing like that? And to a nice oul' fella like Martin?"

Blade considered the scene of the crime. Why, indeed?

Nothing fitted. The day was warm; the sun sparkled through the trees that ringed the ivy-covered mill wall. There was a sense of peace about it all: the old abbey close by, its shell restored by caring hands. Carlingford had not known violence for many centuries. You could have been forgiven for thinking that it had forgotten how to kill.

Until now.

Four

You can easily miss the turning for Ravensdale; it's in a bend of the N1, where lush trees overhang the hard shoulder. Once on the winding country lane, you've left the traffic behind, and Ravensdale tugs you back a century or two to a time when all rural Ireland was like this. Never mind the modern bungalows: you barely notice them, distracted as you are by the green-and-purple slopes of Annaverna Mountain that rear directly ahead. Even Sweetman was caught up in the serenity of it all; she slowed the car as they passed Crilly's filling station and market, looked in wonder as Ravensdale wove its spell.

"Left at the stop sign," Blade said.

"It's beautiful. How long did you say your uncle's been living here?"

"Fifteen years or thereabouts. Some old relative left him the house in her will. It's a massive thing, according to Jack, but more trouble than it's worth. Falling down around his ears. It'll take a million to put it right. Just a bit here beyond the post office."

"Janey, a million. Has he got it?"

Blade smiled. "If he has then he's telling nobody. He's a secretive old bugger—always was."

"Are ye close?"

"No. I haven't seen him in donkey's years. This is it. On the right."

The gates hung slightly askew and seemed to be held upright solely by a tangle of undergrowth. The car's tyres protested as Sweetman turned confidently onto a cinder-and-gravel driveway that had been laid for horse-drawn traffic. The trees formed a dark tunnel; a grey squirrel bounded from their path. Breaking out into the sunlight again, they caught their first view of the house.

It *was* massive, though not quite as big as Blade had expected. He didn't know much about these things but thought it Georgian, probably built towards the beginning of the last century. It was fronted by ten windows and a portico of neo-Roman columns around whose base weeds and wild flowers grew in abundance. Beyond the two-storied facade rose the roofs and windows of a third floor. As they drew closer Blade saw that the tall chimney stacks had pots that supported the nests of big birds whose offspring were long flown. The chimney stacks looked downright dangerous; they and the house itself were in sad need of repair. A million? he thought. More like *two* million pounds would be needed to restore Annadangan to its former glory.

Sweetman saw the house with other eyes. Its bulk and grandeur had made a deep impression. When she stopped the car on the large semicircle of gravel that lay between Annadangan and the fertile field of short grass the house overlooked, she half-expected a liveried footman to come hurrying out to open her door and Blade's too; she half-expected to see a latter-day Mrs Danvers together with an obsequious line of staff drawn up for the arrival of Max de

Winter and his new bride.

Instead the tall front door opened slowly and a solitary, stooped figure emerged.

Jack Macken. Uncle Jack.

My Jesus, Blade thought, he's aged a century, poor old codger. What was it now since he'd last seen his relative? Twelve years? More? He made a mental note to keep in more frequent touch with the rest of the Mackens; there were so few of them left.

But his uncle wasn't stooped, as Blade had thought; Jack had been inspecting something on the porch. He straightened now and regarded the visitors with interest. He peered keenly at Sweetman through a pair of thick-lensed glasses as she swung her long legs out of the driver's seat. I was wrong, Blade thought: the old bastard is as spry as I am, and he's seventy if he's a day. Jack Macken turned his attention to his nephew. He squinted into the sun and beamed broadly.

"Blade!" he roared. "Is that yourself?"

"Hello, Jack."

"Is this your fancy piece?"

"You old shite," Blade replied with a grin; "you haven't changed one iota. For your information, this is Detective Sergeant Orla Sweetman, my assistant."

Jack appraised Sweetman's trim figure with a wintered eye.

"Hmm," he said. Then: "I'd have one of the staff fetch your bags, Blade—only I haven't got any staff."

"So it's true then," Blade said, glancing up at the towering bulk of the house, "you're on your owneeyo here? How do you manage, Jack?"

"I get by. I suppose you and the *detective sergeant* are a bit peckish?"

"No, we had a bite to eat in Dundalk. Thanks all the same."

"Good. You'd better come in then." He looked up into an almost clear blue sky. "It looks like rain."

He led the way into a hall that had Blade whistling in appreciation. It must, he thought, have been magnificent in its day. It was still imposing. The floor was made up of giant granite flagstones; those nearest the twin-doored entrance had been polished by generations of boots; some had sunk to several millimetres below the level of their fellows. The walls were half-timbered in dark oak, carved by a master hand. Above the timber the walls were a pale, leaf green, a restful and subdued background for the six great eighteenth-century hunting canvases that hung there. There were chairs, whose wood was even darker than that of the wainscoting. Blade noted that they were held together not with screws but with wooden pegs. He whistled again; he'd seen such workmanship before and guessed that the chairs must date from the seventeenth century, perhaps before.

And that was all. There was nothing else in the vast hall except for a chandelier high up under the beamed ceiling. Two tall doors led off left and right; ahead rose the main staircase. Jack threw open the left door, to disclose an unexpectedly bright and cheerful interior. The drawing-room.

"Make yourselves at home," he said. "I'll go and put the kettle on. Coffee all round? Right."

He went out, leaving the door ajar.

"Janey, he's everything you said he was, Blade. It's—"

"Ssh," Blade cautioned. "He claims to be as deaf as a post but he hears only what he wants to hear."

But Sweetman was inspecting the room and its contents. It was as though she'd stepped into a museum. Wherever she looked she saw fine china and oriental porcelain, glassware that astonished with its beauty and craftsmanship. She was afraid to touch anything, half-expecting to see a sign that prohibited her from doing so. All the same, she couldn't help running a hand over the moss-green upholstery of one of a pair of chaises longues; the material felt like silk.

The light fell from three windows that faced south and from a pair of french windows facing east. It was reflected from the foliage beyond the windows, and bathed the room in muted, restful tones of yellow and green. Those colours were dominant too in the carpets and wallpaper. Even the wood of the grand piano set close to one wall had a mustard tinge.

Jack returned shortly with three chipped and steaming mugs, joined on a silver tray by a small plate of digestive biscuits.

"So you've come about the murder then, have you, Blade?" he said, pulling a chair up to the coffee-table.

Macken glanced at Sweetman.

"Who told you that?"

"I put two and two together. I didn't flatter myself by thinking you'd want to spend a few days here for my company alone. Am I right?"

"You're right. But it's good to see you, Jack, it really is."

"Hmph." He reached for a biscuit, bit off a portion, then returned the rest to the plate. "Gone stale, I'm afraid. Sorry about that. It's the dampness."

"Did you know Mr O'Neill?" Sweetman asked. She sipped her coffee.

"Old Martin? We all did. He was well-liked, you know, was Martin. A great fellow for the stories. Bit moody, though."

"Was he a Carlingford man? I mean: was he from the area?"

Jack Macken shook his head. "He was a blow-in—or a 'runner', as we say in these parts. He'd lived here twenty years, but he was still a runner as far as the natives were concerned. That's Cooley for you."

Blade tried his coffee. It tasted of old dust but he made no comment.

"So he was a blow-in," he said. "Any idea where he blew in from?"

"Certainly. Martin used to be a primary-school teacher in Newry before his retirement. But he was a Galwayman originally."

"Really?" Blade said. "Your part of the country, Sweetman."

Jack Macken looked at her with renewed interest. Sweetman pulled the hem of her skirt over her knees.

"So what brought him to the Black North?" Blade asked.

Jack shrugged. "I think it was a woman but I'm not too sure. I *do* know that he married a Newry girl. She drowned in the Lough one summer. Tragic."

"Hmm. Children?"

"He only ever mentioned one. A son."

That tallied, at least, with Farley's information.

"Any idea where we can find him, Mr Macken?"

"Please! Call me Jack. No, I never met the lad but old Martin told me he was teaching somewhere. Following in his father's footsteps, don't y'know. Martin approved of that."

Sweetman was making notes. "He'll be here for the funeral, I suppose?"

"I suppose so. But they never got on, you know."

"Why was that . . . Jack?" Sweetman said.

"No idea. But you know what families are like. How's your mother, by the way, Blade? Still as batty as ever?"

"She's grand, Jack. She sends her love."

The elder Macken grinned. "I don't believe a word of it—but thanks for the kind thought."

Sweetman stood up, leaving her coffee half-finished. She reached for her bag.

"I'm off. I'll leave you two to catch up on the family gossip."

"You're not going already, surely?" Jack said. He was on his feet too. "You must stay for dinner. I have a rabbit on—skinned it myself."

Sweetman tried to hide a grimace. "It sounds delicious, but I really have to get back to Carlingford. They're expecting me at the hotel. Thanks all the same, Jack."

"You really should have let me put you up here, my dear. Bags of room. It seems a shame to throw away good money on a hotel."

"That's very kind of you but I wouldn't want to put you out. Thanks for the coffee anyway. Blade, I'll be in touch in the morning. I'll let myself out."

And she was gone, leaving the Mackens to their history.

Five

Macken and Sweetman followed the directions they'd been given at the garda station. They ascended on foot a street that rose to the west of the little market square of Carlingford, pausing to gaze in wonder at the splendour of the Mourne Mountains that rose on the other side of the Lough. The sky was a deep, almost cloudless blue, the waters still, and the green peaks were reflected perfectly in the estuary. Again Macken wondered at the incongruousness of Martin O'Neill's murder; it seemed so unseemly that violent death should have intruded upon this peaceful community, that such horror should have disturbed these magnificent surroundings. Yet he knew that *there*, across the water, in the towns and villages beyond those pleasant slopes, worse crimes had been committed.

They turned onto yet another side street that looked down on the Norman bulk of King John's Castle, the fortress that had once stood guard over the Lough. They found the cottage without difficulty. It was tiny; it couldn't have contained more than two rooms. There was no front garden, just a small area of cement abutting the street. A very old Renault 5 with a bad respray job was parked with two wheels on the cement. There were pretty curtains on the windows of the cottage and each had a box of flowers. Many were withered, neglected, and Sweetman thought that a pity.

"Have you got the key?" Blade asked.

She nodded and reached into her bag. She turned the key in the lock—and gave a little start when the door was abruptly pulled open from the inside. A tallish man, fair hair, horn-rimmed glasses, early thirties, stood in the opening. He was fairly nondescript, the type of man you'd pass in the street without a second glance.

"Who are you?" he demanded.

"Who are *you*?" Macken countered.

"I live here."

"Oh. Sorry, we must have the wrong house."

His tone softened. "That's okay. Who were you looking for?"

"The O'Neill house."

"This is the O'Neill house." His glance fell on what Sweetman held in her hand. "How come you've got a key for here?"

Sweetman's handbag was already open. She reached in and produced her ID.

"Dublin Special Branch. This is Detective Superintendent Macken. We're investigating Mr O'Neill's murder."

"You must be . . . " Blade began.

"Jim. Jim O'Neill. Martin was my father."

Blade hadn't expected this. He appraised the man, attempting to relate him to the eyeless corpse; it required mental acrobatics beyond his capability.

"I'm so sorry, sir. It must have been a terrible shock for you."

Why, Blade wondered, do those dozen words always

trip off the tongue in a situation like this? They sounded so *standard*, so glib, so hypocritical.

O'Neill nodded coldly. "I suppose you'd better come in— since you were all set to come in anyway."

The living-room was tastefully decorated, though Sweetman could see at a glance that a *man* had lived here alone. The cushions on the chairs were utilitarian; there were no knick-knacks on the mantelshelf or the sideboard. The prints on the walls were of buildings: French, eighteenth century. A shallow glass case near the door contained various specimens of the angler's fly-tying art. A pair of worn boots stood in the hearth.

"I've made some tea," O'Neill said. "Would you like a cup?"

"That's very kind of you, sir," Blade said. Sweetman nodded.

Macken noted that the air was stale, though the back door was open. While their host was rattling tea things in the minute kitchenette, he cast an eye over the rest of the living-room.

There were a great many books in a low case that took up almost the length of one wall, more books than you'd expect to find in a room of that size. The case was so full that not a single space remained for an additional volume. Then Blade remembered that Martin O'Neill had been a schoolteacher. Retired too—with plenty of reading time.

He glanced at the titles on some of the spines. They were a mix of thrillers, espionage, detectives, and biographies of movie stars. They offered no clue to the personality of their owner. There were several hardback books: the complete works of Shakespeare in a single volume, children's classics such as *Moby-Dick*, *Ivanhoe*, *Gulliver's Travels*, *Tom Sawyer*. Blade deduced that these were relics from O'Neill's schoolteacher days, and well-thumbed copies of *Peig* and *An t-Oileánach* reinforced his guess. He noticed there were a great number of foreign-language dictionaries as well, far more than you'd expect to find in such a book collection.

But no "Republican" literature, Blade thought. No *Jail Journal*; no *Guerrilla Days in Ireland*; no Gerry Adams memoirs.

"Milk and sugar?" Jim O'Neill called from the kitchen.

"Just milk, please."

"Same for me, sir."

"The way I drink it too," O'Neill said, setting the tray down on a low table with a formica top. He looked keenly at Blade.

"So you're Special Branch. From Dublin, is it?"

"Yes, sir. Look, this is a bit embarrassing. They told us down at the station that the house was vacant. I'd no idea you'd be here."

"So you came to snoop around. Well, snoop all you like, superintendent. I think you'll find that my father had little to hide from the police."

"Look, sir, we can go if you wish. We'd no intention of disturbing your privacy at a time like this. I'd just as—"

"Please, please, sit down, sit down." O'Neill's manner had changed. "Forgive me if I seemed rude. It's all been too sudden. I'm not myself."

"That's perfectly understandable, sir."

O'Neill sat down opposite them and the light from the

window fell behind the lenses of his spectacles. His eyes were bluer than they'd first appeared to Macken. Kindly too. There was a lot of hurt there.

"They asked me to identify the body, superintendent," he said. "I hope nobody ever asks you to do a thing like that. Not your own father's body. And not in that state. Sweet God in heaven—why? Why, I ask you? Dad was such a . . . such an *ordinary* man. I mean, he'd have had his faults, like everybody else, but you'd never hear a bad word said against him. By anybody."

"Were you close, sir?" Blade asked.

O'Neill paused long before replying. "No. No, I wouldn't say that. We never really got on, him and me. I suppose it was a generation thing."

Blade nodded in understanding. "Was this a recent development or was it always like that? I'm sorry to be asking these personal questions, sir, but I'm wondering if you yourself ever came in contact with anybody who bore animosity towards your father."

"Never, superintendent. No, I can't say I ever did, no."

"Really? Everybody has enemies of some kind."

"Not my father. I'm not saying he was a saint—far from it. But he always behaved himself outside the house; a proper gentleman. In the *home* . . . now that's a different matter entirely."

"I don't want to pry, sir," Blade said again. "You don't have to tell us anything you don't want to."

O'Neill sighed. He picked up a packet of cigarettes and offered it to Sweetman. She shook her head. Blade licked his lips but refused as well. O'Neill lit one for himself. Sweetman could see he was wrestling with something. She hated this part of the job. Sweetman was a very private person, always loath to invade the privacy of others without good reason.

"Perhaps I do want to," O'Neill said at last. "Perhaps I do want to tell somebody about my father and me. It's not a pretty story." He saw their look. "No, no, it's not what you think. There wouldn't have been what you'd call *real* abuse—either physical, sexual or mental." He smiled without humour. "I'm sure that must be a bit disappointing. I'm sure it would help you no end if I were to tell you that my dad was a monster who repeatedly abused his son from an early age."

"I wasn't thinking that at all, sir," Blade said.

O'Neill looked at him strangely. "Weren't you, superintendent? But let it pass. What I'm saying is that my father was a cold person, perhaps the coldest man I've ever met in my life. Me, I think there's something monstrous about a man like that. Somebody who was never able to show feeling. Give me a child abuser any day—at least there's passion involved there, even if it's the wrong kind."

He stopped then, clearly embarrassed.

"No, I didn't mean that. What a terrible thing to say! Forget I said it."

The turn the interview had taken was making Sweetman uncomfortable. Macken, for his part, was finding himself more and more in the psychiatrist's chair, and it was a position he'd no intention or inclination of assuming. This was a disturbed individual; he was certain of that. There was something distinctly vulnerable about the man who sat across from them. It most certainly wasn't because of his size: he was about six foot tall and built like a gym instructor. The horn-rimmed glasses were incongruous, as though they belonged on another, more timid, face. A bit, Macken thought idly, like Clark Kent and Superman.

"Would you like to go for a stroll?" O'Neill said suddenly. "I was planning one before you came." He looked about the room. "This place depresses me; it makes me claustrophobic. And it's a sin sitting indoors on a day like today."

Blade looked at his watch. It wasn't yet three o'clock; time appeared to pass more slowly in Carlingford than elsewhere. The offer was unusual yet Macken shared O'Neill's opinion of the little cottage: it was oppressive. Perhaps the broad outdoors might stimulate O'Neill into divulging more. And Blade was, he reminded himself ruefully, officially on leave as and from today; by rights Peter and he should have been arriving at the self-catering cottage on the shore of Lough Bray at about this time.

"Why not, sir," he said. "Where do want to go?"

"Not to the old mill anyway," O'Neill said with a grimace. "Have you ever done the Táin Trail?"

"That's hardly a stroll, sir; that's a *hike*."

"Oh, I don't mean we'll do the whole thing. Sure that'd take us to Connaught. No, I mean just up the side of the mountain. It's easy going, and the view is fantastic. I'll let you see some of the place."

They finished their tea and Blade stood up. "Fair enough. Ready when you are."

Sweetman too was pleased to go along with O'Neill's suggestion. The tiny cottage was having a depressing effect on her as well. It wasn't due only to the sense of its once being the home of a murdered man; she'd been in many such houses. Nor was it due to the smallness of the cottage. Sweetman had the notion that the place held secrets that were anything but pleasant. Or perhaps her uneasiness was caused by the present occupant; he didn't fit there. He was too tall and broad for the confines of the living-room. He had to duck through the door when returning to the kitchenette with the tea things. He seemed more of an intruder in his father's home than Macken and she were.

She wondered idly about his own home. Did he live alone? She thought so; there was something about the practised way he'd prepared and poured the tea. So he wasn't in digs; more likely than not he owned or rented a flat, somewhere in Northern Ireland. He was definitely a loner, a bachelor. She didn't think that his life was a happy one.

On an impulse she asked a question, the answer to which she already knew: "What do you do for a living, sir?"

"Me? I'm a teacher."

"Like your father."

"No, secondary. I teach English and history at the grammar school in Kilkeel."

"Hmm," Blade said. "That's out beyond Rostrevor, isn't it?"

"Aye. It's not much of a place. Fishing town really. Though there isn't a lot to be made with the fishing now. Half the men would be on the bru."

"Big drinkers, are they?"

O'Neill looked blank for an instant, then surprised Macken with a great bellow of a laugh. He swore he felt the window shake.

"The 'brew'; that's a good one. No, it's what we call the dole up north, superintendent. Short for Basic Rate of Unemployment, I believe."

Blade was pleased to see that the laughter had cheered O'Neill up considerably; he was smiling as he let them out by the front door. Then they were descending the short distance to the town square.

A coach party had stopped off in Carlingford. Blade heard American accents as they headed across the square in the direction of the trail. The tourists were elderly and numbered about fifty. Sweetman did not approve of their dress sense.

"Irish-Canadians," Jim O'Neill said. "They make a sort of pilgrimage here in the summer. This is where Thomas D'Arcy Magee was born you know. He was the one who fled to Canada."

"The one . . . ?" Blade said.

"The United Irishmen. He was one of the founders."

And they listened with genuine interest as the history teacher from Kilkeel educated them on the noble deeds of the district's most famous son.

Six

An obelisk stands overlooking Carlingford Lough, close to a lazy bend in the road where the outlying houses of Rostrevor merge with those of Warrenpoint, County Down. The monument commemorates the life and army career of Robert Ross, the district's most renowned fighting man, who lent his name to the village. The shoreline to east and west of the pebble beach is private property.

Another old soldier, Colonel Paddy McKittrick, retired, was writing his memoirs. His bungalow was a good place in which to do it. His study window provided a splendid panoramic view over the Lough. McKittrick had always lived beside water, ever since he and the sorry remnants of his battalion had waited on the beaches of Dunkirk, enduring the ceaseless pounding of the German guns. Perhaps McKittrick's rescue by a simple English fisherman had instilled in him a love of water. He did not know. Yet he'd found himself drawn to the sea; it figured time and again in his memoirs.

At two in the afternoon he switched off his electric typewriter. The right words were refusing to come. How many words *were* there for "wave"? He thought he'd explored them all in this, his key chapter: billow, swell, surge, heave, angry sea.... None measured up to his own memory of the sea off Dunkirk on that May day in 1940.

McKittrick reached for his stick and his dictaphone. The little machine, a gift from his wife, was invaluable. Inspiration came at odd moments, and many's the *mot juste* or telling phrase that came to him as he strolled on the shingle under the trees that overlooked the Lough.

The rubber dinghy would have been invisible from the water. Its owner had contrived to conceal it in the shadow of one of McKittrick's trees. The colonel might have missed it as well, because of its colour: a non-reflecting black. But the metal parts of the outboard motor at its stern *did* reflect the bright sunlight.

McKittrick saw at a glance that the motor was a powerful one. It would have carried him and his men speedily to safety, beyond the reach of the guns in 1940. This dinghy would have ridden the turbulent, tempestuous sea—yes! that was the phrase he needed—with ease.

Whoever owned the dinghy had abandoned it with all its contents. That puzzled the old campaigner. He suspected a mischief. He'd alert the RUC.

McKittrick was trembling with excitement as he made his way back to the bungalow; life still held the promise of action. But he hadn't lost sight of The Work. Before he reached for the phone he thumbed the RECORD button of his dictaphone.

"My wretched comrades and I," he told the machine, "were at the mercy of a turbulent, tempestuous sea."

Jack Macken had business to attend to in Carlingford on Monday afternoon. What that business was he hadn't said, leaving Blade guessing, but he'd been delighted to drive his nephew to the town for his meeting with Sweetman.

Blade had had a night to sleep on the news of the dinghy but that night had resolved little. He pondered still the report he'd received from Chief Superintendent Farley.

According to the RUC in Warrenpoint the little inflatable craft had been found abandoned near the pebbled beach, its contents—oars, first-aid kit, flares, pump—intact. The Yamaha outboard motor, built with a larger host vessel in mind, would have given the dinghy a rate of knots to rival any speedboat's. Apart from that, there'd been nothing out of the ordinary—except for the shell suit. Its black colour had camouflaged the bloodstains; only when the constables had examined it at the station had they seen that the front of the garment was caked with dried blood. A great deal of it. As though, Ed Farley had said, its owner "had worked in a slaughterhouse".

They'd agreed that the dinghy had played a part in Martin O'Neill's murder. The fact that it had been found on the northern shore of the Lough seemed to reinforce the possibility of Loyalist involvement, something they'd already rejected. Farley still wasn't convinced, however, of its having been a paramilitary execution and Macken shared his doubts. So where did that leave the investigation? Somebody had flung them a red herring; Macken was sure of that. But why? And why had that somebody gone to such lengths to dispatch an old, and seemingly harmless, man? Blade had spoken to Linda Doyle of Forensics that morning. They'd examined the Yamaha outboard motor for clues to its ownership. They'd been stymied: the owner had filed off the engine number, yet another example of the killer's thoroughness.

Why not simply have killed O'Neill in his bed? Or made the murder look like an accident. Easiest thing in the world to do: old men are unusually accident-prone.

Jack suddenly interrupted his nephew's train of thought.

"Did you know, my boy, that that used to be a volcano?"

Blade shook his thoughts free. He'd been silent during most of the fifteen-minute drive from Ravensdale, turning these vexing questions over in his mind. Now Jack was pointing to a mountain that rose on their left. Its shape differed from the other, gentler, contours of the Cooley Mountains: its peak was ragged and scant of vegetation. At its foot nestled the town of Carlingford.

"Slieve Foye," Jack went on. "Used to be called Slieve Teinne in the old days. That's Irish for 'Fire Mountain', in case you didn't know. Not a bad name for a volcano, don't you think?"

"I didn't know we *had* any volcanoes in this country."

"Didn't you? You'd be surprised. They were all over the planet at one time: from here to China. This was before the Ice Age, I hasten to add." He craned his head for a better view. "Must have been spectacular when it was still active. Of course it's been dormant a long time now."

"That must be a comfort to the people of Carlingford."

Jack Macken chuckled. "Though who can say when it'll start up again."

"Are you serious?"

"I am. A volcano never dies, my boy. Oh, it'll look as though it couldn't erupt in a million years. Remember Montserrat in ninety-seven? Appearances are deceptive." He gave a nod in the direction of the ragged peak. "What you see above ground is only the tip of the iceberg—if you'll pardon the oxymoron. Down below—under the earth's crust—that's where all the activity is taking place. Molten magma, swirling around, just waiting for a chance to escape. And there, under Slieve Foye—indeed under Carlingford itself—are seas of magma, only below the surface in geological terms. The volcano's chimney is still intact. All it needs is a minor disturbance and you've Ireland's answer to Vesuvius."

Blade brought his gaze down to Carlingford, its cottages and little streets meandering down from the lower slopes of the mountain to the waters of the Lough. Was this how Pompeii had looked, sleeping peacefully on the shore of the Bay of Naples? Had the green slopes of its own fire mountain lulled its citizens into a false sense of security? Probably. Some of those buried beneath the ashes had been caught almost literally with their pants down. The fire from hell had engulfed them so suddenly that their bodies had been petrified for ever in their final acts. Some had been eating, drinking, napping.

And evidently something else had been boiling beneath the surface of placid, peaceful Carlingford. Had Martin O'Neill been lulled into a false sense of security as well? What, Blade wondered, would we find were we to scratch beneath the surface of O'Neill's life? If we were to disturb the bones. . . .

"What do you mean, Jack," he asked then, "by 'a minor disturbance'?"

"Oh, movement of the Eurasian plate—that's the tectonic plate we're situated on. Plate movement is responsible for most volcanic activity. It goes on all the time, though most of it happens at the bottom of the ocean, where two plates converge.”

“So we’re reasonably safe then?”

“For the time being, yes. Unless, of course, something happens that could affect the earth as a whole. . . .”

“Meaning?”

“Umm, any number of things. Increased solar activity, a giant meteor falling to earth, collision with a passing asteroid—that sort of thing.”

Blade laughed. “God, you’re a cheerful soul, Jack.”

“Oh, but one has to be realistic, my boy. It’s a violent universe out there, and don’t you forget it.”

Blade reached for a peppermint and popped it into his mouth. He bit into it, and felt a slight twinge of pain. You can’t win, can you? Give up the smokes to save your throat and your teeth go to the blue bejayziz.

“How do you *know* all this stuff, Jack?”

“I suppose it’s because I never watch television.” He swung the wheel. “Well, here we are: Carlingford. Don’t tell any of the natives what I said, mind. You never know how they’d take it.”

“I won’t. Where’s PJ’s, by the way? That’s where I’m meeting Sweetman.”

“No better place. It’s through here.”

He turned onto a narrow street, drove beneath a medieval arch, and stopped at a little pub on the corner of the town square.

“What time do you want me to pick you up?”

Blade looked at his watch. “Say, five?”

“Fine. Try the oysters. They’re marvellous.”

"No thanks. On a day like this the only thing I'd like swimming around inside me is a pint. See you later, Jack."

The interior was dark and authentic, right through to the grocery shop that took up part of the front area. Blade pushed open a door that led into the cramped bar, nodding pleasantly to the early-afternoon drinkers who sat watching a rerun of an Australian soap, though the volume of the television set had been turned down to a whisper.

He found Sweetman at a table in the courtyard at the rear. Its walls were decorated with naive murals, one showing an ornate map of the town. She was alone in the yard, save for a small group of young tourists seated at a table in the sun, engaged in animated conversation. Germans, by the sound of it.

"Blade! You found it."

"Thanks to Jack. He's some business or other in town. I'll be glad when Duffy sends the car up."

"Couldn't you hire one?"

He made a face. "You know Duffy. 'Budget, Blade, budget. We're overstretched as it is.' No, it'll be in Dundalk tomorrow. Raymond Hughes is bringing it." He ordered two coffees from the waitress.

"I had Linda Doyle of Forensics on the line this morning. They're taking the dinghy apart."

"That was quick."

He nodded. "The RUC were really on the ball there. They put the whole shebang on the Dublin train last night. Linda and Michael are giving everything a good going-over. Maybe they'll come up with something."

"What's happening with the shell suit?" Sweetman asked presently. "Have they analyzed the bloodstains?"

"Yeah. They're AB positive. The very same as O'Neill's."

"The very same as half the world's, Blade."

He looked annoyed. "Well, Linda says she'll be doing a DNA test later today. That'll give us a match."

"What do you think, Blade? This business with Rostrevor. From where I'm sitting it looks like a hit from the North. A Loyalist hit squad executes O'Neill and goes back home. They go by water to avoid any checkpoints at the border. It makes sense, don't you think?"

"Maybe, Sweetman, maybe. But I'm keeping an open mind on that angle."

He was also keeping his eyes and ears open, had been idly observing the young tourists on the other side of the yard. There were four of them: all looked to be in their late twenties or early thirties. He'd seen a wedding band on the pretty, blonde woman and guessed, from the way she sat next to her dark-haired companion—the one wearing the sunglasses—they were husband and wife. The others, both male and blond, were well-built, bronzed and athletic-looking. They wouldn't, Blade mused, have looked out of place in Hitler's SS. But that was racism; it came of reading too many war comics when a youngster.

Now something caused Blade to pay the party more interest than they were due. The waitress was taking their order of coffee and sandwiches and the dark-haired man was speaking in English. Blade caught the word "murder", and was immediately alert.

"It's only dreadful," the waitress was saying. "He used to

be in here all the time. I still can't believe it happened."

"We did not," the dark-haired German said in excellent English, "expect a thing such as this in Ireland. In Northern Ireland, yes, but not here in Carlingford. Tell me, miss, was Mr O'Neill a member of the IRA?"

The girl laughed without humour.

"Old Martin? You must be joking. Sure he wouldn't hurt a fly. Was it two salad sandwiches you wanted?"

"Yes, and tea for me in place of coffee, please."

She was collecting their empty cups. "But the Guards don't believe it was terrorists who did it. They think that was just a trick, like. To cover up."

"Really?" It was one of the blond men. "Joachim and I, we were sure that it must have been a political assassination. Such things happen all the time, do they not?"

The waitress seemed anxious to terminate the conversation; Macken saw that it upset her. And why wouldn't it? This was—had been—Martin O'Neill's local, according to Jack. He'd been well thought of, by customers and staff alike.

The girl left the table and the tourists resumed their lively conversation. Blade understood a few words, thanks to his former career in the British Army. He'd been stationed for a time near Stuttgart, in the mid-seventies, when the Cold War seemed far from thawing. How quickly we forget a language, he thought. The conversation went over his head. Among the words he thought to understand were *Verdächtige*, "suspect" and *hier bleiben*, "remaining here". It seemed to Blade that the Germans were arguing about cutting short their holiday in Carlingford. One wished to stay on; the others demurred.

And who could blame them? He considered how he'd

feel in their position. You're on holiday abroad, in one of the most picturesque, picture-postcard parts of the country. Then Paradise sours when the Serpent slithers out of the undergrowth and shows its fangs. No, he wouldn't stay if he'd the chance of moving on.

Sweetman had been assessing the party too. She'd been quite taken with the dark-haired man; he was strikingly handsome. The sunglasses he wore didn't suit him. But he'd taken them off for a few seconds when speaking to the waitress and Sweetman had at last had a chance to see his eyes. They did justice to his handsome face.

A shame, she thought, that the colours of the pupils didn't match. . . .

Linda Doyle's findings arrived at Annadangan in the form of a fax from Harcourt Square. It was nine in the evening and Blade was about to finish what he was doing and call it a day.

The fax was four pages long and closely typed. Blade made himself a sandwich, placed it on a tray together with the fax and joined his uncle in the library.

"I was thinking, Blade," Jack said. "When you've sorted this out you could do worse things than spending your leave here in Cooley. Bring young Peter along. There's lots to do. He could investigate the adventure centre for instance. And there's no reason why I couldn't billet the pair of you here."

Blade set the tray down and smoothed out the fax.

"That's very good of you, Jack, and I might just take you up on it." He sighed. "But I don't know. Duffy was hopeful that Sweetman and I would have this thing wrapped up by today—or have made enough progress be able to hand it over to the Guards in Dundalk."

"But there are complications, is that it?"

"That's it, Jack. Somebody's gone to a lot of trouble to put us off the scent." He looked up from the fax. "What do you know about boats?"

"Not a thing, and that's how I intend keeping it. We crawled out of the water two hundred million years ago and I see little advantage in trying to reverse evolution. Me, I'm looking to the stars, my boy. That's where our future lies."

Blade smiled to himself. There was something very boyish about his uncle: a man in his twilight years with the optimism of a teenager. He turned again to the fax.

It had been sent by Detective Sergeant Joe Cunningham. Doyle had passed her forensic evidence to him and he'd made some inquiries about the dinghy.

The craft, it appeared, was of French manufacture; the model was generally used as a tender by yacht owners. It was expensive, as was the powerful Yamaha engine attached to it. Joe Cunningham had been in touch with Interpol in Lyons, and efforts were being made to establish the place where both had been bought. The fax did not give Macken cause for optimism; according to Cunningham this particular dinghy was exported widely, even as far as Australia. The hunt could be a lengthy one.

Blade frowned and bit into his sandwich. There was yet another aspect of the investigation that troubled him, as it had troubled Sweetman. The shell suit. It was the false note, the thing that didn't belong. Forensics had found brain tissue and a couple of hairs on the suit. They were no more than fibres, but almost certainly belonging to the wearer; their DNA matched neither that of the brain tissue nor the blood. Linda Doyle had added a margin note here: the match, though not precise, was unusually close.

Blade tried to imagine the sequence of events that followed O'Neill's murder. The killers—at least two, according to the Carlingford gardaí—depart the scene by water, in a dinghy waiting somewhere between the harbour and the marina. They head across the Lough. It's night. There's a small chance they'll be picked up on the radar aboard the British naval vessel that patrols the Lough, if it happens to be cruising the channel at that time. But they aren't spotted; they reach the far shore, below Rostrevor. Once there, the man who pulled the trigger removes the bloodstained shell suit.

And leaves it behind in the dinghy.

Why? Why not weight it and drop it overboard halfway? Or hide it in any of a number of places where it might never be found? It didn't make a lot of sense.

Blade considered a number of possibilities. Perhaps the killers were surprised upon landing at Rostrevor, and had to make a run for it. Perhaps they'd simply overlooked the garment, shrugged off in the dinghy and all but invisible in the darkness. Yet that seemed unlikely; this was a murder planned meticulously, right down to the plastic the killers had wrapped around their shoes so that no identifiable footprints could lead the authorities to them. And the RUC hadn't recovered the plastic.

"May I ask you something, Jack?"

His uncle shut his book. "Ask away, my boy."

"Supposing you'd just murdered a man. Blown his brains out. The clothes you're wearing are covered in his blood, and they more than likely carry tiny traces of your own skin, hair, et cetera. Enough to identify you if the Guards catch up with you. Why would you deliberately leave those clothes to be found?"

Jack Macken fingered the book in his lap and Blade saw now that the illustration on the dust jacket was of two stylized chess pieces: a white king and a black king locked in mortal combat.

"My guess, for what it's worth," Jack said at last, "is that somebody is attempting to lure you into a game that goes one level higher than the one you *imagine* you're playing. I would say that that somebody is a clever strategist, and that he's sacrificing an important piece at the start of play, with the aim of winning a greater prize when the game is advanced."

Blade swallowed a piece of his sandwich. He looked at Jack strangely.

"What are you telling me?" he said. "Are you telling me that this character *wants* to be caught?"

"Not at all, my boy; not at all. I'm saying that this character of yours is deflecting your attention from his real motive. But he's bragging as well—if what you say is true about his leaving the clothing to be found. A third possibility is that he's leaving behind a clue that he wants you to interpret."

"Hmm."

"You think that's nonsense?"

"No, I don't. In fact, you've confirmed my own suspicions. I'm going for the third option. I think our murderer *is* handing us a clue on a plate. It's not uncommon, Jack. I could show you any number of investigations where the villain went out of his way to provide us with a piece of evidence that could lead us to him. It's a sort of hubris really. Like the criminal who's unable to stay away from the scene of the crime. It's as though they're on a high when they've done the deed, and they want that high to last."

Seven

Sweetman did not share Macken's fondness of bars. It wasn't that she was a teetotaller; she simply found them gloomy and depressing places, especially on a summer's day like this one, when the early-afternoon sun shone brightly outside, and inside the air was thick with the smell of stale stout and cigarette smoke. The bar was occupied by four elderly locals and a young female tourist who seemed to have become separated from the rest of her party. She was strikingly pretty and the barman was enjoying her company.

Macken and Sweetman had got to PJ's a little after noon on Tuesday. Blade made an enquiry at the counter and was directed to the man they sought.

"Mr Donegan?"

"That's me."

Liam Donegan was a contemporary of Martin O'Neill. He'd known him for almost twenty years, for as long as O'Neill had lived in the town. The local Guards had assured Blade that Donegan had been O'Neill's best friend. If anyone could shed some light on the murder then it was Donegan. The Guards had informed him that he could be found most mornings and afternoons in PJ's.

Donegan seemed willing to talk. It was as if he was trying to unburden himself. But Blade recognized this willingness for what it was. It was driven by fear: what had happened to a friend could happen to you.

"You and he were close; am I right, Mr Donegan?"

"We were. It's a terrible thing altogether."

"Had he enemies, sir?"

"Martin? Not that I know of. He was the gentlest soul you could imagine. Wouldn't harm a fly."

"That's what we heard, yes. But people make enemies all the same. Maybe without them even being aware of it. Did he quarrel with anybody—ever?"

"Och, we had our arguments, him and me. But it was mostly about the usual things: sport and politics—and women."

Sweetman had to smile. Liam Donegan was at least eighty.

"How did he get on with the rest of the people here?" Blade said then. "Did he have many friends?"

"Well, now, he wasn't what you'd call the life and soul of the party. He kept to himself, so he did. But don't get me wrong now—he wasn't unfriendly or anything. But he'd come in here, and sit right over there. You see that chair? That's where Martin always sat. So sometimes you'd go over and say 'Hello, Martin. How's the form?' and he'd nod and invite you to have a drink with him. And sometimes he'd look straight through you with those quare eyes of his, as if you weren't there at all. That's when you knew that it was better to leave him be. He'd his problems, you see. That's what I always thought. I didn't ever want to pry. I thought: If Martin doesn't want to tell me, then that's all right with me. I was never one to pry you know. Will you have a drink itself?"

"I won't, sir, thanks. I'm on duty. Do you know if Martin had many visitors?"

Donegan scratched his head. "I don't think he had, to be honest with you. He'd be away a lot himself, you see—he'd take the old Renault of his down to Newry. That's where his old friends were. There was the son, of course; he'd be here every other month. Nice enough lad. Lives up above in Kilkeel."

"Yes, we've met him."

"Did you know he was seeing a doctor? Shame altogether. Martin was a bit worried about him."

"Oh, what's the matter with him?" This was news.

Donegan studied his glass. "Now," he said, "when I say he's seeing a doctor I don't mean his GP. No, it's very sad, so it is. The young fella suffers an awful lot with his nerves. You'd never think it to look at him, mind you. But isn't that always the way? It's the silent ones you have to look out for."

So Jim O'Neill's "moods" go deeper than I thought, Blade mused. "Seeing a doctor" and "suffering with your nerves" were the old rural euphemisms for mental disorder. It could be anything: depression—or worse. But this was not the reason why he was talking to Liam Donegan.

"Anybody else, sir?" he asked. "Did Martin have any other visitors?"

Donegan had to think hard. The barman was making progress with the pretty foreign girl; they'd discovered a shared interest in the recorded work of Brian Kennedy.

"Yes," Donegan said at last, "yes, there was one fella I remember. God, it must have been about two or three years ago now. Martin brought him here one night. He didn't seem to want to talk to anybody else, just this fella."

"Could you describe him, sir?" Sweetman asked.

"Ehh, in his seventies, I think. Well-dressed. He looked like a professional man—a barrister or something. But I wouldn't be able to tell you any more about what he looked like. He didn't seem to get on very well with Martin."

"Oh . . . ?" It was Blade.

"Well, they were pally enough when they came in, but as the evening wore on I heard them arguing. It seemed to me like this fella was criticizing Martin for something. I'm a bit deaf, you see, so I couldn't make out what it was."

"You heard nothing of what was said?"

"Ah, I didn't say that; I didn't say that. I heard enough to give me my suspicions, like."

"Why were you suspicious, Mr Donegan?" Sweetman asked.

The old man lowered his voice. "I think the fella might have been IRA."

Sweetman looked sharply at Macken. How much was fact and how much was fiction? Donegan seemed a nice old sort—as harmless as he claimed his dead friend had been. But nice old men were, in her experience, prone to exaggeration—or to the telling of tall tales. It made their autumn years seem more interesting than they actually were.

"Why do you say that?" Blade asked carefully.

"Because I heard Martin tell the fella that he wanted to be left in peace. 'I've done my bit for my country,' says he. 'Let the younger men carry on the struggle now.'"

Sweetman was writing in her notebook. "You're sure of those words, Mr Donegan?"

"Ah, yes. Martin was practically shouting at that stage, so I heard him well enough. That was what he said: 'Let the young men carry on the struggle now.'"

"Interesting," said Blade. Being a seasoned policeman and analyst of witness statements, he hadn't failed to note the fact that Donegan had given two slightly different versions of the stranger's words.

A detail, yes. But details could sometimes prove to be of more significance than at first supposed.

"Please allow me to buy *you* a drink, sir," he said with a smile. "A Bushmills and water, wasn't it?"

Eight

It rained on the morning of the funeral. The sudden change in the weather took the town and its visitors by surprise. Sweetman managed to buy the last two umbrellas on sale in a drapery store on the square. Blade drove them to the church. He knew the way, had been there before: the little road where the Táin Trail begins runs alongside the church.

The building sits on a hill at the eastern end of Carlingford, with a view over the Lough and a backdrop formed by the slopes of Slieve Foye. It's a relatively new church, faced with granite and having a glass-and-wood porch whose architecture is more in keeping with a municipal building or museum. But its stained-glass windows are a credit to their designer.

The car park was full when they arrived, a testimony to Martin O'Neill's popularity in the town. Several of the cars bore northern registrations. Blade parked outside.

"I want you to do something for me, Sweetman," he said. "I want you to make a note of some of those Ulster number plates. We'll find out who they belong to."

"Right."

"And for God's sake be discreet."

Sweetman found him standing in the back of the church, in the gloom formed by the choir gallery; it afforded them an opportunity to observe the mourners. It was tactful too:

you didn't want a conspicuous police presence at a funeral. Blade spotted Guard O'Donnell and a colleague among the congregation; they were out of uniform. He also recognized the grey head of Liam Donegan, bowed in prayer and, seated close by, Martin O'Neill's son.

Beside him, Sweetman was making the sign of the cross. He saw her lips move, and wished then that he shared her faith. For him churches were dismal places, though it must be said that he found himself warming to this one. He took in the design on the window to his left; it bore a resemblance to Mondrian's later work.

He glanced around as the door behind them opened and another latecomer entered. It was an old clergyman dressed, with the exception of a white dog-collar, from top to toe in black, his shoulders sparkling with raindrops. Macken assumed that he was one of the celebrants but this proved not to be the case. The man genuflected in the aisle, then settled into a pew at the rear. He cupped his hands in front of his mouth and bent his head. Blade paid him no more heed.

He was glad when the service had ended. He motioned to Sweetman and they slipped out unobtrusively. They waited in the car as the hearse emerged through the gates, followed by the funeral cortège. They brought up the rear.

The cemetery is relatively new and lies a little distance from the town. The plots on the left of the central walk are filled and fresh burials take place in the shadow of tall cedars that border a neighbouring farm.

The rain had stopped and Carlingford Lough, visible beyond the cemetery, shone bluely again. Macken and Sweetman stood under the trees and watched as Martin

O'Neill's corpse was laid to rest. Sans eyes. Blade scanned the gathering.

"Anyone we know?"

Sweetman understood the question. It was standard practice: the interment of a man suspected of paramilitary involvement tends to attract his fellows. The blood sacrifice is a sacred thing; you're obliged to pay your respects to a man who's died for "the Cause". Garda Gary O'Donnell and the other officer stood on the other side of the grave, facing her; she saw their eyes moving from side to side, registering all those present.

"I don't recognize anybody," she said.

"Nor me. But I'm missing someone, Sweetman."

She looked from mourner to mourner and shook her head.

"The old priest," Blade explained. "The one who came and sat at the back. Where is he?"

"He probably has duties to attend to, Blade. Priests have more to do than you might imagine."

"Maybe so. But don't you think he'd give a funeral priority? *I* do."

Sweetman returned her attention to the burial service. The celebrant was blessing the coffin. The ritual was approaching its close.

"I think you're making too much out of it."

"I wonder," he murmured. Yet another little detail to file away. . . .

Macken and Sweetman had arranged to meet Jim O'Neill at his favourite spot, on that portion of the Táin Trail that overlooks Carlingford town. So peaceful was it there on the gentle slope, amid the bright yellow furze, that the vicious killing of Jim's father seemed to belong to a parallel universe that had somehow rubbed up against this one, leaving a faint scuff-mark and a whiff of brimstone. Yet the cemetery where they'd buried O'Neill the day before was clearly visible to the northeast. Jim O'Neill wasn't looking in that direction: he sat staring instead at the Dominican Priory, its restored walls obscuring the old mill beyond. They sat down on the grass beside him.

"How much," Blade said presently, "do you know about your father's past?"

O'Neill shrugged and studied a sailboat making leisurely progress on the calm water.

"There really isn't much to know," he said. "He was a very ordinary man. Born in a place called Knocklone in County Galway; went to study at St Patrick's training college in Dublin. Moved to Newry in fifty-four. Fell in love with my mother soon after."

"And died in Carlingford," Blade finished. "What do you know about his childhood? In Galway."

"Virtually nothing. He never talked about it. Not to me anyway. I always had the feeling he didn't like the place much."

"Oh? Why do you say that, sir?"

"Well, he never went back, did he, superintendent? Not once in over forty years. Or if he did he never said anything about it." He turned to Sweetman. "You're from that part of the country, aren't you, sergeant? Don't you think that's odd? I mean, even if you had any amount of rows with your family and neighbours, you'd still go back and visit every once in a while. Wouldn't you?"

"Yes," Sweetman said decisively, "I would. Tell me, sir: weren't you ever curious about your father's roots?"

"Certainly. I mean, they'd be *my* roots too, after all. And if you're going to ask me if I've ever been to Knocklone, the answer is 'yes'. I went there some years ago, if only to get a sense of the place where my father's people came from. The thing is: I didn't."

"Didn't what, sir?" Blade said.

"Didn't get any sense at all. It's all changed, you see, since my father's day. There's nothing left of the old village; it's all new houses and shops now. Well, when I say 'new', I mean they'd be all post war."

"And family? Relatives?"

O'Neill shook his head.

"No one. Nobody even remembered him. Oh, they remembered some O'Neills right enough. One ould fella even knew a second cousin of my father's. But that was as far as I got. It seems that any O'Neills who'd lived there had either died out or gone to the States. It wasn't very pleasant, superintendent. I mean: we all need our roots, don't we? They tell us who we are. . . . "

They do, Blade thought. What he was trying to ascertain at that moment was: Who in the name of Christ was Martin O'Neill? What exactly *had* they buried the previous day?

Most of the registrations Sweetman had noted belonged to cars owned by residents of Carlingford. Two were owned by Newrymen. Both had known the murdered man, though not intimately. Martin O'Neill had played bridge with them one evening a week, a pastime he'd begun in his school-teaching days and continued. They knew him as a "pleasant enough man" but one who didn't talk much about himself, if at all. Of "real" friends of his they'd known nothing.

Sweetman opened her bag and withdrew a small manila envelope, shook out something it contained. A photograph. It was in black and white and showed the face of an elderly man three quarters on. It was a reasonable study.

"Did you get that at the station?" O'Neill asked without much interest. "That's the one I gave the sergeant."

"It's not a great picture," Sweetman said. "We'd like a better one."

"Then you're out of luck. That's the only one we could find."

Sweetman looked at him keenly.

"What? Are you telling me that this is the only picture of your father in existence? I find that hard to believe, sir."

It *was* hard to believe. Martin O'Neill had walked the earth for more than eight decades. Cameras are everywhere: at weddings, christenings, parties, school outings and ceremonies, in photo booths. It was inconceivable that O'Neill's image hadn't been recorded more than once.

Where were the photo albums? The holiday snaps? The passport photo? The driving-licence shot?

Sweetman thought of her grandfather. He'd been about Martin O'Neill's age at the time of his own death. She remembered her parents taking possession of Grandda's "few bits and pieces". There's been a great many of them: testimonies to a relatively long life. His war medals, awarded for distinguished service during the North African campaign; his collection of pipes and other artefacts; his diaries, his

letters, his financial accounts—such as they were. But above
of all were the photo albums, some mildewed with age: a
visual record of the life of an ordinary farmer. Grandda going through the Seven Ages of Man, from the cradle to dot-
age. Her mother had had two of the best portraits restored
and framed.

"I took that one myself," Jim O'Neill said. "Just last
year. That's the cottage in the background. Dad would have
been notoriously camera shy. He wouldn't pose for me so I
snapped off the one shot. It's not great, is it?"

"It's not bad," Blade agreed. "I suppose it'll do for our
purposes anyway. Look, sir, are you absolutely sure there
were no others? It's extremely odd."

"My father was an odd person."

"Well, we'll have to see about that. I think you should
know, sir, that I'm extending the investigation to Galway,
beginning in Knocklone."

"You won't find anything there, superintendent. I looked."

"Perhaps," Blade said, "you weren't looking in the right
places."

Nine

The trail began in St Malachy's church in the village of Knocklone. It's a nondescript building, as country churches sometimes are. It stands on an acre and a half at the south end of the village, enclosed by a low wall. There's a grotto to Our Lady of Fatima to one side of the gravelled forecourt; a line of slim yews separates the church grounds from the adjacent building: a tall, three-storied, grey-plastered affair. It's the biggest house in the village—and must therefore be, Macken reasoned in the light of experience, that of the parish priest. He rang the doorbell, introduced Sweetman and himself. They were ushered into the reception-room.

"Martin O'Neill?" said the parish priest presently. He studied the photograph and shook his head. "No, the name doesn't ring a bell, I'm afraid. And you say he's from these parts, superintendent?"

"He was a Knocklone man," Blade told him. "Would he be in the parish records? Birth, baptism, perhaps."

"He might. What year are we talking about?"

"Nineteen seventeen."

The priest whistled.

"Now, that's going back a bit. In fact, this church wasn't even built then."

Blade hesitated, beginning to have his suspicions.

"But was there a church here before that?"

"Of course, superintendent. It was much smaller, built long before the Famine. It fell into disuse then. The people cleared out, you see, in the eighteen forties and fifties. There wasn't enough of a congregation so the bishop amalgamated the parishes of Knocklone and Kilty."

"I see. So if somebody was born here in nineteen seventeen where would they have been baptized?"

"I suppose in Kilty. Yes, I'm sure they would have been."

"Thank you, Father. You've been most helpful."

"Not at all. God bless now."

Two hours later, as Sweetman turned the car onto the road that led to the neighbouring village, seven miles distant, several questions were going through Blade's head.

Uppermost was the matter of Martin O'Neill's birthplace. Their own findings had confirmed Jim's words; no trace remained there of his father; he might never have existed as far as the villagers were concerned. They'd made inquiries at the local garda station, at both pubs, at the grocery shop. To no avail. Not even the "ould fella" who'd known a second cousin of Martin O'Neill could be found; the impression Macken received was that he too had passed away a long time before. Their only chance now of discovering clues to the early life of the elusive Martin O'Neill lay in Kilty.

It is somewhat older, and larger, than Knocklone. It knows some affluence too: there are two churches, one Catholic, the other Church of Ireland. There's even a small hotel on the main street. A plaque in the lobby announces proudly that the village shared in the Tidy Towns awards of

1986. After a coffee and a sandwich, Macken and Sweetman
called on the parish priest.

His youth took Blade by surprise; he couldn't have been
older than twenty-five. Blade had expected a much older
man; one whose age was in keeping with the surroundings.
Father Joyce was affable and helpful, even took them into
the sacristy, where they consulted the parish records together. He seemed excited by the idea of assisting a police investigation. Eagerly he turned to the entries of births, marriages
and deaths in 1917.

They were incomplete. More than that.

"There's a page missing!" Joyce cried.

"Are you sure, Father?" Sweetman said.

"See for yourself. *This* page ends on the twenty-second of
February—and *this* one begins on the tenth of September.
Look: you can even see where it's been torn out."

Martin O'Neill was becoming increasingly elusive.

"Are there any other local records?" Macken asked. "Is
there any other way of finding out who was born here during those months?"

"Not unless you try the Custom House in Dublin."

"We will," Blade assured him. "Though I believe the register is in Lombard Street now."

The young priest was thoughtful for a moment. Then he
said: "Look, superintendent, why don't you have a word
with my predecessor. Old Father Boyle. If there's anybody
in the parish who knows what's what then he's the man.
He's what now? . . . eighty-five I think. Knew everybody in
the district. He's baptized, married and buried four times
as many people as I have members in my congregation. He

could write a book on the place."

"Where can we find him?" Blade asked.

He was given directions.

It was the third priest's house that they'd visited that day. It wasn't as imposing as the first two; it was no more than a cottage, situated in a cul-de-sac at the foot of a small hill on the outskirts of the village. The little garden was a riot of colour: rose bushes in at least ten varieties, pink and blue chrysanthemums and violet bugles of penstemon. There was a small Child of Prague statuette behind the fanlight.

No housekeeper answered Sweetman's ring. They had to wait almost a minute before the door was opened by a wizened old man. His face was startlingly pale, and grooved like an elephant's kneecap. His body was shrunken; he came barely to Blade's chest. What was left of his hair consisted of white wisps on a skull that was cadaverous. Yet his eyes, though yellowed and shot through with red tracery, were intelligent.

And filled with mistrust.

"Father Boyle?"

"Yes. . . . "

"We're from the Special Branch, Father. We'd like—"

"The *what?*"

"Special Branch. The Guards."

"Hmm. I see."

"We're conducting a routine inquiry, Father, and the parish priest suggested we speak to you."

The old man scowled.

"Oh, he did, did he? Very well, come in then. And be sure you wipe your feet."

The cottage was spotlessly clean; Sweetman suspected that the venerable cleric had a daily help. The little sitting room resembled the convent cell of her older sister, Fidelma, if a little bigger. It was the room of an ascetic. A metre-high crucifix dominated one wall. Another displayed a gilt-framed oil showing St Martin de Porres being visited by a radiant member of the heavenly host.

"And why," Boyle said when they were seated on two uncomfortable chairs, "did young Father Joyce refer you to me?"

"He thinks you may know something about a certain Martin O'Neill," Blade told him.

"Never heard of him."

But Blade had noted the hesitation that preceded the reply. He hadn't put it down to the priest's age, or defective memory. He didn't have the impression that there was anything defective about Boyle's memory. Quite the contrary: he felt certain the old man was fully compos mentis. Moreover the reply had been more brusque than was necessary.

Interesting.

"Mr O'Neill", Blade proceeded evenly, "was born in Knocklone in nineteen seventeen."

"That wasn't today or yesterday."

"No, Father, indeed it wasn't. But there's no record of the birth or baptism in the parish records here. I understand that the two parishes were amalgamated."

"Yes yes, that's true." Father Boyle appeared slightly irritated. "But that was *long* before my time. I'm not Methuselah, you know."

"No. But we were going over the records with Father Joyce,

as I say, and it would appear that the relevant page was torn out. The one that might have given Martin O'Neill's date of birth and baptism."

There was silence then. Blade saw the old man's lip twitch slightly and his brow grow several more deep furrows.

"Is that a fact?"

"It is. And I believe that it's something more than coincidence that that very page is missing."

The priest shrugged. "These things happen. We never had to lock the church in my time. You could leave it open day and night and nobody would *dream* of touching anything. Things are different now. They'd steal the tabernacle itself if they thought they could flog it somewhere. People have no respect any more."

"No, Father. It's shocking."

"But tell me, Mr . . ."

"Macken. Detective Superintendent."

"Hmm. Tell me then, Mr Macken. Why are you inquiring about this . . . this Michael O'Neill?"

"Martin. I'm afraid he's been murdered, Father."

"Murdered! Dear me. How? When?"

"A week ago. In Carlingford, County Louth."

"Carlingford. That's terrible, terrible."

"So we're trying to find out why. We're looking into his background—perhaps he had an enemy here. But you say you never knew him?"

"No. I didn't. There was a family of O'Neills once, but as far as I can remember they emigrated to America. That must have been about sixty years ago now."

"I see. Well, we'll just have to check the records in Dublin.

Thank you very much for your time, Father." He got up. "No no, stay where you are. We'll let ourselves out."

They re-emerged into the sunshine. Blade felt he'd come out from Darkness and into the Light. He'd found the cottage cold and oppressive—more so than that of the late Martin O'Neill. He'd found the interview with the old clergyman strangely unsettling too. He'd an inkling that Father Boyle knew more than he was telling.

Blade didn't see the curtain part as he shut the front door. Nor could he have seen Father Boyle shuffle to the little hall and open a book on the table. The priest ran a finger down a list of addresses, then reached for the telephone.

Ten

The group met only in the evening or at weekends, and always at the same location. They met outside working hours because each was an industrious man who used to the full each hour God gave him. They met at the same location because they were a quasi-secret organization and liked their privacy.

The bishop was tired of sitting in the car. The thought had occurred to him to drive the short distance to Knock Airport and board a flight to Dublin. But he dreaded flying. He was eighty-six and had sat only once in a plane; the experience was not one he would forget easily.

So here he was in the back seat of his chauffeur-driven Daimler. The car had every comfort and luxury imaginable, including a minibar, yet the bishop was weary after the two-hour journey here to the little township in the shadow of the Hill of Tara. He watched the sun sink behind the place that had been the seat of Ireland's High Kings in earlier times, and where St Patrick had secured the hegemony of the Christian Church.

The group had given the chauffeur excellent directions. He found the entrance without difficulty and soon the wide tyres of the limousine were crunching on the gravel driveway. The bishop sat impassively as the house loomed into view. It was a Palladian mansion of more than fifty rooms, built of granite quarried locally; much of its stone facing lay concealed behind a thick growth of ivy. There were lights in four of the downstairs windows. The front door opened as the Daimler drew up and a young man, dressed soberly in dark grey, went to assist the passenger. The chauffeur depressed the switch on his dashboard that raised the boot of the car.

"Good evening, your grace, and welcome."

"Thank you."

"Was your journey pleasant?"

"No."

"I'm sorry to hear that, your grace." He helped the old cleric up the steps. "They're waiting for you in the dining room. Would you care to freshen up first?"

"No."

"As you wish, your grace."

The young man motioned to the chauffeur to place the bishop's bags in the hall. Then he threw open a pair of high doors and escorted the old man through.

The eleven men rose as the bishop entered. He waved an impatient hand and they resumed their places at the long dining-table. It was laid with a silver service, fresh flowers and linen napkins. A chandelier sparkled above. The young man helped the bishop to the vacant seat at the table's head, nodded to the assembly and left quietly.

The bishop peered at the men from under thick, white eyebrows. He saw a group of well-dressed, well-fed individuals whose average age was fifty or older.

A man with a kindly face rose a second time from his chair

at the opposite end of the table. He addressed the bishop.

"On behalf of the Society, I take great pleasure in welcoming your grace to our table tonight. I trust the accommodation will be to your liking." The bishop nodded gravely. "Perhaps, before we begin our meal," the man continued, "your grace might care to lead us in a decade of the rosary?"

There were murmurs of agreement from the others.

"I think," the bishop said, "a simple grace-before-meals will suffice."

The man nodded, picked up and rang a little bell. Moments later, a side door opened and a procession of young women entered. Each bore a tray of comestibles, some decked by silver. Each wore a plain, sober dress that reached to the ankle. They wore no make-up and their hair was tied severely back. They kept their eyes fixed on the floor as they glided to prearranged positions behind the diners.

Grace having been said, the meal began.

"It's a bad business," one of the group said, halfway through the meat course. "I thought that particular ghost had been laid to rest for ever, but evidently not."

"I'm surprised," said the bishop, "you know anything about it. We're going back fifty years now. Longer."

"There are documents. . . . "

"Which would have been destroyed long ago if I'd had my way," said the bishop, accepting a slice of roast beef from a handmaiden. "But it's too late now for recriminations. We just have to make sure it doesn't go any further. The hierarchy simply can't afford any more scandals. The paedophile priests and blackguard bishops were bad enough; if this were to come out now then we'd lose the small bit of dignity we have left to us."

"Do we know who's conducting the investigation, your grace?" another asked.

"A Detective Superintendent Macken. We have reason to believe he's Special Branch."

A man with silver-grey hair coughed politely.

"Blade Macken," he said.

"I beg your pardon?"

"Blade Macken, your grace. He's attached to the Dublin Metropolitan Area."

"I see. Blade. That's a rather peculiar name. Not, may I say, a *Christian* name."

"He's a rather peculiar man: has his eccentricities, if you understand. But he's very good, very thorough. You're up against one of the best men in the Special Branch—if not *the* best."

"I see," said the bishop again. "So we've our work cut out for us."

"Macken isn't working alone I presume," said the man with the silver-grey hair.

"No, there's a girl involved too. A detective sergeant. A slip of a youngster. In her twenties. Her name's Sweetman."

"Doesn't ring a bell, your grace."

"She's a local girl; grew up in the parish of Kidafane, which falls within my diocese. That's the trouble you see, gentlemen; that's what worries me. We're a bit clannish in north County Galway; whenever an outsider comes nosing around then we tend to close ranks. But if it's one of our own . . . "

"I see what you mean."

Someone spoke from down the table. He was not much

younger than the bishop. In contrast to the others, he was small and frail; the food on his plate lay largely untouched.

"Your grace," he said, "it seems to me that the trail begins and ends at the Franciscan House in Galway City. Somebody said just now that we're dealing with events that occurred more than fifty years ago. Surely there's nobody left in the community there who'd remember anything."

"I've made enquiries on that matter," the bishop said. "And it seems there *is* one man. He's advanced in years but his mind's as clear as a bell. All it needs is for this *Blade* Macken and his detective sergeant to question him and the game is up. He'll spill the beans and the Church will be called to account."

He wiped his lips with a napkin.

"You'll have to remember that things were different in nineteen seventy, when that busybody Butler was trying to stir things up. Nobody cared; nobody wanted to know. But they're just after having another war out there and that's still fresh in people's mind. If Macken starts raking over the coals now it'll do the Church irreparable damage."

"This friar, your grace," somebody said, "could you arrange for him to be posted elsewhere? Out of the country."

The bishop shook his head.

"I have no power whatsoever in that direction. The Franciscans are run from Rome and are subordinate only to His Holiness himself. In order to have the Brother transferred I'd have to speak to his superior in Galway, who in turn would have to apply to his General in the Vatican. And I ask you: what possible reason could I offer for my request?"

"Then we have to make sure Macken and Sweetman stay

clear of that Franciscan House."

"Agreed," said the bishop. "And how do we go about doing that? That's the question."

"You say Sweetman's a local girl, your grace?" said the man at the end of the table. "What do her people do?"

"They're farmers."

"Hmm, that's interesting."

"In what way?"

"Well, your grace, as a banker who has many dealings with the farming community it's my experience that farmers fall roughly into two categories: those who rely heavily on banks and those who have little need of them, aside from a place to deposit earnings and assist with their investments. Now: is the father a small farmer, would you say?"

"Quite definitely, yes."

"Good. I'll look into his affairs. The small farmers of Ireland, God bless them, are a vulnerable lot, your grace. They depend to a great extent on the flexibility of their local bank manager."

The bishop smiled thinly. "And should that local manager suddenly *lose* his flexibility . . ."

"Precisely."

"You do what you have to then. But on no account must the Church be seen to be involved in any way."

"You have my word on that, your grace. So, that's Sweetman settled. What about Macken? He's the main threat." He turned to the silver-haired man. "Any ideas?"

There was a long pause.

"Macken's another kettle of fish entirely. One doesn't interfere with impunity with a man of his rank."

"But it can be done?"

"It can be done."

"Use any means, fair or foul," said the bishop. "I shall leave the means to your own discretion. You know best."

The man at the other end of the table beamed. "Rest assured that it'll be taken care of, your grace. That is what we're here for—we, the lay-soldiers of Christ. Divide and conquer: isn't that the soldier's way? I think you know what I mean. Now, I suggest we move next door; the port should be at just the right temperature by now."

Eleven

The business park in Swords is a ten-minute drive from Dublin Airport. The location was chosen for this reason by the board of directors of Mnemos, one of several Irish companies having a franchise to manufacture the powerful Pentium III computer processor. Mnemos's customers were far flung, some as distant as Australia. It might be thought that exporting to such distant markets would be uneconomical, yet this was not the case: the smallness of the chips made their transcontinental freight costs a more than viable proposition. And such was the profit margin on those chips that Frank Naughton, founder of Mnemos, had seen his own investment capital of £200,000 grow by more than one thousand percent in a span of six years. He and his fellow-directors had floated the company, with great success, in 1996.

Terry Cahill liked his job. It was certainly an improvement on his previous one, when he'd driven a taxi in Dublin. He had stories to tell—what cabdriver hasn't? There'd been good times, certainly: he could boast about having had some big names in the entertainment world in the back of his cab.

Yet by and large it was hard slog, at times dangerous, and Terry had been pleased to be able to exchange it for the job at Mnemos ("Minnows" to him). The work was clean and the pay was good. It entailed the driving of a lorry-load of processors to Dublin Airport each week, with some other light duties thrown in.

John Meegan, his trainee, was new to the company. He was a good lad, in Terry's opinion, but a bit too keen for the older man's liking. On their first run Meegan had explained that he'd a degree in computer programming, and that he'd taken the driving job solely to get "a foot in the door", as he put it. This admission had placed an unbridgeable gulf between Terry and him. Terry knew nothing about computers, still less about their components; for all he cared, the boxes stowed in the back of the van might just as easily have contained Mars bars.

"Did I ever tell you," asked Terry, as he negotiated the first roundabout on the Dublin road, "that I once picked up Sinead O'Connor at the Berkeley Court?"

"You did," said John. "Twice."

"She was wearing a blonde wig. And dark glasses. You'd never have recognized her at all. And she was with . . . what's this his name is?"

"Bill Clinton?"

"Don't be so fuckin' smart. And light one of those for me, will you? Make yourself useful for a change."

"That's against regulations, Terry."

"Jayziz, would you listen to that! 'That's against regulations, Terry.' And who the fuck's to know, eh? Tell me that. Just light the shaggin' thing, would you?"

"Can I open the window?"

"Yeah, open the bleedin' window."

John did as requested. He was just about to light Terry's cigarette when something very big and very heavy collided with the van on the driver's side.

"Jesus Christ!" Terry shouted.

Another van, larger than their own, had moved up alongside and was keeping pace with them. A Hiace, John noted, despite his panic. He saw its passenger window wind down and a head appear. It wore a balaclava.

"Terry . . . " he said.

Terry looked. And almost lost control of the wheel. The man in the balaclava now held a gun, pointed at Terry's head. With his other hand he was motioning for them to stop. Terry obeyed, shaking. Headlights of cars passed, their drivers oblivious to what was taking place.

"Oh, fuck," Terry moaned. "Oh, fuck." To John he said: "Let them have what they want, do you hear me? Don't for fuck's sake antagonize them in any way."

"I–I won't, don't worry."

The door on John's side was wrenched open. More guns, more balaclavas.

"Is the back locked?" a voice demanded.

"Yes," Terry said.

"Keys. Quick now."

Terry handed them over, and leaned back in his seat, praying under his breath and staring straight ahead. His companion was breathing hoarsely. Terry smelled urine.

"Keep looking where you're looking," said one of the men. "Straight in front of you. If you turn your heads . . . bang! You got that?"

The raiders were thorough, knew exactly what they were doing. Each man removed his balaclava in the lee of the Mnemos van. To the passing motorist there was nothing untoward about the transfer of a score of cardboard boxes from one vehicle to another. It took a little under two minutes.

The same man returned to John's side, disguised as before. John was quaking.

"Put these on your friend." He held out a pair of handcuffs.

"I d-don't know how to use them."

"For fuck's sake. You just slip them on his wrists and press!"

Terry offered his hands. John's own hands were shaking so much that the cuffing operation took much longer than it should have.

"Now roll up that window," the raider ordered.

"Please. Don't k-kill us. My wife's expecting our first baby."

"Nobody's going to kill anybody. Now roll up the fucking window."

John obeyed. Then the raider produced a second set of handcuffs and secured John's wrists. An impatient horn sounded from behind the van.

The raider put away his gun and took something from a pocket. A metal canister. He punched its lid; smoke began to billow out. He tossed the canister in between the two men and slammed the door shut.

As the van filled with gas the vehicle behind it moved out onto the roadway and departed at speed. Inside the van Terry and John struggled to open the doors as their eyes smarted and their windpipes burned. Both passed out in less than a minute.

Knock-out gas is tricky stuff. Ask any anaesthetist. It must be administered in precise doses: too little and it's ineffective; too much and it can kill.

John was fortunate; he had youth and health on his side. With Terry it was otherwise. Two minutes after he'd lost consciousness his heart gave out, and Terry lost his life.

Matt Sweetman had put on his best suit for the occasion. It wasn't often he visited Tuam, the big town in the middle of County Galway. The market was what usually brought him here. Now it was his bank manager.

Matt didn't understand it. He was worried; bank managers didn't phone you out of the blue, requesting the pleasure of your company. No, something was up. Matt didn't like it.

As he turned the off-road vehicle into the car park behind the offices of the Ulster and Connacht Credit Bank he again mulled the possibilities over in his head. He'd been late with the repayment in May—but only by two weeks, not even that. Doherty wouldn't wish to see him about something so trivial; after all, he'd been late before and Doherty had been generous about it. And why, Matt thought, wouldn't he be? Wasn't the fecker getting nine-and-a-half percent interest every month. Crippling. But Matt had needed the loan; the house had been falling down around their ears. If he hadn't spent the money *then* on the rebuilding it would have cost twice that now. He'd worked it out.

And what else could it be? Doherty had sounded very cool and businesslike—as though they were strangers, as though Matt Sweetman and he hadn't practically shared a childhood. Same school, same friends—practically the same women too, come to think of it. He was puzzled. Well, he'd find out soon enough. Matt pushed open the glass front door and entered the bank. John Doherty's office door was open and he saw Sweetman.

"Come right in, Matt," he called, cupping a hand over the mouthpiece of his telephone. "I won't be a minute."

The bank manager was as good as his word. Thirty seconds later he replaced the receiver, got up, shut the door and returned to his desk. He offered Sweetman a cigarette. Sweetman accepted it, bit the filter off and lit up.

"How's the family?" Doherty asked.

"Grand."

"Little Orla? Still up in Dublin? We don't see much of her."

Matt Sweetman studied his cigarette. "She'll be down tomorrow, as it happens."

"I know."

Sweetman looked up quizzically.

"You know? How the blazes could you know? I didn't know meself until this morning. Just before you rang me, in fact. And I didn't tell a soul other than herself."

The bank manager, like Blade Macken, had recently quit smoking. He liked to keep a packet on his desk, to be able to offer a client a cigarette, as he'd offered one to Matt Sweetman. It strengthened his resolve to continue and—let's be honest—it gave him a tremendous feeling of holier than thou, the common weakness of the reformed smoker. But John Doherty was no longer feeling smug. He pondered how he could broach the delicate subject. It wasn't easy; Sweetman and he went back a long way.

"Look, this is a bit awkward for me, Matt. . . ."

"Mmh?"

"We've always been friends, right?"

"John, I wish to God you'd get to the bloody point, and not be behaving like a young fella on his first date. Spit it out."

"All right. The fact of the matter is . . . you've put me in a very embarrassing position."

"I what?"

"I want you to understand this, Matt. It's not me. It's head office in Galway."

"Right, right." Now Matt Sweetman was irritated. Why couldn't Doherty simply get to the point? It wasn't like him. "What about them?"

"They've asked me to review the terms of your loan."

Doherty breathed a sigh of relief when he'd said it. There. It was out and, like the verminous contents of Pandora's Box, couldn't be returned.

Sweetman paled. He knew what those words meant. It was like asking a politician caught with his hand in the till, or in bed with the wrong woman, to "consider his position". The axe was being sharpened. But he remained calm.

"Why? I haven't fallen behind or anything. I'm up to date with my payments—have been from the beginning."

"It's not the payments, Matt. It's the collateral."

"I don't understand."

"Jesus, Matt, don't make this any more painful for me than it already is."

"I'm not. I just don't fecking understand."

"No? Well, I'll spell it out for you." He went to a heavy,

dark-green filing cabinet and returned with a dossier. Breathing hard, he opened it.

"On the twenty-third of March this year you sold ten acres of land to Willie Higgins."

"That's right. I did."

"It wasn't yours to sell."

"Don't talk shite, John. It was my land. Why shouldn't I sell it if I wanted to?"

"I repeat: It wasn't your land to sell. It was the *bank's* land."

"Are you out of your fecking mind?"

"No, I'm not. And I wish to God you'd keep your voice down. This is hard enough for me as it is."

"Sorry, sorry. Now: explain yourself."

"Right." Doherty held up a document. "This is the contract you signed five years ago." He turned the back page round so that Sweetman could see it. "There's your signature at the bottom, along with my own."

"Yes."

Doherty turned back a few pages and folded them. He laid the document in front of Sweetman.

"And these are the terms of the loan. According to them, you put up your land—fifty-and-a-half acres—as collateral on the loan."

"I did."

"Do you know what that means, Matt? It means that you delivered your land into our hands—for safekeeping—until the loan was paid off. The bank became trustee for the land—all of it. It wasn't under your control any more. At least, not to sell. You should have notified me first."

"Ach well, what of it? I'm notifying you now."

There was a polite tap on the door. A young woman dressed in the dark-green uniform of UCCB came in and placed a note on Doherty's desk. She nodded pleasantly on recognizing Matt Sweetman, and left. The bank manager leaned back in his chair.

"I wish it was that simple," he said. "I really do. But you've put me in a spot. As I say, head office were in touch with me yesterday—and they're looking for blood. You should have come to me first, Matt. I could have adjusted the loan."

"That's all very well for you to say. It was hard enough keeping up the repayments last year. I lost half my fecking harvest. Rained out, so I was."

"I know. And you weren't the only one. I understand these things, Matt. Jesus, no better man." He leaned forward again, picked up the cigarette packet from force of habit then tossed it back on the desk. "But head office, now, that's a different kettle of fish. They're not farming men, the majority of 'em. They want to go by the letter; they want to recall the loan. All of it. They've given you thirty days, as of now."

The reality was beginning to sink in. Matt Sweetman was doing some rapid calculations in his head.

"Are you saying I've a month to find nearly twenty grand? Is that what you're saying?"

Doherty nodded. "Either that or the bank puts your land up for auction. I'm very sorry, Matt."

Sweetman's pallor had given way to red. He was seething with anger. "You know what you are, John? You're a fucking gombeenman, that's what you are."

"Now just a minute . . . "

"No, *you* 'just a minute'. You're talking about my bloody livelihood. You're out to ruin me."

"It's *not* me. It's—"

"No, it's 'head office'—the great, faceless head office. Ach, isn't it grand being able to hide behind your mammy's skirts. You fucking Jewish moneylender!"

"You were happy enough to take our money five years ago," Doherty, now also red in the face, countered. "There was nothing wrong with our money then."

"Ah, yes. That's typical gombeen talk. And I know all about it. My wife's people had experience of your sort. I'm going back to the Famine now, but nothing has changed I see. They ruined her family. They doled out loans right, left and centre; loans they knew could never be repaid. And then they took everything—just like you're doing now. You bastard!"

Matt Sweetman was on his feet, heading for the door.

"Matt, wait . . . "

"And you can stick your loan up your arse!"

He stalked out of the office and slammed the door hard. Customers queuing in the public area stared. He was already out on the busy main street when Doherty, out of breath, caught up. He took Sweetman by the arm.

"Take your dirty, money-grubbing paw off me!"

Doherty looked swiftly about him but kept his hand where it was.

"Matt, we have to talk."

"Fuck off."

"No, Matt, listen. Listen now. Walk a bit with me, will

you? I'm on your side."

"Like hell you are." Yet he allowed himself to be escorted down the street.

"There's something you should know, Matt. You didn't give me the chance to tell you back there. Jesus, I know how you must feel. But there's a way out of this mess. And it won't cost you a penny either."

"Hmph!"

"It's all to do with Orla—your daughter. You have to talk to her."

Twelve

"Damn and blast! A pox upon all assistant commissioners. May their daughters marry tinkers and their sons die of the Peruvian clap."

"Am I right in thinking you're a little upset, Blade?" Jack Macken asked. He set a tray of drinks down on the table in the library and tidied the cord of the telephone.

"No, Jack, I'm just passing the time of day. Of course I'm bloody-well upset. I've just been told to drop the O'Neill investigation and go back to Dublin in the morning."

His uncle passed a Scotch. "That's a bit sudden, isn't it? You've barely started."

"That's the whole point, Jack. I've hardly scratched the surface. I haven't a single thing, to be honest with you. In fact, I don't even know who the fuck Martin O'Neill *was*."

He swallowed half his whisky.

"I shouldn't be telling you this though. Don't let it go beyond these walls, okay?"

"Red-hot pincers applied to my private parts couldn't induce me to divulge a single word."

"Yeah, well let's hope for your sake it doesn't come to *that*, Jack. Christ, I honestly don't know what to do. How do you think it'll look? The Dundalk gardaí call me in to help them and next thing they know I've dumped it back in their laps the exact same way I found it."

"Surely not."

"I've fuck all, Jack. I don't know when or where O'Neill was born, or where he grew up. For all I know he could have been the deposed crown prince of Transylvania hiding from the tax collectors."

Jack Macken settled himself into an easy chair and nursed his drink.

"Since you've broached the subject anyway," he said, "you might as well go the whole hog. Do you want to tell me precisely what you've found out about old Martin? I do find it rather intriguing." His eyes twinkled. "There we were thinking that nothing ever happens in our little neck of the woods and now it seems we've been harbouring the Lord knows what. It goes to show: you can never judge people by appearances alone."

Blade refilled his glass and gave his uncle a resumé of what little the investigation had uncovered thus far. Jack allowed him to finish uninterrupted. He brooded quietly for a few moments then said: "I see what you mean. You couldn't hang a cat with that."

"You couldn't string up a dead mouse in an advanced state of decay with it!" Blade said angrily. "And that galls me, Jack; it really does. Call it professional pride if you want, but it goes against my nature to have to leave an inquiry like that."

"I understand. But what's so important about this new investigation? Can you tell me that?"

"I suppose you may as well know that as well." Blade told him of the robbery.

"I see. Now I won't pretend I'm as well up in these matters as I should be, but I'd have thought that murder took priority over manslaughter."

"It *is* murder."

"Really? But they didn't mean to kill the driver, only knock him unconscious."

"Same difference, Jack. We're talking about a felony here: armed robbery and an attempt to cause bodily harm. According to the law if you attempt to harm somebody and he ends up dying then that's murder."

"Hmm, I didn't know that. How many processors did they make off with?"

"According to Duffy it couldn't have been more than fifty thousand or thereabouts."

Jack whistled. "My goodness. That's a fortune."

"Chips? How?"

"Allow me to enlighten *you* now, my boy," Jack said. "You really must make an effort to keep abreast of these things. Take a leaf from your old uncle's book. You know that little machine I have upstairs? The Apple."

"Yes."

"It cost over two thousand pounds. But half of that was for the chip that drives it, the processor. Take that away and you'd be left with a lump of scrap metal and plastic. Agreed, it's a pretty expensive piece of equipment but most good computers are fitted with a chip that would cost you about five hundred pounds in the shop, were you to buy it singly."

Blade did a quick mental calculation.

"Jesus, can that be right? I make it twenty-five million!"

"The thieves wouldn't get anything near that on the black

market of course," Jack said. "But if they got even a fifth, then that's still five million pounds. A good night's work, you'll agree."

"So that's why Duffy's doing such a song and dance about it. It makes more sense now. Still, I can't help thinking that he could have had somebody else handle it. I've no great urge to go back to Dublin."

"That's what *I* said fifteen years ago, my boy, and I've never looked back. But I'll be sorry to see you go—you and Miss Sweetman. You've brightened up an old man's autumn years."

He toasted Blade and reached for the Scotch bottle.

"By Jesus, you've just given me an idea, Jack."

"I have?"

"Duffy didn't say anything about Sweetman. He'd assume she'd be coming back with me. Now, what if I left her to handle the O'Neill business alone? She'd be reporting back to me so I'd still know what's going on."

"Hmm."

"You don't think it's a good idea."

"I didn't say that, my boy. But d'you think Miss Sweetman is up to it? She's awfully young."

"Don't let that fool you, Jack. Sweetman's a lot tougher than she comes across. No, the more I think about it, the better it looks. Now, if she isn't out gallivanting with the local talent, I should get her at her hotel."

He reached for the phone.

Thirteen

Kidafane, mused Orla Sweetman, hasn't changed one little bit. Nor will it ever. Only a number of new cars parked on the main street suggested that the small village in north County Galway had entered a fresh millennium. The pubs and shops bore the same names—and the same paint, it seemed, in some cases—they'd had when Sweetman was a child. The church at the end of the street was completely unaltered, as was the office of the Credit Union fifty metres farther on.

She turned right at the crossroads and started along the narrow, winding road that led to the family farm.

There was no sign of life at the bungalow when she turned in at the gate. Not even Rusty, the family collie—who didn't recognize Orla any longer anyway. The door was open as usual. She'd given up talking to her parents about that. They were stuck in a time when every door in rural Ireland stood permanently open in welcome. The Sweetmans could not believe that that time was long flown; not even the horrific murder of a neighbouring farmer—an aged bachelor who'd been knifed in his sleep—could convince them otherwise.

Orla let herself in, headed for the kitchen, filled the kettle and placed it on the stove.

The pictures in the front room had remained unaltered

too. There was Matt, the eldest, at age fifteen, captaining the junior hurling team. Now he was a father, married and living in Toronto. Matt had "done well for himself", as Orla's father continually reminded everybody. Yet so had the Sweetmans' second daughter: Orla smiled on seeing again the black-and-white photograph of her attestation to full garda, taken at Templemore training barracks.

But not, she mused, as well as Fidelma. No, Fidelma had been accorded pride of place between the photographs of Pope John XXIII and John F Kennedy, the twin Saint Johns of Roman Catholic Ireland. Fidelma Sweetman looked out modestly from under the grey veil of her nun's habit. A Guardian of the Peace was secondary to a Bride of Christ in the parish of Kidafane.

The kettle was boiling. Orla was about to go to the kitchen when the front door opened. An elderly man, dressed in a work shirt, old corduroys and green wellingtons, wiped the soles of his boots on the mat.

"Daddy!" she called out happily and went to him.

If Matt Sweetman was pleased to see his daughter then he didn't show it. Rusty, at least, was more honest. The collie growled deep in his throat on sighting the visitor. Ears laid back on the head, tail limp, the dog brushed up against his master's leg. Matt Sweetman tapped him lightly with a palm.

"Shut up with your oul' nonsense now," he ordered. "To Orla he said: "So you're here. Will you be staying?"

"For a couple of days. How's Mammy?"

"She's grand. She's over with Mrs Kearns, helping out. She hasn't been well."

"Who? Mammy?"

"No, Mrs Kearns. It's the arthritis. She can't leave her bed, poor oul' divil."

"She's getting on. Would you like a cup of tea, Daddy? The kettle's just boiled."

"Yes. But no sugar. I'm not allowed any."

There had never been much show of affection between Orla and her father. But the same applied to all the household. To be charitable, Orla thought, they come from a different time, my parents; they're products of another way of life. And life hadn't been easy for Matt and Mary Sweetman. It would probably have been better if Matt *hadn't* inherited the few acres of land from his own father. He'd have taken the boat to England, just like his brothers, rather than continue the struggle to make a living from some of the poorest land in the county. The struggle had left no room for affection, let alone love.

He's a *good* man, Orla thought: the best there is. When she saw him like this, growing old and frail, suffering now from heart trouble and diabetes, she wanted to put her arms around him and hug him. Yet she knew how he'd react to that. He'd think her stupid and mushy, would be reinforced in his opinion that "the Dublin ways" had ruined his daughter.

"There's talk, Orla," he said after a few minutes.

"There always is. Who's been gossiping now?"

But Matt Sweetman wasn't smiling. "No, not that sort of talk. This is more serious. You've been asking questions over in Kilty."

Orla froze.

"Who told you that?"

"Never mind. It's true, isn't it?"

"That's garda business, Daddy. I'm not at liberty to discuss it."

Matt Sweetman set his mug of tea down on the table with a crash; some of it spilled onto the tablecloth.

"Would you listen to that! 'I'm not at liberty to discuss it'! Jesus, Mary and Joseph, what have I raised at all?"

"Please, Daddy—your heart."

"To hell with my heart! I've never taken cheek from any of yiz, and I'm not about to start now. So don't play the madam with me. You're not too old that I can't still take a strap to you." Rusty growled from his basket in the corner.

"Daddy, please. You know I'm not allowed to discuss a case. Not even with you. I would if I could but I can't. Please try to understand that."

This seemed to mollify her father; his face lost some of its redness. Then Orla saw that, behind the anger, there was something else.

Fear.

"What is it?" she asked. "There's something very wrong, isn't there? You're never like this."

Matt Sweetman shut his eyes. He looked more vulnerable and frail than ever.

"They're threatening me," he said softly.

"Who are?"

"I can't say."

She went to him and knelt beside his chair. She was about to take his gnarled hand in hers, but thought better of it.

"Daddy, you have to tell me."

"The Boys. The Boys are threatening me."

The capital letter was unmistakable. Here in north County Galway they were a long way from Ulster. There was no paramilitary activity in these parts. That, at least, was the public perception. Yet Orla knew that Republicanism was not a movement that confined itself to Northern Ireland. There were no official figures available but it was widely known that almost one third of members of illegal organizations were recruited in the South. Orla had grown up in a staunchly nationalist community, had heard of young men training with weapons in sparsely populated parts of the countryside. She knew that "the Boys" was a euphemism for the IRA. She knew too that you antagonized the Boys at your peril. Years before, the fiancé of a girl she knew had disappeared; the talk at the time was that he'd "crossed" the Boys in some way.

"But why, Daddy?" she asked. "Why should they be threatening you? What have you done?"

Her father opened his eyes and looked at her in an odd way.

"It's not what *I've* done, Orla. It's *you*. Listen, I don't know what's going on. All I can say is that you're poking your nose into something that should be left alone, that's all."

Martin O'Neill. A harmless, retired schoolmaster, born in a tiny village in County Galway. Murdered at the age of eighty-two in another town, ostensibly by a hit-squad of Ulster Loyalists. So why were the IRA, through her father, warning Orla Sweetman off the investigation? It didn't add up.

"I'll have to report this," she said.

He was angry again, and Orla feared for his heart.

"Will you for heaven's sake listen to me!" he shouted. "Drop it, Orla. Whatever it is, drop it. It doesn't concern *you*—it doesn't concern *me*. Don't get involved in something that probably started before you were born. God bless us and save us—for all I know, before *I* was born. Let those people fight it out between themselves."

She was silent. Then said: "Did they threaten your life?"

"They threatened my livelihood, Orla—and I don't know which is worse. They're out to ruin me—and your mother too; let's not forget about *her*. Now: will you promise me you'll forget all about this, go back up to Dublin, and pretend it never happened?"

She didn't reply in words. How could she? Her father was asking the impossible. She nodded, and patted his shoulder.

"Will I warm that up for you?" she asked.

He smiled gratefully and passed the mug.

Fourteen

Frank Naughton was what Blade called "a dignified gentleman". He was older—late fifties—than Blade had expected; he'd assumed that the chief executive of a semiconductor plant would be much younger; such had been his previous experience of that sort of enterprise. Yet Naughton's office suggested a mind that lived very much in the present. Blade smiled knowingly on recognizing the application of the dictates of Feng Shui: not a single sharp edge or indeed right angle was present in the furniture; Naughton's desk was a glorious expanse of gently contoured pine; it called out to be touched. He sat with his back to the wall with no objects above head level, and looked out through a broad window that framed the poplars ringing Mnemos's patch. The chair he indicated to Blade was pine too, and its cushions gripped the body in all the right places. Naughton knew his stuff.

"You've already been to the scene of the crime, superintendent," he said.

It wasn't a question. No beating about the bush here, Blade thought.

"I have, sir. There wasn't much I found out that I didn't already know."

"Tragic about the driver. I hardly knew him, but I'm told he was a good man."

"How long had he been with Menemos, sir?"

"That's 'nemmos', superintendent. The 'm' is silent, as in mnemonic. As a matter of fact, they both have the same root. You see, Mnemostyne was the Greek goddess of memory. And we began by manufacturing *memory* chips. It was my daughter who came up with the name; she's studying Classics at Trinity. Very clever, wouldn't you agree?"

"I would." The proud father, Blade thought.

"It's a useful name as well, within a marketing context. Once you see it, or hear it, you're not likely to forget it."

"In other words, sir, it's memorable."

Naughton seemed to enjoy the weak joke, though Blade guessed he'd heard it and others like it countless times.

"Who knew about the weekly delivery? Apart from you and your staff."

"Well, the cargo people at the airport, of course—and our customers. But they'd only know about arrangements at the other end, not here."

"And the shipment was always at the same time and the same day?"

"Certainly not. It was always on either a Monday or Tuesday, but we made sure to vary the times. Anything between six and ten in the evening."

"I keep wondering about one thing, sir. Maybe you can explain it for me."

"I'll try. . . ."

"Why didn't you use Securicor or some other outfit? From what I gather your van hadn't any protection at all."

"That's easily answered. We didn't wish to attract attention to ourselves. As far as the outside world was concerned the two men in the van might have been engineers making a call. Nobody would have guessed that the van carried such a valuable load. That's how we've done things right from the beginning. It was a calculated risk." He smiled ruefully. "I suppose we're paying for it now."

"You won't be much out of pocket though, if we can't retrieve the chips. The insurance'll shell out, won't they?"

"No, superintendent, I'm afraid they won't. You see, we weren't insured."

Blade was as a man pole-axed.

"Just a minute, Mr Naughton. How much was that shipment worth?"

"On today's market? Twenty-five million. No, more."

Blade made a mental note to congratulate Jack Macken on his uncanny insight into the value of computer chips.

"Are you telling me, Mr Naughton, that that shipment was worth more than twenty-five million quid—and it wasn't insured?"

"That's correct."

"But you're going to lose a fortune if we don't recover it!"

Naughton swivelled slowly three hundred and sixty degrees in his chair; when he returned to face Macken he was smiling.

"Oh, we'll lose money all right. But not as much as you think. Those chips can't be sold, superintendent—at least, not to bona fide companies. Each and every one has its own serial number, you see. Only it's stamped on twice. You can see one of the numbers with the naked eye but the other one you can't. You see, that other number was engraved using an electron microscope. You can't see it with the naked eye—

you can't even see it under a magnifying glass. But it's there all the same. And it can't be altered. Not unless you go to an awful lot of trouble and expense. I won't tell you how it's done either. That's a trade secret."

"I won't pry either, sir, because I'm sure it'd go over my head in any case. But let's see if I understand this properly. You didn't insure the chips because you knew they couldn't be sold to anyone else. Am I right so far?"

"Yes. And also the insurance premiums we were quoted would have eaten into our profit margins. We're a relatively young company, superintendent, in a field that's changing not from year to year but from month to month. We've no way of knowing if we'll even be in business this time next year. So you understand that we have to make our killing while we can."

Blade thought the metaphor grossly inappropriate, given the circumstances. After all, a man had died during the transport of Naughton's precious cargo. He studied the managing director, and wondered about the man's priorities: what was more important to him, the loss of his chips or the death of a van driver? He hadn't detected much sympathy for the dead man. Then again, Naughton didn't seem too upset about the robbery either. A cool one perhaps. Blade decided to reserve judgement for the time being.

"You didn't," he said, "use a security vehicle for transporting the processors because you didn't want to call attention to the shipments."

"That's right. It would have been like painting a sign on the side saying 'Here be booty'."

"All the same, sir, that was quite a gamble."

"I know. And it looks like somebody called our bluff, eh?"

"Indeed. Let me put a question to you, Mr Naughton. What do *you* think is going to happen now? I'm asking this because your business is unfamiliar territory to me. I know very, very little about it—and even less about computer theft. It's not my department."

Naughton nodded slowly; he seemed to be assessing Macken. Then he said something surprising.

"Did you know I asked for you specially, superintendent? Your reputation precedes you, you see. Plus the fact that your commissioner and I know each other very well. He agreed at once."

So that's it, Blade thought; I might have known. He was aware that Duffy had a wide circle of friends and acquaintances. Top men in top positions. Blade's assignment to the investigation was beginning to make sense. He swore inwardly, thinking of Duffy's high-handedness. Fuck him, anyway; I should be with Peter now, throwing a line into Lough Bray. Instead . . .

But Naughton was speaking again. "I think we'll be hearing from the raiders very soon," he said. "They'll be offering to sell the chips back to us. Isn't that what *you'd* do, superintendent, if you were in their shoes?"

"Yes, I suppose it is. And will you be buying, sir?"

"If you don't catch the culprits, yes. What choice do we have? We'll lose a great deal of money of course. I wouldn't like to say how much but it could be as much as ten per cent of the market value of the chips."

"Two and a half million pounds. Your shareholders won't like it."

"They certainly won't." He caressed the soft contours of the desk, as a man in love would caress his partner's skin. "So what are your plans, superintendent? You can be sure of the cooperation of myself and everybody here. Anything you wish to see, anybody you wish to talk to, and we're completely at your disposal."

"Thank you, sir. I'll take you up on that. Could we start with the factory itself?"

"Of course. But don't expect anything resembling a factory. I think you'll find it's more like a laboratory."

Blade had once toyed with the idea of becoming an astronaut. Not in the recent past: he'd been fifteen at the time. He'd been enthralled by the idea of donning a spacesuit and riding a rocket into the cosmos, the sensation of weightlessness, taking a god's-eye view of the earth and the other planets.

Now he was experiencing something akin to the reality, and it didn't match the dream. It wasn't quite a spacesuit but felt like one. It was white and spotless with an integrated helmet and visor. The boots isolated you from any remaining contact with the outside world: you felt as though you were walking on soft cushions. It was eerie.

Naughton, similarly attired, conducted him through an airlock that led into a brightly lit room. It was spotless. Literally, Naughton assured him; not a speck of dust could be tolerated here. White-suited men and women sat at white benches, eyes fixed to microscopes, fingers nimbly working with components too small for the eye to see. All were young.

"We may look like a small outfit, superintendent," Naughton said as he led Macken past his employees, "but don't let that fool you. We're the second-largest processor producer in the country—and one of the largest in the world. Four out of every ten Pentiums in the world were manufactured here."

"Those are the chips, are they?"

"That's correct."

"But you make no secret about it?"

Naughton laughed.

"Why should we? We're not a top-secret defence organization or anything like that. This is, as I say, only a factory."

Or, Blade thought, a laboratory, as you said as well. He didn't much care for the place; there was something unsettling about the silence in which the workforce operated, almost as automatons. He'd have preferred an old-fashioned sweat shop, with its racket of machines and a blaring radio tuned to 2FM.

A phone rang. It was for Naughton. He listened, frowned, and replaced the receiver.

"Well, superintendent," he said, "things are moving more quickly than I expected. They've made contact."

It was an extortion note—though unlike any Blade had ever seen. It wasn't written using cut-out letters affixed with gum. It wasn't even written on paper. The note had dropped into Mnemos's electronic letterbox; it appeared now as a short email on a computer screen in the office of Frank Naughton's secretary. Not surprisingly, the sender hadn't identified himself.

"They want two and a half million, Mr Naughton," she said.

He nodded and read the message. Blade joined him at the monitor. He read.

Our apologies for the van driver. We did not mean that to happen. We have the chips and it will cost you two and half million pounds (£2.5m) for their return. Do not on any account involve the gardai. If you do then we will destroy the chips. A second message with instructions will follow.

"Short and to the point," Blade said. "And you were right about the amount."

Naughton grunted, eyes still riveted to the screen. Blade could see he was grinding his teeth.

"You know about these things, sir; I don't. Can we trace who sent that message?"

Naughton turned, frowning.

"That's exactly what I was thinking. Either we're dealing with a complete amateur—or somebody who really knows his stuff. Of course you can trace an email address, superintendent. This isn't like buying a stamp and popping your letter in a postbox."

"You'd better explain, sir."

"To send an email you go through a service provider. These are people who rent the service to you. Then you pay for every time you use the service—for example, to surf the net or send an email—and that's charged to your bank account or credit card."

"So all we have to do is get in touch with this service provider? It's as easy as that?"

"It is. They'll have a record of the exact time of transmission." He turned to his secretary. "Eileen, I want you to get onto Eircom, Indigo, Ireland on Line and the rest of them. Find out if any of their customers sent this."

She applied herself to the task.

Blade was thoughtful. "What if they're using a stolen card?"

"Unlikely," Naughton said. "The owner would have reported it, maybe in a couple of hours." He gestured at the screen. "These people would have to open an account, get an address and a password. All right, you can do that very quickly nowadays. But I ask you, superintendent: isn't that a very stupid way of doing things? If the owner cancels his card then that botches up their whole operation."

"It does," Blade agreed. "And I see what you mean about them either being a bunch of wankers or very clever operators."

"Mr Naughton . . . ?" It was Eileen.

"Yes?"

"They went through Chorus."

"Hmm. That's our own service provider, superintendent. Well, do they know who it is, Eileen?"

"Yes. It's us."

"What do you mean?"

"Ehh, it's like this, Mr Naughton," Eileen said a bit sheepishly, "we seem to have sent that email to ourselves."

Sweetman had thought it preferable not to meet Macken at Harcourt Square. He'd suggested his favourite pub in Purcell Street but she'd declined, preferring the more sedate ambiance of the Westbury Hotel, off Grafton Street. He was already enjoying a coffee in the lounge when she arrived, some thirty minutes late.

"Sorry, Blade, I couldn't get parking. And there was no end of hold-ups. There's repair works on the M4 again."

"Hmm. That's what they get for building a motorway on a bloody bog. Coffee?"

"No, tea'll do grand. My nerves are jumpy enough as it is."

She related the events at her father's farm. Blade took the threats even more seriously than she'd done.

"I don't like that one little bit, Sweetman. No, I don't like it at all. Are you sure your dad had it right though? It was the O'Neill business?"

"He didn't mention names, but what else could it be? It's the only thing I'm working on at the moment."

"That's true. Remind me, Sweetman: Did we make inquiries about anything else in Galway? Maybe something of a local nature? You never know. It happened to me once before. I was investigating this guy who was involved in a robbery and somebody else thought I was after *him*. Stupid, because we put the two of them away in the end. If the second guy had just lain low then we'd never have been onto him."

"No. No, I'm sure it's not like that, Blade. You were there. We only asked about O'Neill." She frowned. "You don't think there are *two* Martin O'Neills, do you? A case of mistaken identity?"

"Christ, Sweetman, one is enough to be going on with. If we could get the story on *him* we'd be laughing." He finished his coffee and wiped his lips with a napkin. "Now, let me get this straight. Somebody—'the Boys' as your dad calls them—puts pressure on the bank manager who, in turn, puts the screws on your dad. Am I right?"

She nodded.

"Then I'd start with that bank manager if I were you. Find out what he knows. Give him a taste of his own medicine. Ask him—"

"I can't do that, Blade."

That took him aback. This wasn't at all like the Sweetman he knew. He studied her, looking for clues. Couldn't find any. He felt as though a portcullis had dropped between them.

"And why not?" he asked cautiously.

"Because I don't want my father involved any more than he is. It'd kill him. If I start questioning the bank manager who knows what that might lead to. I can't risk it."

"I understand that, Sweetman. But you know yourself you can't give in to threats like that. We'd never be able to do our jobs if we did."

"So what do you suggest I do? Give up the inquiry?"

"Certainly not. I'm as determined as you are to get to the bottom of it. But I'm a little worried, Sweetman. My guess is that this goes beyond anything local. Look at it this way: somebody knew we were asking questions in Galway, and that same person knew those questions were connected to a murder investigation in County Louth. So unless he's Padre Pio and can be in two places at once—"

"That's not nice. You shouldn't say things like that."

"Sorry if I was disrespectful. What I'm saying, Sweetman, is that whoever's putting the frighteners on your family knows what's going on in several parts of the country. He knows about you, your background and your movements."

"Janey, are you saying it's somebody on the Force?"

"No, I'm not. But don't rule it out. Keep an open mind. All I'm saying is that this somebody is clearly in a very powerful position. And you're not, Sweetman. You may be carrying a deadly firearm in that handbag of yours but you're still only one woman."

She frowned.

"Ah, don't get me wrong now. I know you're tough, but I'd feel better about it if we assigned a second detective to work with you. Failing that, I'd sleep better if there was a uniform around."

"A man of course."

"Well . . . yes."

"Thanks for the vote of confidence, Blade."

"Ah, come on, Sweetman! You're being unrealistic now. You don't know what you're up against."

"I think I can handle it perfectly well myself, sir."

"And let's not have that bloody 'sir' bit. I know all too

well what that 'sir' of yours means."

Sweetman crossed her legs and arms, propping a fist under her chin. She looked him in the eye.

"Let's see if I understand this properly," she said coldly. "Are you ordering me to accept a bodyguard?"

"For fuck's sake, Sweetman—" He lowered his voice as a well-dressed and well-groomed couple turned to stare. "No, nobody's ordering anybody to do anything."

"No, you're just being patronizing." Her voice had risen too. More faces turned.

"Well, to hell with you, Detective Sergeant Sweetman! If that's what you think then *don't* take a uniform along."

"Right. I won't." She stood up. "Thanks for the tea, Blade. If you need to reach me, you have the number of my mobile."

Her haste to leave had surprised him. There were many more matters he'd wanted to discuss.

"Where are you going?" he asked.

"Back to get a few things at the flat. Then I'm off to Galway again in the morning. I'll be in touch."

Blade watched her go. He knew that both were right and that the row had been unnecessary. He'd mentioned at the beginning of their conversation an experience he'd had many years before. He'd told Sweetman only half the truth. The thief had been small fry compared with the other individual his investigation had drawn out of the woodwork. It was true: he'd put both men away for life, but he'd almost lost his own in the process.

Now he feared for Sweetman. He knew her to be a very level-headed young woman who could moreover keep that level head in a real emergency. He also knew that she could be excruciatingly sensitive when her abilities were called into question. She resented what she saw as male chauvinism.

Had he overstepped the mark? He didn't think so. What mattered though was that Sweetman thought so.

He vowed to keep in touch as frequently as possible—while not appearing to meddle.

But crossing the river Liffey on a tightrope was, he decided, an easier proposition.

He walked back to Harcourt Square, taking the short cut through St Stephen's Green. The park was thronged on this warm August afternoon. Blade heard many languages: mostly Spanish and French from the lips of Dublin's annual influx of residential students. The Germans, he noted, were much in evidence this year too. Four young people seated on a bench took him back to another afternoon, one spent with Sweetman in Carlingford. Again, three men and a woman. But they were arguing about money—he understood enough of the language to know this. They were complaining about Dublin's high prices, and debating the wisdom of moving out of the capital and heading for County Kerry.

Farther along the path Blade stopped at another bench. Two old men sat there in the shade of an elm, a chessboard placed between them. Their game was in the opening stages of play. He thought of Jack Macken.

He moved on. He was at the southeast end of the park. He paused to look at the group of bronze statues that served as a reminder of the devastating Famine. On the grass close by, several groups of people were picnicking. Some were sunbathing. Blade paused again on noticing two girls who'd removed their brassieres. We're turning into real Europeans, he thought with a smile of approval.

"Blade!"

He turned. It was Assistant Commissioner Duffy, out of uniform for a change, dressed now in a linen suit.

"That's against the law, isn't it?" Blade said, nodding at the topless girls.

"I won't complain if you won't," Duffy said. "It's too nice a day. But I'm glad I ran into you, Blade. I was just on my way to the Shelbourne. Would you like to join me?"

"No sir, I won't, thanks. I wanted to check a couple of things at the Square."

"Hmm. Have you spoken to Frank Naughton?"

Blade didn't like this. St Stephen's Green on a sunny afternoon didn't strike him as being the most appropriate place to discuss an investigation. And not with Duffy. Not that he didn't trust the assistant commissioner; Duffy had stuck by him in the past, had consistently taken the professional, as well as the fair, line. He would almost—if not quite—trust Duffy with his life.

Yet Naughton had made it clear that he'd used his friendship with Duffy to influence the choice of investigating officer. That rankled. And not least because the holiday atmosphere of the park reminded Blade keenly that he ought to be enjoying his own leave of absence.

"I'll have my report on your desk by this evening, sir," he said curtly.

Duffy hesitated. Then he mumbled something resembling approval, and was off to enjoy whatever-it-was in the grand hotel directly opposite the memorial to the Famine victims.

Some fifteen minutes later Blade was at his desk again. He missed having Sweetman's presence in the office. He liked her feedback, her way of pulling him down to earth again at those times when his enthusiasm threatened to get the better of his judgement. He even, he admitted to himself, enjoyed her criticism.

Blade swept a space clear and began making notes. It wasn't long, however, before he came to the conclusion that he was out of his depth with Mnemos. Armed robbery with violence was no stranger to him. He could run through the modi operandi of known criminals and maybe find something to follow up on. There might even be forensic evidence from the van—and certainly from the gas canister used in the raid. Progress was possible in that quarter—the physical, tactile, quarter.

It was the business with the email that would prove sticky. He'd definitely need expert help there. Blade made a note: *Talk to Humphrey Bell.*

He made another note and circled it a number of times. It read: *Inside job?*

It seemed the obvious inference to draw. Somebody had known about the deliveries, the times, the route. They'd known the black-market value of the processors as well, could demand a price for their return exactly commensurate with Frank Naughton's own valuation. That person had also been able to use Mnemos's own password to send the email. How secure, Blade asked himself, was a password? He'd quiz Humphrey on that one.

Yet something else was nagging him. The old chess players

in the park had recalled Jack's words two nights before.

My guess, for what it's worth, is that somebody is attempting to lure you into a game that goes one level higher than the one you imagine you're playing. I would say that that somebody is a clever strategist, and that he's sacrificing an important piece at the start of play, with the aim of winning a greater prize when the game is advanced.

It would have been much simpler for the raider to phone Mnemos with his demands. Having seen Naughton and his high-tech enterprise, Blade was convinced he'd most likely have the very latest type of telephone switchboard, one that would automatically log the caller's number. But if the raider were using a call box then that information would be practically useless. Blade would have chosen that method.

So why the convoluted route; why the dangerous gambit of calling attention to yourself if you were indeed a man "on the inside"? Was somebody else playing a dangerous game, drawing Blade onto a higher level? He couldn't even begin to speculate why.

His phone rang.

"DS Flynn here, sir. I'm glad I caught you, so I am."

"Yes, Paddy. What have you got for me?"

"Well, sir, the lads in Malahide found something this morning that might have a bearing on the chip van."

Blade turned in his chair and consulted the map on his wall. The coastal town of Malahide lies to the north of Dublin. It is about six miles from the airport.

"Go on," he coaxed.

"It's a big van, a Hiace. Burnt out. It might be the one the raiders used. We got that much from the co-driver. He swears it was a Hiace.”

“Hmm. I’m surprised he’d even have noticed that, Paddy. But I suppose little details stick in your mind when you’re up against it.”

“Apparently he’s a bit of a motor freak, sir.”

“I see. Was there a reg?”

“There was, only it’s fake. But the chassis number matches one that was nicked in Finglas on Sunday.”

“Anything else, Paddy? No chance of prints I suppose?”

“They’re working on it, sir, but they think it’s unlikely.”

Or next to impossible, Blade thought. Burn out a vehicle you use in a robbery and you burn any evidence that might connect you to that vehicle.

But the site of the burning might be important. There was also the Finglas element: it could place the raiders’ stamping ground on Dublin’s north side.

“If Duffy asks, I’m in Malahide,” he told the detective sergeant.

“Fair enough, sir.”

“Oh, and if he wants to get me this evening, tell him I’ll be at my uncle’s place.”

“Right. Er, where’s that, sir?”

“Ravensdale, County Louth. He has the number.”

And that, Blade thought, is only an hour from Malahide. He’d weighed up this investigation against that into Martin O’Neill’s death, and had concluded that Mnemos took second place. Duffy could like it or lump it; Macken was staying close to Carlingford.

If only, he thought, to keep a tutelary—if discreet—eye on Orla Sweetman.

Sixteen

The wreck of the Hiace reminded Blade of any number of burned out vehicles he'd encountered during his career as an army officer. Whoever had torched it had been thorough: not even the colour of the paintwork could be identified.

"What I don't understand," Blade told the garda inspector from Malahide, "is how nobody spotted the blaze sooner. Or smelt it for that matter. The tyres would've stunk to high heaven."

"You'd think so, wouldn't you, sir. Only there weren't any tyres to burn. These boys were clever: they took the wheels off before they set fire to the van."

Clever isn't the word, Blade mused. You can tell a lot from tyres, even burnt ones. Most times the fire destroyed them utterly, but he'd known fires to burn out, leaving a portion of the tyre unscathed: the portion that rested on the ground. Tests could determine where the vehicle had been in the recent past, perhaps from the presence of an unusual type of stone lodged in a tread, little things like that.

The men who'd torched the van had driven it into a field on the outskirts of Malahide, far from the villas and other expensive homes that made up much of that prosperous community. Fires were a common sight in the vicinity at this time of year; farmers burned stubble in the wake of harvesting.

One more fire would not have attracted notice, and certainly not when the van was out of sight of the road, behind the tall hedgerows.

"So what do you make of it, inspector?" Blade asked as he looked into the rear of the wreck.

"Well, we found two other sets of tyre marks so they must have used two cars."

"Cars? Not vans?"

"Yes sir, we're certain of that. The tracks were narrow."

"I suppose it'd be asking too much to get a make on those."

"It would. We haven't had a drop of rain in days now; the ground's as hard as a rock." He pointed to the gate that led into the field. "They must have hid the van here the night before last, and then come back yesterday. They'd have transferred the boxes into the cars—and the wheels as well. Then they doused the whole shebang with petrol and set her alight."

"Hmm. Who found it?"

"The man who owns the field. He was away in Dublin at the time. Got back only this morning."

"That was very convenient."

"I know, sir. That's why we thought they might be local lads. We don't have all that much crime in these parts but we do have our share of tearaways all the same. But we've made inquiries in that quarter and we've ruled them out."

As had Blade Macken. This, he suspected, wasn't the work of common thieves. This was an operation planned and executed at a high level.

"What's the word on Finglas?" he said. "I know the van was stolen there. Have you followed that up?"

"We have. Finglas is another story altogether. That's bandit country over there, superintendent. It wouldn't be the first vehicle stolen and used in a raid."

No indeed, Blade thought. He knew that Finglas contained some of the least salubrious areas of the city, housing estates where only the toughest Guards ventured—and never, ever on foot.

He was inspecting the blackened interior of the van. It was a mess of fused metal and surfaces that gleamed like obsidian. There was nothing recognizable.

Yet an aspect of the floor of the van troubled him. It wasn't quite level, as you'd expect had the van been completely empty prior to the torching. There was a shallow bed of charred matter, pitted as the craters of the moon. Plastic.

"I want that removed, inspector," he said. "All of it, if possible. Have it sent to Forensics in the Park."

"What do think it could be, sir?"

"I haven't the foggiest," Blade answered truthfully.

Jack Macken was taking the air on the bench in front of the house when Blade drew up. He joined his uncle. They sat in silence for a minute or two, enjoying the lingering warmth of the afternoon. Somewhere beyond the trees two sheep bleated to each other across a distance. The first swallows of evening had appeared in the sky; one fast-flying bird attempted to drive a rival from its insect-rich territory. Jack lit a pipe.

"It's beautiful, isn't it, Blade?"

"Mmm."

"Still missing the smokes?"

"If you must know, yes. Thanks for reminding me."

"You're doing well, my boy. Keep it up." He puffed contentedly on his pipe.

"I'd like to ask you something again, Jack. You seem to be well up in computers and the like."

"Not as much as I'd wish to be, but if I can be of help . . . "

Blade told him of his visit to Mnemos and of the curious demand note sent by electronic mail. Jack listened gravely, nodding at intervals.

"I called to see Humphrey Bell," Blade said. "He's in charge of the IBM we have up in the Park—you know, where we store all our records. He wasn't much help, though. No, that's unfair. I'm sure he knew what he was talking about but it was all a load of gobbledegook to me. I came out of there as much in the dark as when I went in."

"I see. Well, try me. What's the problem?"

"Right. Supposing you want to send an email using somebody else's account, how would you go about finding out his password? Can it be done?"

"Of course. Every code can be cracked. But are you certain somebody used the same account? It's relatively simple to fake an email address."

"No, I asked Naughton about that. Someone had genuinely used the Mnemos account."

"Hmm. That makes it a little more difficult. But not that much. All you need is time or, failing that, a bit of luck."

"Explain."

"I shall do my best, my boy. Most email passwords use seven or eight letters; any more and they're hard to remember. And most people tend to use somebody's name, maybe one of their children's names, or that of a fictional character. Scrooge or Pickwick or something along those lines."

"So the possibilities are endless."

"That's what you'd think, isn't it? But it doesn't work that way in practice. If you're clever then you can make a shrewd guess as to which name a person chooses. Try his wife's name. Or his favourite daughter's, as I say. Or even the name of his mistress. Come to think of it, that might be a better bet. You see, Blade, he can't write it down so he can't afford to forget it. That's why you don't get many people using Tsychoalu or Kruplemsh."

"And what the fuck are *they*, Jack, if you'll pardon my Spanish?"

"I just made them up. And if you were to ask me to repeat them in five minutes' time I couldn't. No, people tend to stick to the familiar. Unless, of course, they've something important to hide. In that case they'll choose from the whole ASCII range of characters."

"Askey?"

"That's short for American Standard Code for Information Interchange. All computer systems use it. Now, ASCII includes all the letters of the alphabet, small letters and capitals, so that's fifty-two letters in all. So if you have a password of six letters then an attacker has—"

"An attacker?"

"That's what they call a code-breaker these days. Anyway, an attacker has less chance of breaking that code as you or I have of picking the six winning numbers in the lottery."

"About fifty million to one."

"Probably far greater odds than that, Blade, if it's seven

letters. Off the top of my head, I'd say multiply that by five and you'd be closer. But we've only started. If Naughton used the entire ASCII range of characters he'd have included the numbers as well: nought to nine. That makes sixty-two possibilities. Then there are the punctuation marks. So add, shall we say, another thirty. Have you any idea how long it would take to decrypt a password of ten characters, using the fastest search engine available today? One that can make one million attempts at decryption per second?"

"I've a nasty feeling you're going to tell me, Jack."

"About twenty-six thousand years."

"You're not serious."

"Never more so. That's the reason many governments are trying to muzzle encryption programmers. They're worried that such people can have too much power."

"I don't blame them. So Humphrey Bell was right—though I didn't understand one tenth of what he was telling me to-day. Thanks for explaining it in plain English, Jack."

"My pleasure."

Blade fell silent then, thinking, as the sky began to redden in the west and rooks, black and raucous, settled in the oaks and chestnuts of his uncle's estate. Rooks in the treetops, castles in the air.

Again he had the unsettling feeling that somebody was playing games with him. It would have been much simpler and more straightforward for that somebody to have telephoned Naughton with his demands. Instead he'd gone to enormous lengths and taken a foolish risk. Blade had no doubt now that it was an inside job. The staff of Mnemos merited investigation; he'd have one or two of the lads at

Harcourt Square look into it. Discreetly. There were employment records, perhaps even police records. No one need know of the inquiry. He'd agreed with Naughton that there'd be no garda involvement; ostensibly the deal would be conducted between Naughton and the raiders.

So there was little he could do before contact was made again. His thoughts returned to the vexing question of Martin O'Neill. There'd been no word from Sweetman. He considered calling her but decided against it. He'd give her some breathing space.

"Any word," Jack said suddenly, "from Miss Sweetman?"

"You read my thoughts, Jack. No, she said she doesn't want to bother me with that other business. She wants to handle it by herself."

"She seems very young to me, though, to be taking on all that responsibility."

"Orla's a lot tougher than you think."

"So you told me. Very pretty too. You haven't ever . . . ?"

"*No*, Jack, I haven't."

"Hmm. *I'd* certainly have tested the waters there."

"I know you would've, you old goat." He stood up. "Listen, I did some shopping in Dundalk. Nothing fancy, but I can throw a chicken salad together. Hungry?"

"As a homeless tapeworm. PG Wodehouse."

"Cute," Blade said. He went to the car and returned with a bag of groceries. The phone rang. It was Linda Doyle of Forensics. Agitated.

"The canister's disappeared, superintendent."

Macken had to do a mental somersault. He'd been concentrating on Frank Naughton's mysterious email, to the neglect of the one, tactile, piece of evidence they'd recovered from the Mnemos van: the murder weapon.

"You're sure about that, Linda?"

"Very. Michael ran some tests on it yesterday and swears he put it away safely under lock and key. But he might be mistaken. We're a bit understaffed at the moment—the holidays, you know—and he's under a lot of pressure."

"I see. When did you notice it was missing?"

"Just now."

"Who was there today? Apart from the usual people."

"That's just the problem, superintendent. We'd no end of visitors. Prize-giving day."

Blade cursed. He knew the form, had been present at garda headquarters on several occasions when the commissioner presented awards and decorations earned for distinguished service in the line of duty. The place would have been thronged with media people, as well as the spouses and other relatives of the men and women who represented the Republic's finest law enforcers.

But, he asked himself, who'd have the neck to swipe something from right under the noses of the cream of the gardaí? That someone would have to be very, very clever indeed.

The same someone who'd cracked Naughton's password and masterminded the raid.

Seventeen

Thursday morning found Orla Sweetman at the garda station in Tuam. The superintendent gave her a small room to herself, with a phone, and telephone directories that covered all areas of the country. A cup of tea—the first of many that would materialize at regular intervals—appeared on the table in front of her, accompanied by a Jacob's Club Milk bar. She thanked the officer and he smiled pleasantly. The detective sergeant from Dublin was "one of our own".

Orla uncapped her ballpoint, reached for a sheet of paper and began to make notes.

She wrote a date at the top of the sheet: 10 July 1917; then another—6 August 2000—at the bottom. Eighty-three years, a considerable lifetime. Now she would attempt to account for those years. She took her notebook from her handbag, turned to the relevant entries, and transcribed some of the data to her "chart".

Martin O'Neill had taught at St Kevin's Primary School, Newry, from 1954 until his retirement in 1979 at the age of sixty-two, and moved to Carlingford. He'd married a girl named Margaret Donovan in 1960, and they'd produced a son, James, in 1964. Margaret had drowned thirteen years later. There'd been nothing suspect about that death; Orla had checked the records in Dundalk.

But that left thirty-seven years unaccounted for. From 1917 until 1954 the life of Martin O'Neill was a blank. Sweetman had tried to reconstruct that life, beginning with the year of O'Neill's birth, but had come up with nothing. She decided now to work backwards instead, from the time O'Neill began teaching in Newry.

She tried a number in Carlingford. No answer; Jim O'Neill wasn't at his father's cottage. Her backtracking would have to be put on hold for the moment.

The next call she made was to the Register of Births, Deaths and Marriages in Joyce House, Lombard Street, Dublin. She asked the clerk to ring back with the information. He did, some twenty minutes later.

"There doesn't appear to be any record, detective sergeant."

"None?"

"We have a John O'Neill, born in County Galway in nineteen seventeen, but there's no mention of a Martin. Are you sure about the name?"

"Yes. Ehh, this John O'Neill . . . did he have any other Christian names?" It was a faint hope.

"Let me see. Yes: John Patrick Mary."

"Mary?"

"That's what it says here. Lovely handwriting they had in those days."

"Hmm. Thanks for trying anyway."

"No problem, detective sergeant. Give us a ring again if we can be of any more assistance."

So Martin O'Neill hadn't even been born. Not, at least, according to official records.

Orla tried Jim O'Neill again. This time she was successful.

"Mr O'Neill, do you happen to know where your father taught before he came to Newry?"

"In Dublin. That's all I know. Why do you ask?"

"I'll tell you when I see you, sir. Are you in Carlingford this evening?"

"No, I'm away to Belfast. I'm seeing Dr Brophy."

"Your psychiatrist."

Shit. She hadn't been thinking, had been correcting one of her notes. The words had slipped out. Sweetman bit her lip in annoyance.

There was a pause on the other end of the line. "How did you know that?"

"A little bird told me."

"Detective sergeant, I don't like you making inquiries about me behind my back." He sounded very irritated. "But yes, you're right. Except Dr Brophy wouldn't be the man I usually see. He's a hypnotherapist; my doctor referred me to him."

"I honestly didn't mean to pry, sir. It just came up."

"It doesn't matter. Forget it. Anyhow, he's going to try regression therapy."

Then O'Neill's tone changed with a rapidity that surprised Sweetman.

"I'm a little on edge, sergeant, to be honest with you. I've never done anything like this before."

"I'm sure you'll be grand, sir." She meant it.

She hung up. O'Neill had sounded very nervous. And why wouldn't he? It's not every day of the week that somebody probes deep into your past. Orla would have hesitated as well. But here she was, probing into the past of another. And getting nowhere. It was like chasing a ghost in a graveyard.

Another phone call. This time to a contact at the Department of Education in Marlborough Street, Dublin.

"Brian? It's Orla Sweetman. Yeah, I'm fine. Listen, I'm trying to trace somebody who taught in Dublin in the early fifties. In a primary school. Can you lay your hands on that sort of information?"

"It all depends. What school?"

"We don't know."

"Oh, great. You see, Orla, the problem is this: half the primary schools in Dublin have updated their records to the computer, and the other half haven't. So if your man happened to work at one of the schools that haven't, then you're talking about a lot of phone calls and a lot of legwork. Look, why don't you try the income-tax people? If he was teaching then he was paying tax. They're sure to have him on their books."

"Now why didn't I think of that? Thanks, Brian."

"Any time."

The Revenue Commissioners had eleven Martin O'Neills on file, yet it wasn't long before they gave her details on the one she was investigating. Yes, a Martin O'Neill had indeed worked at a primary school in Dublin. From September 1953 to June of the following year. And yes, they had his date of birth: 10 July 1917. Orla called Brian again.

"He was at St Patrick's National School in Drumcondra in nineteen fifty-three."

"Well, that's something, at least. Oh, shit."

"What?"

"I just remembered. They knocked the place down sometime in the seventies. Oh, there's a new school there now, but I don't know whether they'd be able to help us."

"Great."

"Wait, now. Not so fast. That's where the teacher-training college is. They're bound to have him on their books; they send their student teachers to the national school to get practical experience."

Orla's contact was proven correct. The secretary at the college informed her that the institute still had O'Neill's dossier. Orla waited while the woman consulted it. It contained little: an ancient and faded Roneoed copy of a teaching diploma, and a handwritten report by the then headmaster of St Patrick's National School.

There was also a letter of introduction from the principal of St Mary's Primary School, Kilty, County Galway.

Orla again rang her friend at the Department of Education.

"Sorry to be such a nuisance, Brian."

"That's okay."

"Look, let's suppose that I'm a primary-school teacher, and I'm applying for a job in nineteen fifty-three. What papers would I need to show?"

"Well, you'd need a teaching diploma."

"Yeah. What else? What about identification? Would I need to show a birth cert—or would a baptismal cert do?"

"It would. They were more or less the same thing in the fifties. The Church had equal status with the State in those days—maybe even higher. Sure: you'd get by with a baptismal cert. And you'd need references of course."

"Who from?"

"Oh, a couple of local 'dignitaries' would do. Your GP, say, and the parish priest."

"I see." So, thought Orla, we're back to the parish priest. "Brian, you're an angel."

"Thanks. Does that mean you'll be ringing me again today? The girl on the switch probably thinks we're having an affair. Not that I'd mind. . . . "

"No, I think I've enough to go on now. Thanks again."

The blanks were being filled in. Orla wrote the name of the primary school next to the year 1953. Only thirty-nine more years to account for, she thought. Progress. She needed air. Picking up her bag, she left the station and went for a stroll.

Something didn't add up. They'd been to Kilty five days before and had spoken to a retired priest. Martin O'Neill, when he died, would have been about the same age as Father Boyle. Yet the old priest claimed never to have heard of him. Orla Sweetman had attended primary school in a village almost indistinguishable from Kilty. It would have been inconceivable had her headmaster and the parish priest *not* known each other. As it was, they'd been as thick as thieves.

Or as thick, for that matter, Orla mused, as any other kind of criminal you cared to mention.

Back at the garda station, she made a call to Detective Sergeant Paddy Flynn at Harcourt Square. Paddy, she knew, was a mine of information.

"Orla! The bould. How goes it?"

"Grand, Paddy. Listen, tell me this: how do you go about forging a birth cert?"

"Nothing simpler," he told her. "You can scan a real one, fake the details on your PC then run it off on a colour printer. They're very sophisticated these days. A man on a flying horse couldn't tell the difference."

"No, Paddy, I'm not talking about these days. How would someone go about forging one dated nineteen seventeen?"

"You're codding me. Now who'd want to do that?"

"Somebody did. I think. And I think it must have been a long time ago too. Say, forty-eight years ago."

There was a long pause.

"It'd have to be done by hand of course. But that would have involved printing blocks and suchlike. The best way would have been to get yourself a blank cert and just fill it in. But you'd need to have had somebody on the inside, somebody in the registry office who could slip you the goods."

Sweetman was thoughtful. The stroll had cleared her head—and had allowed her to mull over the suspicion that was taking root there.

"What about a baptismal cert, Paddy? How would you go about forging one in those days?"

"Ah! Easiest thing in the world. Any priest would have hundreds of blank ones. You'd just get your hands on one and fill it in. No bother at all if you knew the right buttons to press."

She thanked him, hung up the phone and sipped her tea.

Eighteen

"Now I want you to relax, Jim," Dr Brophy said. "Are you sitting comfortably?"

"Yes."

"Good. Warm enough?"

"Fine, thanks."

Brophy angled the reading lamp on the table so that its light fell between him and the patient in the armchair. Then he removed his gold wristwatch and dangled it loosely by the strap. It swung gently to and fro.

"I want you to look at the watch, Jim." His voice had dropped in volume. "I want you to follow its movements. Don't think about anything. Just look at the way the light falls on it."

The watch swung. Jim O'Neill's eyes followed its course, backwards and forwards, backwards and forwards.

"Feel your body relaxing," Brophy intoned, the modulation having left his voice. "Relaxing . . . relaxing . . . as you keep your eyes on the watch. Relaxing more . . . relaxing more . . . and more. Do your eyes feel heavy, Jim?"

"Yes. . . ."

"Then let them fall shut . . . as you relax . . . more and more."

O'Neill obeyed, and Dr Brophy quietly placed the watch on his wrist once again.

"I want you to imagine, Jim, that you're standing at the top of a long flight of stairs. Can you do that?"

O'Neill nodded.

"Good. Now you're feeling perfectly relaxed . . . and at peace with yourself. You don't hear any sounds from outside this room. You hear only my voice. You're very relaxed now. Can you feel your breathing?"

"Yes. . . ." O'Neill answered languidly.

"Good. I want you to breathe slowly . . . and to concentrate on every breath. Out . . . and in; out . . . and in."

He saw with satisfaction that his client's breathing had deepened and slowed.

"You're standing on the top stair and looking down. And breathing very slowly . . . in . . . and out. The stairs are so steep and long that you can't see the bottom. Only darkness. But you don't feel at all uneasy about this darkness. No, it's almost a welcoming darkness. You're in perfect control of your body, Jim . . . as you breathe very slowly . . . in . . . and out."

Brophy observed that the man in the armchair displayed the telltale signs of somebody who'd entered a light hypnotic trance. He nodded to himself. The difficult work was beginning.

"Now, Jim, I want you to take a deep breath and, at the same time, place your foot on the next step. You understand?"

"Aye."

"Now breathe in . . . that's the way. And out . . . and take the first step."

His client was responding exceedingly well.

"Now, continue to walk down those stairs . . . taking them very, very slowly. And, as you walk down, slowly, breathe out. That's the way. You'll notice that the more you go down, the deeper your breathing will become. That's the way . . . in . . . and out . . . another step . . . in . . . and out."

Brophy leaned forward in his chair and took O'Neill's left wrist gently between thumb and forefinger. There was no response. He raised the limp wrist and allowed it to fall back on the armrest of the chair. There was no sign of perturbation in his client. Brophy nodded to himself again.

"What do you see?" he asked.

There was a long pause.

"It's dark."

"Yes, it's dark, Jim. Very dark . . . as you walk slowly . . . one step at a time . . . down the stairs. And you breathe in and out. And, as you breathe, you inhale more and more deeply. The lower you go on the stairs . . . the deeper your breathing becomes."

He waited another minute, observing O'Neill keenly, then said: "Is there a door? Do you see a door?"

"Ummm . . . no."

"It doesn't matter, Jim. We've all the time in the world. But it's not as dark as it was, is it?"

"No. . . . "

"There's light at the bottom of the stairs. It's very dim at the minute . . . but the more you descend, the brighter it becomes."

"I can see a door," O'Neill said drowsily.

"Good. That's very good, Jim. What sort of door is it?"

"I don't know. It's shut."

"Is there a doorknob?"

A pause.

"Aye. . . . Aye, there is."

"Turn it. Turn the knob, Jim . . . and open the door."

"I–I . . . I can't."

"Yes you can, Jim."

"I'm afraid."

"There's nothing to be afraid of, Jim. Go on: turn the knob and open the door."

Yet another pause. Then O'Neill's breath caught.

"What is it, Jim? What do you see?"

"My father," Jim said—to the mirror.

Nineteen

Frank Naughton called Blade at Annadangan shortly after lunch on Friday. The noise of traffic in the background told him that the head of Mnemos was using his carphone.

"It's safer this way, superintendent," he said. "If they know my password then there's every chance they could be listening in on my phone calls as well."

"I agree, sir. And, speaking of passwords, how many characters are there in yours?"

"Fourteen. And it's not my wife's maiden name or anything as obvious as that. All random letters."

Blade whistled, recalling Jack's extraordinary calculations. Fourteen letters.

"So it's virtually impossible to decrypt."

"It is. You know what I think, superintendent? It's my belief we might be dealing with one of my own people. It's the only explanation that makes any sense."

"I think you're right, sir, and it's a line of investigation we'll be pursuing. But you're not ringing about that. They've made contact again; am I correct?"

"Ten minutes ago. Another email. Have you a pen handy, superintendent?"

Blade took one from his pocket. Jack read the cue and fetched a notepad he used for his grocery lists.

"I suppose this is how these things are usually done," Naughton said. "They want me to deliver it in person, and they want it in used notes, all fifties. That's a tall order in itself. It'll probably take at least a day for my bank to arrange that. But we have until Monday—that gives us three days."

Blade made a note. "Did they say where they want to make the trade?"

"Yes. And this is the *un*usual part, superintendent. I'd have thought they'd want to use some out-of-the-way place, like a deserted warehouse or something. Or maybe I've been watching too many bad films."

Blade smiled. "So what did they arrange?"

"The *airport*, would you believe. I'm to drive there in my own car, and leave it at the short-stay car park, with the boot unlocked. That's where the money will be of course."

Blade was intrigued. The short-stay car park at Dublin Airport was the last place he'd have chosen for the "drop". It consists of a multistorey complex and outdoor parking. It's busy at all times of the year but in August exceptionally so. Moreover it can be exited only at one point, through one of several tollgates with barriers.

"Did they give a specific time, sir?"

"Yes. Ten in the morning. They were very specific about the place as well. I'm to park in a no-parking zone directly opposite the airport police station."

In broad daylight. Somebody was either extremely daring or extremely stupid.

"And they'll hand over the processors?"

There was a pause. "I'm afraid not, superintendent. I'm supposed to take this on trust. The arrangement is that once the money is handed over, the processors will be returned to the plant. What do you think? Should I go along with it?"

Blade had written the words *2.5 million, used fifties*. He added another note below them: £2,500,000. Seen written out in full, the amount acquired a higher status.

"I don't know, Mr Naughton. That's the best answer I can give you. You're talking about two and a half million pounds of your own money. Who's to say that if you pay up they won't simply send you another demand for another million or two?"

Naughton paused long.

"On the other hand," he said at last, "if I don't pay up I'll lose those processors."

"There is that. Look, Mr Naughton, I'd like to advise you but I can't; it'll have to be your decision. Have you any way of getting in touch with them—to give your answer?"

"No. If I show on Monday, they know the deal is on. If I don't, then that's that."

"And *will* you show, sir?"

There was another long pause; Blade heard only the sound of traffic. Then: "Yes, superintendent. What choice do I have?"

Twenty

"Blade?"

"Sweetman! Where are you?"

"Carlingford. The Village Hotel again."

She sounded upbeat and that cheered Blade.

"How are you getting on with the O'Neill thing?"

"That's why I'm ringing, Blade. Look, can we meet? I've things to discuss with you. I wouldn't say I've made a lot of progress but . . ." She left it hanging.

"Right. I'll see you at the hotel."

He did, and Sweetman brought him up to date. Then she told him of her intention of visiting Jim O'Neill.

"Regression therapy? I'm not sure if I like the sound of *that*, Sweetman."

"Don't knock it till you've tried it."

He smiled. "Or, as a certain relative of my mine would say: 'Condemnation without investigation is the highest form of ignorance.'"

It was Sweetman's turn to smile. "That *has* to be Jack. And he's right. Anyway, O'Neill says it's the goods and, who knows, maybe it'll help get to the bottom of his father's identity."

"Maybe," Blade said without a trace of conviction.

* * *

"My father was a sadist," Jim O'Neill said. "He was a sadist, superintendent. I didn't know it before—or maybe I had known it and didn't want to face up to it. But I can face up to it now."

"Look, you're upset, sir," Blade said gently. "Maybe you should—"

"I'm not upset. I'm . . . relieved. Aye, that's it: I feel a great sense of relief. Isn't it funny? You'd think I'd be horrified. But I'm not. It's like as though a weight had lifted from my chest, as though I can breathe freely again."

"It worked, then—the hypnosis."

He nodded. "There go all my preconceptions about hypnosis. Paul McKenna has a lot to answer for, so he has."

"What was it like, sir?" Sweetman asked.

"Weird. He brought me back."

"Dr Brophy?"

"To when I was wee. Unbelievable. I would have been four years of age, sergeant. I mean, *really* four years of age. I felt it. I sounded it. I even *thought* like a four-year-old—at least, part of me did. The other part of me was observing the whole thing. Weird."

He stuffed his hands into his pockets and went to the bookshelf. Idly he took out a dog-eared paperback and studied its cover. It was a child's storybook.

"And my father. He was a young man. It's funny: you never think of your parents as being young when you're wee. They always seem ancient. But I saw my dad as he must have appeared when I was four. Dark hair, masses of it. He was built like a house as well. The bastard!"

"What did he do, sir?" Blade asked quietly.

"What did he *not* do, you mean, superintendent. He beat us black and blue—in the most sadistic way—me and my mother. He always said I took after her, that there were two of us against one of him. I suppose I *was* more like her—thank God for that. You know what I think? This is just my theory, you understand."

"Of course, sir."

"My mother drowned—over in Warrenpoint—when I was thirteen years of age. My dad never wanted to talk about it. Never. I'd always assumed it was because it broke his heart. Now I think differently. I think it was suicide. I think she drowned herself. I think he drove her to it."

So the records in Dundalk were wrong about that, Sweetman mused. Swimmer drowns in Carlingford Lough. There are currents, many of them treacherous; who was to know that the swimmer had taken her own life, had chosen the fatal current or undertow with care?

She might have left a note though—most would-be suicides do. Could her husband have read it, then destroyed it? A suicide in the family is the worst kind of dirty linen. . . .

"Was it really that bad, sir—the beatings?" Sweetman asked.

O'Neill didn't reply but rolled up his sleeve. They saw three shallow white depressions in the arm, a little way above the wrist.

"He didn't just beat us," O'Neill said. "My mother always told me that those were birthmarks. But now I know better. They're cigarette burns. My father did that to me when I was four years of age."

"My God."

"That's the kind of man he was, sergeant." He tapped his temple. "It's all still in there—every memory I have of him. I saw him do that; I felt the pain. Jesus, can you imagine: a wain of four? Dr Brophy wants to see me again next week. He says we've only scratched the surface."

"It can't be pleasant for you. . . ."

"No, it's not pleasant, superintendent. But it's better this way. I have to lay the ghost to rest. I can't carry this around for the rest of my life. God, I can see him now! I can hear his voice as clearly as I can hear yours. Swearing like a trooper, face as red as that cushion there. I could hear him as clear as day. But I also heard him saying something I still can't understand."

"Oh . . . ?"

"Aye. Some phrase or other. He said it at least three times."

"Maybe you couldn't understand it as a child," Blade suggested.

"No, superintendent, I don't believe that was the case. As I said, I seemed to be two different people: the kid, and the adult looking on. I'd have understood it right enough."

"What did it sound like?"

"Do you speak Irish?"

Macken shook his head and turned to Sweetman.

"Yes, a bit," she said.

"It's probably Irish then. That was one of the subjects he taught. I'm told he was fluent. I can't speak a word of it; very few schools up north would have had it on the curriculum. Not even the Catholic ones."

"What did it sound like, sir?" Blade repeated Sweetman's question. "Maybe if we heard it . . . "

"It sounded like 'paske mallow'. Does that make any sense at all, sergeant? In Irish?"

Sweetman turned the sounds over in her head. Paske mallow. "Paske" could be *páiste*, she thought: "child"; the pronunciation was close. But "mallow"? Well, there was the town of Mallow in County Cork. Unlikely. Perhaps *meallacht*: stupid. *Páiste meallacht*: Stupid child; that made more sense. She thought back on her schooldays; she'd once been a fluent Gaelic-speaker too. Yet she knew that a language is soon forgotten if it isn't used often.

And there was no guarantee that Jim O'Neill's recollection of the phonetics was flawless. He'd been under hypnotic regression therapy for God's sake. A decade ago the mainstream physicians had scoffed at the notion. Even now it was far from being considered a reliable scientific tool.

"Well, Blade," she said later, as they strolled back to her hotel, "what did you make of that?"

"I don't know. He's a queer fish, isn't he? O'Neill. I can't make him out."

"You don't believe him then? About the therapy?"

"Ah, I didn't say that, Sweetman. No, I'd say he's on the level all right. It's just that I thought he remembered too much of the therapy. What do you think?"

Carlingford was coming to life. A country band was doing a sound check in the bar on the corner of the square; a group of youths loitered against the wall, appraising a sudden influx of young, female tourists.

"*I* was hypnotized once," Sweetman said.

"Really?"

"Ah, it was nothing much. Just a stage hypnotist. He was very good though. He had us doing all kinds of stupid things. He made me think I was a chicken—would you believe it? There I was prancing around the stage, flapping my arms and going *bok-bok-bok*."

"The mind truly boggles, Sweetman."

"I know. I was mortified, so I was. But I really did remember every second of it. And you *do*, Blade. I don't think O'Neill was making it up."

They'd reached the entrance to her hotel. The interior looked inviting. Sweetman saw his expression.

"Have you time for a drink? A coffee maybe?"

He hesitated. "Better not, Sweetman. I want an early night."

"Fair enough." She seemed disappointed. Blade changed the subject.

"Look, about those words of O'Neill's. I know one or two fluent Irish speakers. I'll check with them. They might give us something."

She nodded and was gone before Blade realized that neither had mentioned their altercation in the Westbury Hotel. But there'd been no need to. They had an understanding. That's what he liked about Sweetman.

Twenty-One

"Blade?"

"Speaking."

"It's Maeve. Maeve McCluskey. Look, sorry to ring you so late."

"That's all right."

"You asked me about those words. The ones in Irish."

"Oh, yes. Did you come up with anything?" Blade cradled the receiver and reached for pen and paper.

"I did," his friend told him. "And I think this'll surprise you as much as it surprised me."

"Oh . . . ?"

"Remember you said you weren't sure it was Irish? Well, you were right. I took it to a friend of mine in UCD. He's attached to the Modern Languages faculty. And he was very intrigued by it. He couldn't place it; said it didn't resemble anything he was familiar with. So he showed it to some other people. And guess what?"

"Well?"

"It's Serbo-Croatian."

"You're codding me."

"There's no doubt about it. It wasn't phonetically exact, but near enough to make no difference. And it's quite rude, Blade. Where did you come across it?"

"I can't say. Sorry."

"No, of course not. I shouldn't have asked. Anyway, it's actually *pasce malo*. It means 'dirty little dog'."

"In Serbo-Croatian."

"Right. Serbo-Croatian."

"Very interesting. Thanks, Maeve. I appreciate it. I owe you one."

Thoughtful, Macken hung up the phone. He found his uncle taking the air on his back porch.

"Jack, you mentioned a book you were writing once. The one you never finished. . . . "

"Never even got started. Damned shame."

"Wasn't it about Russia? In the war."

"Indeed it was." He studied his nephew. "Why do I get the idea you want to pick my brains?

Some two hours later Blade went to the phone in the library, dialled the number of the Village Hotel in Carlingford and asked for Orla Sweetman. He made no apologies for the extreme lateness of the hour.

Twenty-Two

Jim O'Neill answered the door in his dressing-gown and slippers. He looked as though he'd slept badly. He admitted Macken and Sweetman, and went to the little kitchenette to put the kettle on.

"And what," he asked presently over a mug of tea, "am I to make of this—this latest revelation?"

"It beats me, sir," Blade said. "But it's definitely Serbo-Croatian. Did your father ever make any mention of Yugo-slavia?"

"None."

"Did he ever go there on a holiday?"

O'Neill laughed. "To Yugoslavia? You clearly didn't know my father, superintendent. A day trip to Portstewart would have been his idea of an exotic holiday. He didn't even have a passport."

"I know. We checked with the passport offices in Belfast and Dublin."

He looked at Macken strangely.

"I could have saved you the bother. I've been going through his things—his 'personal effects' as I believe they call them in such cases—and there's no sign of one. He would have been very much a home bird, superintendent."

"So where could he have picked up Serbo-Croatian, sir?"

"Maybe he did a Linguaphone course. No, I'm being a

wee bit facetious. I honestly can't imagine. Was it really Serbo-Croatian? There's no mistake?"

"No." A thought occurred to Blade. "You don't speak it yourself, do you?"

"Certainly not. French is the furthest I've ever got—with a wee bit of Italian thrown in. You think I might have been fooling myself with the regression therapy, do you?"

Macken threw Sweetman a glance.

"It's possible, sir," he said. "But no. I think, from what you've told us, that Dr Brophy really did regress you. Those memories are genuine."

"So where does all this lead us?"

"I don't know. May I speak frankly, sir?"

"Please do."

"It's my belief that your father was mixed up in something very sinister. I don't know what that something was—yet— but I suspect he was linked to paramilitaries in some way."

"Republicans? But I thought the police had ruled that out. Didn't you say yourself that somebody had tried to make my father's murder look like a sectarian killing?"

"That's true. But now I'm beginning to think otherwise. I'm beginning to think that there are some very big players at work here. And very clever ones at that."

"Go on, superintendent. I'm listening."

"Okay, let's say for the sake of argument that your father was a member of the IRA at one time. Let's say he was a top man, a divisional commander or something similar. I'm go- ing back a few years now—long before the present Troubles began. Let's say the thirties and forties."

"Aye, there would have been a lot of IRA activity then,"

O'Neill agreed. "It could also explain why my dad never talked about his past."

Blade nodded. "Now let's suppose that the IRA needed an undercover agent in Northern Ireland; somebody who was above suspicion, somebody who'd no record as far as the authorities were concerned. Wouldn't a harmless primary-school teacher be just the man?"

"You mean he was a plant? A 'sleeper' I believe they're called."

"Yes, sir; that's what I'm getting at. He'd lead a very ordinary life, but he'd be keeping his eyes and ears open all the time. He could report on what was going on in Newry and arrange for all kinds of movement of arms and explosives across the border."

"It *is* possible, I suppose," O'Neill said without much conviction. "But where does the Serbo-Croatian come in?"

"I'm getting to that, sir. I haven't worked this out properly yet; it's only a theory. I could be a million miles wide of the mark, but it seems to fit all we know at the present moment. Now: if you were planning on having arms shipped into the North where would you do it from? Bear in mind that we're talking about the late forties, early fifties, now."

"From the States?"

"Think closer to home. The war's just ended. Europe is awash with weapons—from France to the Black Sea. And a lot of those weapons are in Communist hands. Am I starting to make sense?"

"You certainly are, superintendent. Yugoslavia was Communist."

"Exactly, Mr O'Neill. It's the start of the Cold War. The

Communists are looking for allies all over the world. They have them in South America; Cuba is about to go Marxist—"

"My goodness! You're very well informed in these matters."

Blade smiled. "Not really, sir. It's just that I've been reading up on it. But it starts to make sense. The IRA want to take the Six Counties back. The Soviets know the IRA are Marxists, so they'll go out of their way to help them. The IRA have very few weapons; the Soviets have millions of them. So they arrange for some to be shipped to Ulster. They don't do it all at once; that would be too much of a risk. No, they have their contact in Newry, just a few miles down the road from Warrenpoint, one of the biggest ports in the North. Martin O'Neill is ideal. He's unobtrusive; he's a pillar of the community. And he speaks their language."

"Serbo-Croatian."

"That's it, sir. The guns wouldn't come from Russia; that would be too obvious and there'd be a careful check made on every Russian boat. No, they'd come from Yugoslavia, by way of the Mediterranean. There's ships delivering oil, maybe machine tools; I don't know. But their skippers are in contact with a man who's learned their language. He speaks it like a native. And there's little danger if telephone or short-wave radio messages are eavesdropped on, because hardly anybody outside the Balkans speaks the language. It's perfect."

O'Neill refilled his mug and stirred the tea slowly.

"I don't know, superintendent. It all sounds so farfetched."

"Does it? How else do you account for the Serbo-Croatian?

How else do you explain that yawning gap in your father's past? He simply didn't exist before nineteen fifty-three."

"All right. I'll go along with this for the moment. But let's go back to the IRA angle. Let me see if I've understood this properly. My father is a high-ranking commander in the south. It's decided to move him up north so he can set up an operation there. He's given a new identity, a new name. He sets up the operation and everything works as planned. Except here I find the first major flaw in your theory, superintendent."

"Oh?"

"If the guns came in then where are they? I know a wee bit more than most about the history of Northern Ireland—I should; I *teach* the subject—and I don't recall hearing about the authorities finding any caches of Soviet-made weapons in the fifties—or later, for that matter."

Macken had to think about this. He snapped his fingers.

"No, sir. They wouldn't. The Soviets wouldn't ship their own stuff. That would draw too much attention to them if they were intercepted. They'd send captured German guns, maybe British ones too. And don't forget about the lend-lease arrangement America made with Russia before they entered the war; all of those weapons were Western made."

"Hmm. It's a bit thin, superintendent, but I'll go along with it for now. But to return to my father. He runs this operation for years. Never gets caught. He retires from teaching and plans to live out the rest of his days in Carlingford. That would make sense I suppose. He's a southerner and, when his time comes, he wants to die in his own country. He can't go back to Galway—or wherever the blazes it is he was born—but Carlingford is the next-best thing. He feels at home here and can nip back up to Newry to see old friends any time he likes."

"Yes. Though so far we haven't been able to find any."

"I'd like to help you there but I can't. I'm afraid he never mentioned any to me—with the exception of Liam Donegan. But if he had friends I didn't know about then he had enemies as well. Somebody who disliked him enough to murder him. Who? And why wait till the year two thousand?"

"That's the part I'm still working on, sir. I simply don't know. But I suspect it was the Provos—or some other group of Republicans, an IRA splinter group; maybe the Real IRA or the INLA."

"That wouldn't make much sense. Why kill one of your own?"

Blade shrugged. "Why, indeed? But don't you see, sir? Let's say it was the Provos, but they don't want anyone to know that. So they make it look like a *Loyalist* killing. Fairly straightforward, you might think. But they go further than that. They make sure the Guards know that it *wasn't* in fact Loyalist paramilitaries; they leave enough clues to tell us that. So we immediately think it's an ordinary, non-political, non-sectarian murder. Only it isn't. It's a paramilitary execution, after all—except that your father was executed *by his own people*."

"But why, for God's sake?"

"I can't answer that, sir. But I've reason to believe that there's a political motive involved here. Who knows, maybe your father became a traitor. Maybe he became a double agent, and the IRA found out."

"So they wait till he's almost ready for the grave anyway before silencing him. No, it won't wash, superintendent."

"Have you a better explanation?"

"No, but I'm not the detective."

"Very droll, sir." Blade got up then and went to Martin O'Neill's bookshelf. He looked idly at the innocuous collection of cheap novels and school texts. He turned.

"I probably shouldn't be telling you this, sir, but somebody is trying to frighten Sergeant Sweetman off this inquiry. Somebody wants her to leave your father's past alone."

"When you say 'frighten', superintendent, what exactly do you mean?"

It was Sweetman who told him, omitting the irrelevant details concerning her own father. When she'd finished, Jim O'Neill's face showed great concern.

"Has this been reported?"

"To headquarters?" Sweetman shook her head, "No. I don't think it'd do much good, sir. These people can vanish back into the woodwork whenever danger threatens. I'll bet you anything you like they've the support of just about everybody in the community. That's always been their strength. It's different in my part of the country. The Boys, as we call them, are local heroes; they can do what they like up north, kill as many innocent people as they want to; it doesn't affect the lives of their own people. It'd be different if there were bombs in Tuam, but Tuam is a long way from the front line."

Jim O'Neill was silent. Macken could see that he was turning the theories over in his mind. He was troubled. His father's violent death had disinterred the skeletons of buried memories, and the hypnosis had put flesh on the bones. We bury our past, Blade thought, hoping that it won't ever rise from the grave to pursue us. But it does, in the end. Jim O'Neill had to confront his past now. What was it Dr Patricia Earley, the police psychologist at Harcourt Square, called it? Catharsis. Healing by the release of repressed emotions.

"Fancy another stroll, sir?" he asked. "The Táin Trail?"

O'Neill nodded. "Aye, why not. You have my head turned, superintendent. You and your theories."

Twenty-Three

They sat on the gentle, gorsed slopes of Carlingford Mountain, the town at their feet. Out on the Lough the naval frigate moved at a slow rate of knots along its borderline course. Sweetman opened her bag and spread on her lap the notes she'd made at the station in Tuam. She sucked on her pen. Macken tilted his head, the better to read her notes.

"You people never stop, do you?" O'Neill said pleasantly. "Don't you ever take a weekend off?"

"It's just that it's all so sketchy, sir," Blade said. "We've so little to go on. Right, I'm reasonably certain now that your father changed his identity somewhere along the line— probably in the forties. Now, along with a new identity goes a new circle of friends and acquaintances."

"New enemies as well, superintendent, if your hunches are right."

He nodded. "But it seems unlikely that your father would have broken *completely* with his past. It's not natural. There must have been somebody from his former life he'd have kept in touch with." He looked to O'Neill for guidance. "Maybe somebody like himself, somebody who wouldn't have aroused any suspicion?"

O'Neill plucked a long blade of grass and chewed on it. "Are you asking me if I remember anybody, superintendent?

From when I was a kid? No, the answer is: I don't."

"Nobody at all? Think now, sir. Think about a person, or persons, who didn't fit into your father's life. Somebody he behaved differently with."

O'Neill creased his brow and chewed harder on the blade of grass. The bright blue of the sky and the Lough was reflected in his glasses; Macken couldn't see his eyes. Then he stopped chewing.

"The abbey."

"What abbey?"

"The one in Galway. The Franciscans."

Sweetman's ears pricked up.

"I should have thought of it before," O'Neill said. "But it would have been a long time ago, in the early seventies. I was only a kid at the time."

"Go on," Blade urged.

"Well now, one thing I do remember about Dad is that he wouldn't have been what you'd call a very religious person. I mean: I don't remember him going to Mass, except on Sundays and holy days. Like most of us I suppose. He wouldn't have had a high opinion of the clergy either, as far as I can recollect. But he went to that Franciscan abbey at least six times."

"In Galway."

"Aye."

O'Neill folded his arms; he was bringing up half-forgotten memories. Sweetman laid her papers and pen on the grass; their presence made her feel like a stenographer.

"He'd say to my mother: 'I'm off to do my retreat.' Then he'd be away for a week, and sometimes longer. This was during the school holidays—when we weren't making those wretched daytrips to Portstewart."

Macken saw that O'Neill was gazing in the direction of the cemetery. He caught himself wondering about the schoolteacher's continued presence here, in the town where his father had met his violent end. Is this, Blade asked himself, on the suggestion of his psychiatrist? Is this part of the cathartic process?

"He'd come back as happy as Larry," O'Neill went on. "All smiles and claps on the back. My mother was delighted to be rid of him—and so was I. She'd say there must have been something in the Galway water." He smiled at the memory.

"Funny that he should have gone all the way to Galway to do a retreat," Sweetman said. "But it fits with what we know. He'd have felt more at home there. And I suppose the odds of him meeting somebody from his past must have been small if he spent all his time in an abbey. If that's where he really did go."

"What do you mean, sergeant?"

"Well, you'd only his word to go on, hadn't you, sir?"

"Not quite."

"Oh?" It was Blade.

"It's funny, isn't it, how talking about one thing from your past triggers another memory?" O'Neill was growing excited. "I'd completely forgotten about this until now. You asked me if he'd ever had visitors who didn't quite fit in. Well, the answer is: he did. The man in the black suit."

"A priest?"

"I don't know. He came to our house one year—it must

have been nineteen seventy-two or thereabouts. Early seventies at any rate. He'd a southern accent; I remember that well. An oldish man, grey hair, very soft-spoken. Dad introduced him as Benedict—'Benedict from Galway'; that's what Dad called him."

"Not Ben?"

"No, Benedict. That's unusual, isn't it? The only Benedict I know of is Benedict Kiely. But this fella, as I say, always wore a black suit. And black socks too. That's what made me think he must have been a priest—or maybe a friar. Plus the fact that he and Dad went to morning Mass together."

"And you considered that unusual, sir . . . ?"

"Four days in a row, superintendent? I'd call that unusual behaviour for a man who'd no time for religion or the clergy."

"I see what you mean. So he stayed at your house, this Benedict?"

"No, I think he was in a B and B somewhere. But he'd spend most of the day with my father. They'd talk for hours in the sitting-room. We weren't allowed in there, my mother and me. I remember that well."

"It *is* odd," Sweetman agreed. "Anything else you can remember, sir? Did he come in the summer? Winter?"

He shrugged. "I can't remember. It's not much to go on, is it, sergeant?"

But Sweetman was thinking otherwise. All roads seemed to be leading back to County Galway. Something had started there a long time ago, long before she was born. At present Sweetman had no notion of what that something could be, yet felt certain that this newfound link with Martin O'Neill's previous "existence" might shed light on the matter.

She knew Galway intimately and was aware that the only Franciscan House in the county was situated in Galway City. That house, she decided, merited a visit.

Twenty-Four

That Sunday Jack Macken generously gave the library over to his nephew. He'd been extra thoughtful as well: when Blade settled himself at the phone table he found that Jack had also provided him with writing paper and a number of sharpened pencils.

The first call Blade made was to Frank Naughton's home.

"Any further contact?"

"None, superintendent. But I hadn't expected any."

"The deal's on then?"

"It is."

"And the money?"

"All taken care of. I'm accepting delivery at eight o'clock tomorrow morning. Ahh . . . have you made any progress from your end?"

"Some, Mr Naughton. Expect me at your office around half eight."

"You'll be discreet of course."

"Of course."

Next Blade called DS Paddy Flynn at Harcourt Square. His instructions were clear and Flynn responded well.

"Consider it done, sir. Now, Joe Cunningham would like a word."

"Good. Put him through."

Cunningham had news.

"It's about the dinghy and the chip van, sir. Which do you want to hear first?"

The "chip van". The label had stuck. "Let's hear what you have on the van, Joe."

"Right. Just a second, sir. I have the report here somewhere. Sorry about this. I'm on me own and the phone hasn't stopped since six. You'd think they'd have respect for the Sabbath, wouldn't you?"

"Take your time."

"Yeah, here it is. It seems the Hiace was nicked by a couple of joyriders. One was seven; the other was eight. Can you believe it?"

"I can." How their feet even reached the pedals of the cars they stole was beyond him.

"But here's the good part, sir. They weren't just stealing it for kicks. They were doing contract work."

"You mean somebody was paying them to nick it?"

"That's it. The Guards in Finglas pulled them in yesterday but of course they couldn't hold them for long, them being juveniles."

"Did they get anything out of them?"

"Very little, sir. These are tough customers. At that age."

"I know. Do you have their details?"

Cunningham duly obliged.

"See if you can have them rounded up again, Joe. I'll be down there tomorrow anyway."

"I'll take care of it, sir."

"Now," Blade said, "the dinghy."

"The lads in Interpol have traced it. It was tough going

too, sir, according to them. It had changed hands a couple of times."

"Right. Give me what you have."

"It's French-made, as we knew. It was bought by somebody in Antwerp in May, nineteen ninety-nine. A certain Paul Takx—that's T-a-k-x."

"Has he form?"

"No, he's straight. A businessman who likes a bit of yachting. Then two years later he upgraded to the newest model, the Viper, and gave the dinghy to his son Vincent, who apparently runs a sort of ferry service in the south of Portugal. He sounds like a young hippie. Probably smuggles dope in from Morocco but the lads in Interpol have nothing on him either."

"So how did it get from Portugal to Ireland?"

"I'm coming to that, sir. It seems that young Vincent came into a bit of money earlier this year, and decided to invest in a new yacht. He bought one and put the old one on sale in the marina in Tarifa—that's near the Spanish border. I looked it up, so I did."

"Good man. Who bought the old one?"

"A German. It was a cash deal, but they'd have to register it all the same. So Interpol checked with the Portuguese port authorities. Nothing. Then they checked with all the other European authorities, including the Germans. No luck there, sir, I'm afraid. The yacht seems to have disappeared."

"How can that be, Joe? I mean, how do you make a yacht disappear? Sink it?"

The Guard laughed. "I wouldn't think so, sir. Maybe if you're rolling in Deutschmarks. We're talking eighty grand or so. No, we think they must have changed the name of the boat and registered it under that name. It's fairly easy to do. It's not like applying for road tax or anything."

"I see. So we've a second-hand—or even third-hand—dinghy that was aboard a boat that could have been moored anywhere between southern Portugal and Bremerhaven. You can look that up as well while you're about it."

The cut was lost on Joe Cunningham. "I will, sir," he said. "That's it I'm afraid. The lads in Germany are still looking into it, but they aren't too hopeful."

"I can imagine. At least we know what happened to the dinghy."

A dead end. He thought again about the shell suit. It was, Linda Doyle had determined, a mass-produced garment that could have been bought anywhere. It could have been made in any of a number of sweatshops from Mexico City to Taipei, such was the scope of operations of today's clothing manufacturers. O'Neill's murderer had been careful to remove the label, though Blade doubted that the precaution had been necessary. The killer could have bought the shell suit at any store and remain anonymous.

He suddenly thought of something else.

"Joe, are we sure the buyer was German?"

"Pretty sure, sir. He spoke German anyway, according to the report."

"Hmm. But would an expat Belgian be able to tell the difference between a German and, say, an Austrian?"

"*You* tell *me*, sir. I haven't the foggiest."

When he'd hung up Blade dwelt on his question. He tried to picture the scene: a young dope-head strikes a deal with a stranger in a sun-blest marina at the southernmost tip of the Portuguese coast. The two men share a lingua franca: German. He asked himself: Could a Belgian distinguish between a native German and a German-speaking citizen of any one of a number of European countries? Blade wasn't sure how many there were, but suspected that the net was wide. It covered most of Europe, from Scandinavia right down to Greece and Turkey.

And what was once the Republic of Croatia.

Twenty-Five

Sweetman made an early start on Monday morning, forgoing breakfast at the Village Hotel, Carlingford. It wasn't yet light when she hit the road to Mullingar, the one that would take her by the shortest route to County Galway. There had been, as she'd expected, very little traffic at that early hour and she'd made good time. She approached her parents' farm from the northeast, bypassing the village of Kidafane.

She'd called her father on her mobile at the "respectable" hour of seven o'clock. He'd always been an early riser—proud to be up each morning at the crack of dawn—but in recent years was in the habit of staying up into the small hours, reading, and breakfasting late the next day.

That phone conversation had been a disturbing one.

"What's the matter, Daddy? You sound funny."

"I'd prefer if you didn't come here, Orla. If you're going to Galway then that's your business, but I'd prefer if you gave us a miss this time."

"Daddy, what *is* it?"

"I'm not saying. And don't ask me to explain either, all right?"

She'd agreed to give the farm a miss. Yet her uneasiness grew with each passing mile. She was convinced that something was seriously wrong. To hell with it, she decided. He can think what he likes but I'm going all the same.

She hadn't expected a welcome at the farm, so it came as no surprise when Matt Sweetman confronted his daughter at the door, wearing a face like thunder.

"I know I promised, Daddy, but I couldn't stay away. There's something very wrong, isn't there?"

Her father's expression changed slowly. Anger was replaced by what Orla read as resignation—or defeat.

"Aw, come in then," he said with a sigh.

She'd never seen her mother looking paler. Dora Sweetman sat in her chair by the unlit fire. Knitting. Orla knew the signs: knitting was her mother's way of coping with grief or great distress. She nodded wanly as Orla followed her father into the room.

"You shouldn't have come, Orla," she said.

"Well, I'm here. So would anybody like to tell me what's going on?"

Her parents exchanged worried looks.

"It's Rusty," Matt Sweetman said. "I found him at six this morning. In the barn."

Orla had never been overly fond of Rusty, or he of her. Yet she knew how attached her parents were to the dog.

Dora Sweetman's knitting needles clicked faster; Orla heard her sniffing.

"They *hanged* him," her father said. "They hanged the poor little creature. Can you imagine that? The bastards went and hanged him."

"Matt . . . " his wife pleaded. She always frowned on strong language in her home.

"My God, that's shocking," Orla said.

"There he was," her father continued, "hanging like a shot rabbit from the beam by the door. Little Rusty, who never harmed a soul in his life—not even so much as a stray sheep."

"Who'd do such a thing, Daddy?"

Matt Sweetman did not reply but went to where his jacket hung, on a peg beside the front door. He took a crumpled sheet of paper from a pocket and passed it to Orla.

"It was a warning," he said. "Rusty. Didn't I ask you to stop whatever it is you're up to in Kilty?" Fear had given way to anger again. "Didn't I? Now look what's happened."

Orla read the message, scrawled in capital letters. It said:

THIS TIME ITS THE DOG
NEXT TIME ITS THE DAUGHTER

Frank Naughton set the black Samsonite suitcase down on his desk. As Macken watched he unlocked it and threw back the lid. His secretary gasped as the neatly packed bundles of banknotes were revealed. Fifty thousand of them: two and a half million pounds.

Blade studied Naughton's face. It was unreadable. He wondered how he himself would have felt, having to part with that amount of money. Mnemos, he thought, couldn't be that prosperous that its loss wouldn't punch a sizeable hole in the company's profits. They'd have to call in the accountants; "downsizing" and "human-resource restructuring" would be among the euphemisms bandied about when it came to balancing the books. The shareholders might even call for Frank Naughton's own head.

Assuming, of course, that the raiders would get away with it.

"They'll know the Guards are involved," Blade said. "If they knew about your deliveries, and could send those emails, then they'll know of my presence here. There's still time to send me packing you know. I won't like it; neither will my superiors. But it's your money, sir. I'll understand."

Naughton shut the case and locked it.

"I'm not stupid, superintendent. I'm aware of the risk involved—but this company wouldn't be where it is today if I hadn't taken risks. No, I know what I'm doing." He looked keenly at Blade. "And I hope you do too."

"Our people are in place, sir. They're professionals. They won't be spotted."

Naughton nodded and looked at his watch. It was a quarter to nine.

"Perhaps you should leave now," he said. "I intend doing everything they demanded. I'll be driving to the airport alone. And I don't want anybody following me, you understand? That's important. It is, as you say, my money."

"You have my word, sir. No tails."

Blade put the binoculars to his eyes as the blue-metallic Mercedes turned into the car park at Dublin Airport. Naughton was alone. The car moved out of sight, behind the multistorey car park, then reappeared in Blade's field of vision from where he sat at a second-floor window of the terminal.

"What time is it now?" he asked.

"Ten to ten," Detective Sergeant Paddy Flynn answered. "He's early."

Blade passed the binoculars. "Does that boot look locked to you?"

Flynn focused on the now-stationary car. "No, sir, I wouldn't say it does."

"Good. Naughton's sticking to the arrangement. How many men have we down there, Paddy?"

"Twelve, including the two airport lads. We've four in the multistorey—you can't see them from here. There's two more in that white Mazda you see looking for a parking space. The others I don't know. If they're there then they're doing a good job of it."

Blade nodded approvingly. Flynn had been as good as his word and had recruited the manpower, drawing on officers at Harcourt Square and the garda station in Swords. They'd been in place long before Blade's arrival.

"He's getting out," Flynn said.

Blade returned his binoculars to the car. Naughton was emerging. He looked about him, then directly at Blade. But he knew Naughton couldn't see him behind the gold-mirrored glass.

Naughton locked the car, glanced again to left and right then headed in the direction of the terminal building.

"Are we meeting him, sir?" Flynn asked.

"No. The deal is that Naughton is picked up by one of his staff. He leaves the car and waits for further instructions."

"D'you know what I think, sir?"

"What?"

"I think they're out of their bloody minds. They'll never pull this off. We'll be onto them like a shot if they go *near* that car."

I agree, Blade thought: it's madness. It was broad daylight; cars were coming and going, passengers parking or collecting their vehicles.

The instructions Naughton had received were specific. The money was to be packed in a plain, black Samsonite suitcase, and stowed in the unlocked boot of the car. So all someone had to do was raise that boot, take out the case and leave. He'd attract no attention; a man carrying a black suitcase was hardly an uncommon sight at an airport.

Yet any thief worthy of the name would guess that Naughton would go to the police. To be sure, he risked losing the two and a half million by doing so, but he stood more chance of recovering the processors—and not having to pay for their return. The raiders would know this.

"What would *you* do," Blade asked, "if you were the villain?"

"Is this a trick question?"

"No, Paddy, it isn't a trick question."

"Well now, I think I'd wait. Yeah, that's what I'd do." He scanned the movement of cars and people below. "I'd figure there was a lot of surveillance here, so I'd wait. I'd wear us down, wait for us to get bored sitting around on our bums."

"Very good, Paddy. That's what I'd do too. Fuck this for a game of cowboys; we could be here all bloody day."

A burst of smoke rose from the ground close to Naughton's Mercedes.

It was followed by another.

"Jesus!" Flynn shouted. "Smoke grenades."

The car park was suddenly blanketed in thick, white clouds of smoke. Pandemonium broke out. Through the triple glazing of the window Blade heard nothing, yet could see the open mouths of men, women and children as they fled the area in panic. He was on his feet and running for the door, Flynn hard on his heels.

The airport police were there before them. So too were a number of plainclothes officers, barking urgently into radios. Macken gestured at one of them.

"Seal off the car park," he yelled. "Get word to the men at the exits. Nobody's to leave."

"No problem, sir. They're our own lads."

Blade's eyes stung and he had to cover his mouth with a handkerchief. He'd feared that the gas might be CS or some other mixture used for riot control. But it seemed harmless enough. Someone had alerted the airport fire service and two small trucks with flashing lights were blocking the route to the departures building. Hoses had already been brought into play. The firefighters remained on standby but were hardly necessary. Even as they watched, the smoke was beginning to dissipate.

Blade cursed then. Flynn and he had occupied the best vantage point, had been able to keep Naughton's car in plain sight. Had they stayed put instead of rushing below then they'd have spotted any movement at the car. He cursed his stupidity again. He'd played right into the hands of the raiders.

Flynn was at the car, holding the boot open with one hand, the other pressing a tissue to his mouth. "It's gone, sir," he said.

"Jesus on a push-bike," Blade said. "From right under our noses." He turned to the other police officers. "Who was nearest? Did anybody see *anything*? Anything at all?"

No one had. Blade looked to where a group of holiday-makers and businesspeople had gathered. Many held suitcases, some just like Naughton's. All were suspects. But good fuck, Blade thought angrily, we can't stop and search every person carrying a black Samsonite suitcase, now can we?

The man who'd taken Naughton's two and a half million could be there, standing among that group of onlookers.

He would have been invisible, admiring his handiwork, and smirking at the helplessness of the gardaí.

"Sir . . . ?"

Blade turned. It was a sergeant attached to the airport police. He held a canister. It was the most innocuous object in the world: a slightly crushed Pepsi Cola can. Yet a thin trail of vapour issued from it.

"This is one of the smoke bombs, sir," the man said. "And this is how they did it."

The sergeant held the can closer. The lid had come off on detonation, to expose a tiny device with a digital readout.

"A timer," the sergeant said unnecessarily. "Somebody just dumped those two cans on the ground and went about his business. They could've lain there all day until the cleaners came and you wouldn't have given them a second glance."

He was right. Blade looked around the car park and saw other discarded cans shimmering in the warm, summer sun. Like Naughton's stolen suitcase the smoke bombs would have been in full view—and invisible at the same time.

And here, in the company of another, clearly a subordinate, came Naughton himself. His expression was grim as he regarded the empty boot of his car.

"Two and a half million pounds," he growled. "Two and a half million pounds, literally gone up in smoke. I'm telling you, superintendent: heads will roll for this."

Blade was lost for words. Naughton was right: there was no excuse. Two and a half million pounds had disappeared from under the noses of thirteen well-trained officers and a detective superintendent of the Special Branch. He'd no idea how it had been done. David Copperfield might have provided a plausible, thaumaturgic, explanation. But Blade Macken could not.

Lough Bray, Wicklow, had never seemed more appealing than at that moment.

Twenty-Seven

Had Rusty's killers expected Orla Sweetman to heed the warning and curtail her part of the investigation then they were very much mistaken. The collie's death served only to harden her resolve. Somebody was determined that she should not visit the abbey in Galway City, and that fact alone drew Orla to the Franciscans as a bear to a honey jar.

The building itself, she saw, was not unlike the convent where her sister Fidelma had taken vows: austere, functional, and grey. A statue to Francis of Assisi, the devout lover of animals, stood a little to the left of the big church adjacent to the abbey. Orla was amused to see that the saint's stone head bore many traces of pigeon droppings, and wondered what the great man would have thought about that.

She'd announced her coming the previous day and was received by the man she'd spoken to on the phone: Brother Alphonsus, secretary to the Father Superior. Despite his robe and sandals he seemed a man as well-versed in worldly affairs as in those of his Order. Sweetman noted that the glasses he wore had thin, blue frames flecked with yellow and purple, an unusual nod to fashion for a man of the cloth. His manner was equally urbane as he led the way into a bright and airy reception-room.

"I'd expected someone older, detective sergeant," he said. "I mean no disrespect by that. Simply that you sounded older on the telephone."

Sweetman smiled sweetly.

"A cup of tea?"

"That'd be nice."

Brother Alphonsus pressed a bell. "Please. Sit down, won't you."

A younger friar appeared when both were seated in two comfortable chairs by the window, a coffee-table between them. The order was taken and the young man departed quietly.

"Now, then," Brother Alphonsus said, "you spoke of one of our men who'd been to Newry in seventy . . . ?"

"Somewhere in the early seventies. We're not sure of the year, but we believe his name was Benedict." Sweetman produced her notebook.

The friar frowned. "Benedict, you say? There's nobody of that name here I'm afraid."

Sweetman's heart sank. How old was Brother Alphonsus? Fifty? Older? Had he been here in the seventies then he'd have known the names of all the men in the community. Jim O'Neill had seemed quite sure of the name with which his father's friend had been introduced, and Benedict is a name you'd remember. But what if it were a pseudonym?

"Might I ask the nature of this inquiry, detective sergeant?" the friar said then. "One is always a little—shall we say—nervous these days when the gardaí start showing interest in a member of the Order."

Sweetman grew a little flustered. "Ehh, no, Brother, it's

nothing like that, I assure you."

"I'm glad to hear it."

"It's just that we believe that this Brother might be able to shed some light on another matter."

"And that being . . . ?

"I'm not at liberty to divulge that information. Sorry."

"That's perfectly all right." He smiled. "We used to have to take a vow of silence ourselves you know."

Sweetman didn't doubt that the well-spoken friar might have experienced difficulty in keeping such a vow.

The tea was brought in; Sweetman was impressed by the speed of its arrival. She sipped hers gratefully; she'd done without breakfast at the hotel and there'd been no offer of tea or other refreshment at her parents' farm.

"I know it's a long time ago," she said presently, "but would there be any way of finding out if any of the Brothers visited Newry in, say, nineteen seventy-two?"

The friar frowned. "That's a very tall order. The Franciscans aren't what you'd call an enclosed community. We tend to be out in the world a good deal, so there's a lot of coming and going. I'd scarcely know where to start looking."

"Aren't there records kept?"

He shook his head. "Only when a man is engaged in work for the Order. A visit to another House, a trip to Rome, that sort of thing." He frowned again. "Of course . . . "

Sweetman brightened. "Yes?"

"I was thinking of the quartermaster's book." He saw her look of incomprehension. "That's what *I* call it. We keep a record of income and expenditure—similar to the sort of record a business firm keeps. There's always the possibility that that might contain something charged to this Brother of yours, the one who visited Newry. How long did he stay there?"

"Ehm, perhaps a week."

"He'd have had to pay for transport. And for accommodation if he wasn't staying with friends or family. He wasn't, was he?"

"No, I don't think so, Brother."

"Good. Finish your tea and we'll dig out those records. Who knows, detective sergeant, we may be in luck after all."

Sweetman sipped. "How many men were here in the seventies?"

"A great many more than there are now," the friar told her wistfully. "Our numbers have been dwindling all the time. There were almost a hundred men in the community when I was a novice here in the early sixties; now we're down to thirty. So far this year we've had only one vocation." He sighed. "We're a dying breed I'm afraid."

"I'm sorry to hear that. My sister's a Carmelite you know. She says the same." She wiped her lips with a tissue and stood up. "Shall we go then?"

She followed the friar down a passageway and presently he unlocked a door marked *House Records*. The air in the long, narrow room was stale. Lines of cloth-bound, ledger-like volumes ran from floor to ceiling along one wall. All were blocked and gold-leafed, indicating the years they covered. Brother Alphonsus cleared some books and papers from a desk, lifted two ledgers from a shelf and laid them side by side.

"It would be a lot quicker if Brother Anthony were here,"

he said. "He's in charge of the records now. But he's laid up for a few days in the infirmary." He opened the first book. "We'll start at nineteen seventy, shall we?"

Sweetman nodded. "If what we want is there, it'll most likely be listed at some time during school holidays: Easter, summer or Christmas."

The friar looked at her quizzically.

"We have reason to believe," she explained, "that the Brother visited a friend of his during those periods."

"Well, that narrows things down I suppose. Grab a chair, detective sergeant. This might be a long search."

"Look, I'm really grateful for this. Are you sure you can spare the time?"

His eyes twinkled behind the blue-framed glasses. "Don't you worry about that. Time is a commodity we have a great deal of in an abbey."

The search was long indeed. They'd pored over the records for 1970, 1971 and 1972, had twice paused for a tea break, when the church bell tolled. Brother Alphonsus rose.

"You must excuse me," he said. "A higher duty calls."

"I understand, Brother. Would it be all right if I stayed here?"

He hesitated for a moment and his brow creased. He shrugged. "I don't see why not. It's unlikely that you'll be disturbed but, if so, say you're here with my permission. I'll be back in about twenty minutes."

Left to herself, Sweetman had more opportunity to study at leisure the day-to-day finances of a well-run Franciscan abbey. Whoever had kept the records had been thorough to the point of fanaticism. She recalled what Brother Alphonsus had said about time. The friar in charge of these records had had plenty of it, it seemed. He'd made entries of every item bought and sold by the community: everything from a new gearbox for the Father Superior's car (£160.15 plus VAT for the parts, £33.50 in labour costs), a CIE rail pass for a certain Brother James (£10), to a replacement washer for a tap in the kitchen (5p). And all recorded in a tiny, elegant hand that would have met with the approval of the monastic scribes responsible for *The Annals of the Four Masters*. So small was the handwriting that Sweetman was feeling the onset of a headache when Brother Alphonsus returned from his prayers.

"Anything?"

"Not yet. I'm almost through with seventy-three. No one seems to have gone anywhere at Christmas that year."

"It can happen." Brother Alphonsus looked at his watch. "Do you know it's nearly two? You look tired. What about calling it a day and coming back tomorrow morning? You'll be fresher then."

It was tempting but Sweetman declined. Jim O'Neill had been convinced that his father's "retreats" in Galway and the visits by the "man in the black suit" had taken place in the early seventies. They'd almost exhausted those now.

"Let's try seventy-four," she said. "If there's nothing there then I *will* call it a day."

Fifteen minutes later Brother Alphonsus gave a little whistle. His eyes shone as he tapped an entry dated 22 July. It read:

> *Invoice bed and breakfast, Mourne Vista,*
> *34 Rock Road, Newry, £43.70, Brother Louis.*

"This, I believe, is what you're looking for, detective sergeant."

Sweetman was elated. She'd had her doubts from the moment she'd heard Jim O'Neill's story. He couldn't have been older than ten in 1974. Yet O'Neill had been correct, or so it seemed. A Franciscan had indeed stayed in a Newry guesthouse for longer than a night: Sweetman calculated that, at seventies' tariffs, the stay might well have been for a week. It corresponded.

So Brother Louis had been the man in the black suit—and the black socks. But was he still alive? O'Neill had described a grey-haired man.

"Brother Louis? Oh, he's alive and kicking. Getting on though, I have to say. He'd be . . . what? . . . at least eighty-two. One of our oldest men in fact."

"Could I talk to him?"

"I'm afraid not, detective sergeant."

"Ah. Against house rules is it?"

"Not at all. The thing is, Brother Louis isn't with us any longer. In fact, you just missed him. Very unfortunate timing."

Sweetman felt suspicion growing. This, she reasoned, was more than coincidence.

"He left two days ago in the company of his nephew. He's been given what you might call compassionate leave. You see, his sister is dying and Brother Louis wanted to be at her bedside. Father Superior was most understanding about it. He's a good man."

"Did Brother Louis leave a forwarding address? I mean: could I talk to him at his sister's?"

Brother Alphonsus smiled wanly.

"You could, I suppose. Only it would be a rather expensive undertaking. The sister lives in Sarajevo."

"What!"

"Oh, didn't I tell you? No, of course I didn't. We call him Brother Louis, but his real name is Luji. He's a Bosnian."

Twenty-Eight

Blade Macken parked his car outside the garda station in Malahide, County Dublin, at a little after two in the afternoon. He hadn't eaten since early morning but wasn't hungry. Three rolls of peppermints had taken the edge off his appetite. Moreover, his meeting with Linda Doyle at the garda depot had put all thoughts of food from his mind. He'd been sorely in need of some trace of evidence that might explain the disappearance of Naughton's two and a half million pounds. Doyle had delivered it. Now he had to talk to Inspector O'Brien.

"Silicon?" O'Brien said.

"That's it. Not, I hasten to add, what the page-three girls use to pad out their Wonderbras. The kind they use in chips."

O'Brien was thoughtful. "So they burned the processors, did they? Twenty-five million quid's worth. Seems a bit wasteful to me, sir."

"Doesn't it? And that's just what's bothering me, inspector. This isn't like a kidnapping, where you get rid of the victim when you have the ransom money. They could still have flogged those chips in any number of places. For the same money they got from Mnemos, maybe a lot more. So why didn't they?"

"I think you're going to tell me."

"Because, inspector, they weren't chips at all. Bear with me now for a minute, will you, while I tell you what a chip is? I'm passing on what I heard from Forensics now."

"I'm listening."

"A chip like the Pentium Three processor—the ones that went missing—is about the size of a matchbox. But that matchbox contains thousands of pieces of circuitry: the transistors and capacitors and suchlike we used to have in our radios—only now they're microscopic. But there's metal in a chip as well; there has to be. And here's the point, O'Brien: we didn't find any metal in that gunge you dug out of the back of the van. In other words: those weren't processors at all. They were just lumps of silicon, the raw material used to *make* processors."

"I see."

"I'm glad you do," Blade said sourly. "Because I sure as fuck don't. All I know is that somebody's been pulling the wool over our eyes, and I want to know why."

He rose.

"You're off again, sir?"

"I am. I'm going to start with that stolen Hiace." He looked at his watch. "The Guards in Finglas have two little desperadoes in custody since ten this morning. They should be thawed out by now—and ready for a good grilling."

"Through here, sir," the duty-sergeant said.

The interview-room reeked of stale body odours. Very stale. Blade deduced that they emanated not from the young woman dressed in sweater and leggings but rather from her charges. He recognized them—or, better said, he identified their generic type. They were the sort of boy you frequently came across in the meaner Corporation housing estates, and he'd been assured by the sergeant that none was meaner than the estate where "Danno" and "Antho" had lived since birth.

Daniel "Danno" Scally was eight, the older of the two. Yet he was smaller than Anthony "Antho" Finn—a scrawny, undernourished boy with very short red hair and freckles. His eyes were pale and darting, eyes that saw the world as an adult would. Blade felt genuine compassion for the two kids. He saw what their future would be, saw the inevitability of petty, boyish crime leading to the real thing. And jail. Then freedom. And jail again. Then . . . The boys had boarded the carousel that would never stop until you shot the horses from under them. Neither boy knew who his father was, but it wouldn't have made any difference had the nuclear families been intact. It was the street not the home that had shaped and would continue to shape these boys.

Blade felt compassion, yes. He had, nevertheless, a job to do. The social worker could pick up the pieces when he'd gone. Her name was Dolores, and she fitted it. Twenty if she's a day, Blade decided, and looks like she's carried the dolours of the entire human race on her shoulders since she climbed out of the cradle.

"I'm Detective Superintendent Macken."

"I know," said Dolores. You're the enemy.

He sat down at the bare, grey formica-topped table, and laid the file on it, unopened.

"I have to ask the lads some questions. It shouldn't take long."

Dolores was prepared to allow that.

He was bemused—though not too surprised—to see that each of the boys stared at him unblinkingly. No fear there. And sure as shite no respect either. He turned to the elder, the boy with the russet hair and pale eyes.

"Now then, Danno, so you like to drive, do you?"

"Have ya gorra cigarette? Aren't yiz supposed a give us cigarettes when we're bein' interrigayreh? Your woman says she hasn't gor any."

"Sorry, I don't smoke," Blade could answer quite truthfully. "And you're not being interrogated. I'm just going to ask you a couple of questions and then you can go home."

"Fuck. I'm on'y gaspin' for a smoke, so I am."

"Well, gasp away, Danno," Blade said. "I don't give a toss. Tell me about the Hiace you borrowed on Monday."

"I fuckin' tole yiz all I know."

Blade opened the file.

"That may be, Danno, but there may also be something you *forgot* to tell us. So I'm here to refresh your memory. Do you follow me?"

He said the last with unmistakable menace in his voice. Dolores frowned; neither Danno nor Antho batted an eyelid.

"I ain't sayin' nuttin'," Danno assured him, "until I gerra bleedin' cigarette."

Blade smiled and continued reading the file, not looking at the boys. Evidently Danno had been more forthcoming than his seven-year-old pal. He'd divulged the fact that the van had been earmarked for theft by a "fella I met down in the chipper".

The "contract" had cost the man little: £20 had changed

hands. Danno had refused to reveal the man's identity.

"I can't give you a cigarette," Blade said. "You're a minor. Besides, it's a bad habit and I've just quit smoking myself."

"Ya don't have ta *gimme* one," Danno said with a sly grin. "All ya gorra do is ger a packet an' I'll help meself."

It was Blade's turn to grin. Bright kid. In different circumstances, had the lad not had the misfortune to have been born in one of the worst areas of the city then Danno could have gone on to become a successful barrister. Danno knew his letter of the law.

"I'll see what I can do," Macken said. Dolores scowled.

He went out and returned some moments later with a lighter and a packet of cigarettes. He opened it and placed it in front of him on the table. Two scrawny hands reached out and emptied its contents, stuffing the cigarettes into pockets. Danno lit one for his pal, then his own. Blade pushed an ashtray across.

"Happy now?" he asked.

Dolores shook her head in disdain.

"Right. So this 'fella' paid you twenty quid to get a van for him. Who was he? Did you know him?"

"Nah."

"Never seen him before in your life?"

"I told ya. Nah."

"What about you, Antho?"

"Antho didn't know him neither."

"Let Antho speak for himself. Well, what about it, Antho?"

"Nah, I didn't know him neither."

"I see. That's a pity now because I think this fella gave you a bad deal. I mean, twenty pounds and you're looking at

I-don't-know-how-long in the juvenile prison. Think about that now, Antho: ten pounds and you could be on bread and water for six months. Not a nice thought, is it?"

The seven-year-old had paled slightly; some of the bravado had left him.

"I didn't get t—"

He didn't finish the sentence, nor was it necessary that he did. Blade had seen the look he gave his companion.

"Just a minute," Blade said.

He left the room again and returned with a Guard.

"Danno will be leaving us for the time being, Dolores," he said. "If that's all right with you? Come along, Danno."

"Okay, son," Blade said when the door had shut, "what was your share of the deal? How much did Danno give you?"

"Ehh . . . a t-tenner. I tole ya."

"It's okay, Antho; you don't have to lie for him. Do you think it's fair that you should do the same amount of time as him if you didn't get the same amount of money? That isn't fair, is it now?"

Antho suddenly looked his age. His small hands trembled; Blade thought he saw moisture appear at the corners of his eyes.

"So what *was* your share? Six pounds? Seven?"

"I on'y got four."

"Four! Jesus, Antho, you were done, weren't you? Four quid. And Danno kept sixteen for himself. You know how many times four sixteen is? Do you?"

"Ehh . . . nah."

"No, I didn't think you would, Antho. Well, it's *four times* four. So Danno made four times the money you made and you both took the same risk. Some friend, eh?"

Antho was quiet. Blade could see he was wrestling with something. But he did not wrestle long.

Ten minutes later Blade was in his car again and heading east, in the direction of another housing estate. It's called Kilbarrack but outsiders know it by its fictional name of Barrystown, the place that gave birth to the Snapper and spawned several other colourful characters. Yet Macken knew that the characters whose trail he followed weren't to be found in the novels of Roddy Doyle. These characters had killed.

It was good to be in control of the game again. He'd met two of the pawns and had allowed one to sacrifice the other. But that was literally kids' stuff. Now it was time to face the higher ranks.

They might lead him to the officers.

Twenty-Nine

The Galway public library, just off Eyre Square, is a good one. Sweetman left her car parked at the Franciscan House and walked the short distance there; after the hours spent in that stuffy room she badly needed air. Moreover her headache was now full blown; she took two Anadin Extra Strong from her bag and washed them down with a palmful of water from a fountain on the square.

It was three o'clock. The library shut at six so she had ample time for the research she had to do. She bought a jotter at a newsagent's.

The assistant librarian was helpful: at Sweetman's request he ducked into the History section and returned with an armful of books. Sweetman found a quiet reading table, opened her jotter, and settled down to acquaint herself with the history of the former Yugoslavia in the 1940s.

She'd filled nearly twenty pages of the jotter when the assistant librarian came to her table to inform her they'd be closing shortly; it was approaching six.

Out again in Eyre Square Sweetman strolled slowly among the tourists; it was the height of Galway's summer season. She heard voices speaking in many languages: French, Italian, Spanish, German and, for some bizarre reason, their speech served to bring to life for her the accounts she'd just studied of the terrible events that had taken place in the Balkans during the Second World War.

Some of the accounts had horrified her by their graphic detail; she'd shuddered at the eyewitness reports of barbarousness and genocide on a grand scale. Sweetman, in common with most outsiders, had known little or nothing about the background behind the more recent Balkan conflict. The books had shown her that violence begets violence, and that the sins of the fathers are visited upon the sons as surely as night follows day.

She took from her bag the little photograph that Brother Alphonsus had lent her. There were at least thirty friars in the group, but it had been taken by a professional and the definition was excellent. Brother Alphonsus had identified Brother Louis; now Sweetman studied that face again. It was, she thought, the face of a saintly man. She found it impossible to reconcile such apparent kindliness with the litany of savagery she'd found in the history books. Brother Louis, she decided, had to have been on the side of the angels. . . .

She realized with surprise that she was very, very hungry. Small wonder: she'd eaten nothing all day. She'd intended returning to her parents' farm for dinner but found now that her hunger couldn't be put aside any longer. First, though, she had to contact Dublin. She found a quiet corner of the square and called in on her mobile phone.

"Joe Cunningham, please. DS Sweetman here."

"Just a moment."

Cunningham was in good form. "Orla! The dead arose and appeared to many. What are you up to? Has Blade been in touch?"

"No, he hasn't. I'm still in Galway. What's the news on the dinghy?"

"Blade has the details but I couldn't give him much to go on, I'm afraid. Oh, and Duffy wanted a word with you."

Sweetman sighed. The assistant commissioner hadn't had her report in over twenty-four hours. Such lapses made Duffy irritable. "I suppose you better put me through then."

"He's not here just now. Look, why don't you call in again around ten? I won't be here but Duffy will."

"Right. Anything else? What about Blade? Where is he now?"

"He's here, there and everywhere. Last I heard he was in Finglas. Where exactly in Galway are you, just in case your mobile's down or something?"

"In the city itself. I'll be grabbing a bite to eat here then I'm off to see my folks."

"In Kidafane, wasn't it?"

"God, you've a great head for names altogether, Joe. Talk to you later."

There's an Italian restaurant on the western side of the square and a light breeze was carrying the aroma of Mediterranean herbs and pasta to Sweetman's nostrils. Her mouth began to water.

She decided that her expense account would bear the cost of a glass of red wine as well.

"His name," Inspector Pat Hughes said, "is Leonard Reilly, known as Titch to friend and foe alike."

"Small, is he?" Blade asked, inspecting the photographs: one was frontal, the other a profile. Reilly reminded him of a younger Kevin Kostner but with coarser features.

"About five six. Listen, Blade, I don't mind telling you this but if you have anything on Reilly then you'll be doing me a gigantic favour. I've been after him for years, him and his mates. Oh, we get them for little things, just to annoy them and let them know we have our eye on them. But that's as far as it goes."

"What are the big things then?"

"Remember when you and me were in Pearse Street together and we had that prostitute thing?"

"The murders? Jesus, that's going back a bit. When were they now? Eighty-two or so? Was Reilly behind them?"

"I think he was. In fact I'm nearly sure he was. And a lot more local stuff. You've seen the place, Blade. There's a lot goes on in Kilbarrack. Did you know that half the dope in the city is supplied from here?"

"No, I didn't."

"And probably half the illegal weapons too. Now, I don't know about the heroin but I do know about the guns. That's Titch Reilly's territory. If I could bust him for that I'd be laughing."

"So show me where he lives, Pat, and I'll deliver you his balls on a plate."

Hughes went to a large-scale map of the area. He pointed to a house on the periphery of a housing estate.

"Right here. But he's seldom at home."

"I don't want him to be at home. Not for the present anyway. Can we find out?"

"No problem. I'll have a couple of the lads cruise the street." He paused, thoughtful. "But tell me something,

Blade. What are *you* looking for that Reilly has?"

"Chips. About twenty-five million pounds' worth."

"Fuck *me*. Is he opening a chain of takeaways or what?"

"Pull up a chair, Pat, and I'll tell you all about it. We've plenty of time. I want to see what's in that house as much as you do, but I want to do it after dark."

Thirty

Sweetman took the road that led from the village of Kidafane to her father's farm. It was already twilight when she passed the boreen that marked the southern periphery of the holding. She switched on her headlights then tuned the radio to the local station. It was playing a sample of the music Sweetman referred to as "diddly-dee", the repetitive fiddle, pipes and bodhran folk tunes that she loathed. She changed to Radio One, and was in time to catch some of the national news. SIPTU was planning industrial action. She silenced the radio.

At the same moment, she saw the lights in her rearview mirror. A car—a large, white BMW—was coming up behind her, travelling recklessly fast. The driver hadn't bothered to dim his lights either, and Sweetman pressed the base of the mirror in order to engage the anti-dazzle device.

There was no room for the car to overtake her; this stretch of the road was extremely narrow. To be sure, there were a number of small lay-bys constructed for this purpose, but Sweetman chose to ignore them. The fecker could just wait, couldn't he?

But the fecker was not in a patient mood. Sweetman jumped as the angry blast of a horn sounded, appearing to come from a spot just centimetres behind her rear bumper.

She was suddenly fearful. She had her gun in her bag, it was true, and she was a well-trained police officer, prepared for many emergencies. Yet she was at the same time a lone woman driving in the darkness of a deserted minor road in the middle of nowhere. She squinted in her mirror, trying to make out who was in the car following her. The headlights blazed as brightly as ever, yet, despite their glare, she discerned to her dismay not one, but three or more dark figures. Sweetman pressed the accelerator to the floor.

The road twisted abruptly.

Sweetman cursed and quickened her pace, bringing to bear all her driving skills. Blade, she thought, if he were in the passenger seat, would be shitting bricks by now. That seat was now occupied by her handbag. She had to get to her phone. Sweetman took one hand off the wheel and reached out blindly for the bag. The catch was on and she fumbled to release it. But she was forced to return her left hand to the wheel as another bend loomed and, when she groped again for the bag, she knocked it sideways, the catch falling out of reach.

"Damn!" Sweetman took her eyes from the road for an instant—just long enough for her to ascertain the bag's location. Then she lunged for it, gripped it, and brought it onto her lap. Her car almost left the road.

She was shaking as she released the clasp and rummaged inside for her mobile phone, promising herself that from now on she'd keep the instrument on the dashboard when driving. She punched in 999.

"Emergency. . . . "

"Gardaí," Orla said, "and make it quick."

Two seconds passed before the police switchboard operator responded.

"Officer in trouble," Sweetman said. "DS Sweetman. Require immediate assistance."

"Yes, sarge. If I could have your loca—"

"North of Kidafane, County Galway. I'm near the Mayo border. Make it quick, will you?"

"We're onto it, sarge. Please hold the line open."

Her pursuers had fallen back somewhat when she'd increased speed. But not for long. The car was again keeping pace with her. Its driver had the advantage of the hunter: Sweetman it was who had to reconnoitre the road ahead, judge bends in a split second, steer accordingly; the car behind had only to follow her every manoeuvre. Sweetman's hands were wet on the steering wheel.

As she exited a bend at speed, she saw headlights from the opposite direction. The vehicle was approaching slowly, yet Sweetman knew there was very little room for them to pass. The road was slightly wider at this point and she decided that, with two wheels on the grass verge, she might make it with perhaps only the loss of a door-mirror. She slowed to thirty and mounted the verge.

The events of the following seconds seemed to Sweetman to take place in slow, nightmarish motion. She heard another blast of a horn, then two more: the headlights on her tail flashed three times: the driver of the car ahead slowed and turned his full beam upon her: the car swivelled and blocked the road: Sweetman slammed on her brakes.

She picked up her phone.

"Repeat urgent request for assistance!"

Nothing. Sweetman heard car doors slamming and saw two men emerge from the vehicle that blocked the road. They carried handguns.

"DS Sweetman here. Request assistance." She hit the central locking of her car.

"Hello? DS Sweetman? We've two units heading your way. If I could just have your—"

The car window on Sweetman's side imploded with a shower of glass fragments that sparkled like gems in the lights of the other vehicles. She felt several bite into her cheek and ducked low in instinct. A gloved hand reached through the shattered window; Sweetman looked on helplessly as the catch on the door was raised.

She glanced around for her bag; it lay upside down on the floor, again out of reach. A thin voice was coming from her telephone; it too lay on the floor, invisible in the well beneath the steering column.

"Out, bitch! Get the fuck out of there."

Sweetman saw the gun and the black balaclava the man wore. She knew better than to argue with an armed man so attired. She stepped out of the car.

There were five of them. Three had shared the car that had pursued her. All wore balaclavas, and together represented one of the most frightening spectacles Orla Sweetman had ever seen. Suddenly she was a detective sergeant no longer, but a defenceless woman at the mercy of five armed men.

She felt her hands being grasped roughly, wrenched behind her back. Then somebody was wrapping a length of strong adhesive tape about her wrists.

"Normally what they do is wind gaffer tape around the

head—*that's the stuff photographers and*—"

"*I know what it is.*"

Orla, again acting on instinct, tensed her muscles and ligaments. Even so, the tape was already beginning to restrict her blood circulation. She knew that her hands would be numb within minutes.

"Get that phone," somebody said. Sweetman couldn't see him.

"What phone?" another asked. She noticed now, despite her fear, that the accents weren't local and tried to place them. Two spoke with what could only be Dublin accents; where the others hailed from it was hard to say, and accents were low on Sweetman's list of priorities at that moment.

"I hear a fuckin' phone," the first voice said. "It's in the car somewhere. Find the fuckin' thing, will ya?"

Some seconds passed. Then: "Yeah, it's here. What'll I do with it? There's somebody on the other end."

"Then wish him a happy fuckin' Christmas and hang up."

"How do I do that? I don't know how to use these yokes."

"Oh, for fuck's sake! Here, gimme that thing."

Sweetman heard the sound of something small plopping into water. Then a hand grabbed her hair and pulled her head back. She stared into eyes that glittered from behind two slits in black wool as one of her tormentors sealed her mouth with a smaller length of duct tape. Seldom before had Sweetman felt so utterly helpless. She felt her bile rising.

"Right, lads, go," came the first, authoritative, voice.

They frogmarched Sweetman to the car that had pursued her. They weren't gentle, and her head collided painfully with the top of the door frame as she was thrust into the back seat. Her thruster got in on one side and was joined by another man, wedging Sweetman in the middle. Two more men slid into the front seats, the driver gunned the engine, reversed into a farm-gate opening, turned the car and roared off, back the way they'd come.

"Get her head down," the man in the front passenger seat ordered. "Shove her head down between her knees. And you lot get your headgear off."

"She was on the phone," the man on Sweetman's left said presently. "She must have been calling for backup."

"Backup, me arse," the man in the front seat said. "You know what these boggers are like. It'd take them the best part of an hour to get here and by the time they find her car we'll be halfway to Dublin."

Dubliners, Sweetman thought: out-of-towners, brought in to do a job. From her painful, cramped position she attempted to make sense of what was happening to her. That she was in mortal danger was clear; men in balaclavas did not mess about. She'd encountered men such as he who sat in the front passenger seat; the leader's voice and demeanour had told her that she was dealing with a seasoned paramilitary, one who wouldn't hesitate to kill at the slightest provocation.

These were the Boys; she'd little doubt about that. Yet she wondered about the purpose of this exercise. The Boys were not in the habit of expending their resources on the abduction of a lowly detective sergeant. There was more.

Though her hands were aching now, growing progressively number, and her head throbbed from the blood pounding in her temples, Sweetman's mind was lucid. She knew that some person or persons had been trying to persuade her to drop the O'Neill investigation. She'd assumed they were locals. Now she was beginning to think that the mystery surrounding the life and death of Martin O'Neill had ramifications that went beyond an old squabble or feud at local level. Her abductors were contract men, sent to County Galway in order to halt the investigation in its tracks. Blade was right: the game was bigger than she'd imagined.

The car had left the minor road. The flash of many headlights and the sounds of increasingly heavy traffic told Orla they were travelling on a main road. To Dublin.

"Get that tape off of her," the man in the front abruptly ordered. "I want to hear how much she knows. But keep her head down."

The tape was ripped unceremoniously from Sweetman's mouth. She swore she'd felt some skin come with it. She gasped with pain.

"Now, Orla dear," the leader said, "I'll be wanting a few answers. And you're going to be a good girl and give 'em to me, all right?"

Sweetman was silent.

"All *right?*"

"Yes."

"Good. Now, this O'Neill fella: who wasted him?"

She paused, wondering. "Didn't *ye?*"

The leader laughed. "If we did then I wouldn't be asking you, now would I? So let's try it again: Who wasted Martin O'Neill?"

"I don't know."

"Come on, Orla. You must have some idea. How long

have you been on the case now? A fortnight?"

"Yes. And I honestly don't know."

There was a long silence, broken only by the intermittent sounds and lights of oncoming traffic.

"I think I need a smoke," the man in the front seat said. But there was something about the manner in which he said it that caused alarm bells to ring in Orla's head. She heard the faint click of the cigar lighter in the dashboard being depressed. She'd shared a car often enough with Blade Macken and his Hamlet cigars to recognize that sound.

"So you honestly don't know?" The voice was ominously calm now.

"No. I swear I don't."

Orla heard another click from the dashboard. Then somebody switched on the car radio. Daniel O'Donnell was giving "Carrickfergus" his best effort; his mother would have been proud.

A hand gripped Orla's pinioned wrists and yanked them upwards. She cried out as her arms were nearly wrenched from their sockets. Another hand—this time a gloved one—grasped the fingers of her left hand, allowing the tips to be exposed.

"No long nails, I see," the leader's voice came. "That's good. Very professional, very businesslike."

The tips of your fingers rank among the most sensitive parts of the body. You can prove this to yourself by trying to take your pulse by pressing your tongue against the artery on your wrist. You'll feel nothing. Yet the tips of your fingers will register what that sensitive organ, the tongue, cannot.

Orla screamed as agony more excruciating than she'd ever endured seared the tip of her middle finger. She almost fainted. Her entire body shuddered. She screeched again as white fire burned into the tip of her exposed and imprisoned index finger. She smelt roasting skin. Then she was blubbering like a baby. She heard her own voice and barely recognized it. It was pleading for mercy.

"Now, bitch," she heard that cold, impassive voice speaking through her tears. "I'm going to ask you again: Who shot Martin O'Neill?"

Her body seemed to have disappeared; only the searing agony in her fingers filled her consciousness. And she *was* conscious, would remain conscious: the doctors would explain later that it's harder to lose consciousness when your head is between your knees and the flow of blood to the brain is thus intensified.

"Please," she moaned. "I don't *know*. Please!"

"The other one," the leader said. The radio was silent, and again Orla heard the click of the cigar lighter as it was pushed home into its socket. Her other hand was held in a tight, gloved grip.

"The *right* hand this time, Orla. We'll start with your middle finger—you know: the one you play with yourself with. No more self-abuse for Detective Sergeant Sweetman for weeks to come. Or you'll have to get the boyfriend to do it for you."

There was coarse laughter on all sides. Sweetman felt hot tears drip from her eyes.

She heard the lighter announce its readiness like the cocking of a gun held against the temple.

"I think she's tellin' the truth." A different voice: that of the driver.

"Like fuck she is."

"No, I really do. I mean, if she knows who popped O'Neill then what's she doin' in County Galway? Eh? Does that make sense to you? It doesn't to me."

There was movement in the front passenger seat. Orla felt a head brush against hers and the voice of the leader spoke close to her ear.

"You hear that, Orla? You've a friend. If you're nice to him he might even let you give him one. That'd make a nice change from your man—what's his name?—John, isn't it? Has he got himself a job yet or is he still burning the shepherd's pie every Thursday?"

John. Sweetman's fiancé of six years. Somebody, somewhere, had been doing their homework, and doing it well. Orla was frightened more than ever. Her damaged fingers still screamed their torment, yet her mind was working full out.

Her father, her mother: somebody with real power and influence had impinged upon their private lives. Now she was discovering that that somebody knew more about her own domestic arrangements than was decent.

Her mouth was sealed with another strip of duct tape and the car sped on into the night, its occupants and its radio maintaining silence.

Thirty-One

Sweetman didn't know what time it was when her abductors stopped the car. Her watch was out of sight, behind her back, where the mutilated fingers of her left hand continued to shoot waves of pain through her body; she still sat with her head between her knees and so had no opportunity of reading the clock on the dashboard. She thought it might be midnight.

"Headgear on, lads," the leader ordered from the front seat and Sweetman heard the soft rustle of wool. Then she was dragged from the back seat of the car. She stood, dizzy and unsteady from her ordeal and her cramped limbs, and breathed cool air.

The street, dark and lifeless now, might have been anywhere, in any town or city. But she knew it was Dublin; the red-black sky told her that, as had the steady build-up of traffic she'd heard on the final leg of the journey. Sweetman had barely time to catch a glimpse of a concrete front yard before she was marched through the front door. One of the men threw a switch and a weak bulb revealed a little hallway with a door leading off and a kitchen visible beyond the stairs. An ordinary two-up, two-down Corporation house.

But not quite. The floor-covering in the hall was a red-and-green carpet with a paisley design and an unusually thick pile. Sweetman looked on in puzzlement as one of her captors went to the door leading to the kitchen, bent and tugged smartly on the spot where the carpet met the door saddle. It came up in his hands. He began to roll it back, stopping when halfway to where the stairs began.

There were bare floorboards, swept clean. There was also the unmistakable shape of a door, complete with steel handle, which was recessed in the wood. The man in the balaclava tugged on the handle and the door opened, revealing blackness below.

Sweetman was seized by a terror she hadn't experienced for many years—not since the age of five. There'd been a cellar in the big house near Tuam owned by her Aunt Aggie. They'd played in the house as children, she and her sister Fildelma and Matt junior. Matt, aged eleven at the time, had been placed in charge of the girls while Aggie was away one evening. They'd explored the house, venturing into the attic where Aggie kept the junk of ages. Exciting stuff. But Matt it was who'd discovered the door to the cellar. He'd been afraid of the dark himself yet had dared Fidelma to go down. She'd chickened out. Orla had been the brave one.

Matt had locked the door, leaving her in the dark for the longest, most terrifying hour of her young life. Orla had never got over it. There'd been invisible, tiny creatures that scurried away in the darkness. . . .

"I'm not going down there!" she told her captors. She tried to back away. She felt as if she were about to pass out.

"You are," said the smallest of the men, and she recognized his voice as that of the man in the passenger seat. "If we have to carry you down feet first, you're going. Now, which is it to be?"

The light switch was located below ground. The steps down which Orla was ushered were of fresh timber. Where they ended was a bare, concrete floor. Three doors led off. Two were shut; she was pushed through the third.

The room smelled of mildew. When the light was switched on she saw it contained no furniture other than an old kitchen table and two chairs. There was a phone on the table. A pile of old magazines and newspapers lay on the floor.

Sweetman saw her five captors clearly for the first time. Apart from the black balaclavas there was nothing out of the ordinary about them. Each wore denims, thick-soled shoes and a lightweight nylon jacket. They varied in build. The leader was the smallest, but what he lacked in height he made up for in build; he looked muscular and very, very fit.

"There's some flex in the shed in the backyard," he said. "Bring it here."

The "flex" proved to be a long length of cable that must have been attached at one time to a TV aerial. At a gesture from the leader the gaffer tape was removed from Orla's wrists. She had no feeling in her hands. It returned now and with it the intense agony of her burnt fingertips; she had to bite her lip to cope with the pain.

He was thorough; he knew his knots. The back of the chair had three supporting rods, and Orla's arms were thrust into the spaces that divided them; then each of her wrists was secured individually to a chair rod so that her hands didn't touch; the cable was then looped again and again, until at last Orla's wrists and ankles were imprisoned by a veritable cat's cradle of TV cable. The leader tested his handiwork with a sharp tug, grunted, then turned to his men.

"Give me a minute, will yiz," he said. "I'm going to call Delta One."

"There's a phone right here."

He looked at Sweetman. "No, I'll use the one upstairs." He left.

Delta One. A codename. Was this the man who'd decide Sweetman's fate? If so, then Delta One had given the order to abduct her, had known precisely where she'd be earlier that evening. She hadn't been followed on her journey to and from the Franciscan abbey. She was certain of that; her car had been the only one on the small road to Kidafane. So that left only three possibilities.

One: her father had informed on her. No, that was in-conceivable.

Two: Brother Alphonsus was a player in the game. She dismissed that theory as well; the friar had shown her every courtesy and, had he been involved, most surely would not have given her access to the "quartermaster's book" but would instead have sent her on her way none the wiser about Brother Louis' identity.

The third possibility sent a shiver up Sweetman's spine. She'd called Harcourt Square.

Joe Cunningham she could rule out: he and Orla went back a long way; Joe was one of the most trustworthy men she knew. He couldn't be bought at any price; several vil-lains doing long stretches in Mountjoy Prison could attest to that fact.

So if Joe was in the clear, who else knew about that phone call? It would have been mentioned in Cunningham's daily report—but Cunningham, she knew, had been on duty from two to ten p.m. Delta One—and Deltas Two to Six; she was beginning to think of her captors in those terms—had been tipped off long before Cunningham's shift ended. Sweetman would demand a full investigation when this was over.

Providing, that is, she survived.

Delta Two had returned. He threw Sweetman a look that was, because of the concealing balaclava, unreadable.

"He's on his way," he said.

He sat down at the table, close to Orla, and studied her closely, fingers tapping irritatingly on the tabletop. It caused Orla to turn her attention to her own hands.

There was something Delta Two had overlooked, thorough though he'd been. The duct tape about her wrists had caused her hands to swell. Now her blood circulation was returning to normal; the cable did not restrict her arteries. The bonds had been tight at the outset but were growing progressively looser as the swelling in her hands diminished. Orla was careful not to move them, fearing that one of the other men might spot the action. Nevertheless she flexed her wrist muscles and was gratified to feel the play in the cable. One weak point in the cat's cradle meant a weakness in the whole.

The trapdoor had been left open and Sweetman heard the ringing of the front doorbell some time later. Delta One had arrived. The Delta Group was complete.

Who were they though? She'd thought at the beginning, when pressure had been exerted on her father, that the Boys, the IRA, were involved. She ruled that out now. This wasn't how the Boys operated; they worked in cells: active-service units comprising three or four individuals. The Deltas were six. There was any number of suspects however. The Irish National Liberation Army; the Continuity Army Council; the Real IRA, the latest IRA offshoot. Or the Provos themselves.

But they might not even be paramilitaries. Any thug or common criminal could cut eye-holes and mouth-holes in a black balaclava, and have access to guns as well—Assistant Commissioner Duffy was forever complaining that the country was awash with illegally-held firearms.

Yet small details in the men's demeanour and behaviour pointed to membership—if not current then past—of paramilitary groups. There was also the codename Delta; apart from civil aviation, the phonetic alphabet tends to be used almost exclusively by armed forces, whether legal or illegal.

Delta One had entered the house. Even through the wood of the closed door of her holding-room, Sweetman heard his loud, if indistinct, voice. It sounded oddly familiar too. And excited. Then somebody shut the trapdoor, cutting off all sound from above. Yet before it closed she'd heard, quite audibly, Delta One's exclamation of either surprise or admiration.

"Be the holy!" he'd said. "Well, well, well!"

Thirty-Two

Northeast of the DART railway station in Kilbarrack lies a grassy expanse of open ground where children play and sometimes semi-wild ponies graze. It will not stay green and open for very much longer; the outward push of Dublin City will see to that. Walls overlook the grass and they in turn are overlooked by the backs of houses, all two-up, two-down, the cramped dwellings of what was once called the working class.

It was dark when Blade Macken, Inspector Hughes and a detective cruised slowly past the fronts of these dwellings. Children still loitered on the street; the flickering light of televisions fell threw the curtains at every window; a satellite dish was riveted to every chimney stack or gable.

Macken, seated in the back of the car, jumped as something thudded against his window. When he looked he saw that a stone had hit the glass, leaving a small, white depression.

"Little bastards," muttered Hughes. "They know who we are. I think they're born with an extra sense that allows them to identify coppers by smell alone."

Blade looked behind. Two boys, who bore a striking resemblance to Danno and Antho of Finglas, stared back at him defiantly. The car had stopped.

"That's the house."

Blade leaned forward. It was the last one on the street. Beyond lay open ground; within a year or two new houses and streets similar to this one would have risen there. But at present it was a good place for headquarters if you needed privacy. Your unpaid gang of young vigilantes would see that you weren't disturbed. Unlike the other houses in the street that of Titch Reilly had no front garden. The small patch of earth had been cemented over. A car was parked there.

"Looks as if there's somebody home after all," Blade said. A light showed in the hall. The rest of the house was in darkness.

"Fuck," Hughes said. "Sorry, Blade, but that ballses up your operation and mine. We can't go in there. We've nothing on Reilly. He'd just laugh in our faces."

But Blade was eyeing another car, parked on the street outside the house. It was a series-seven BMW, white. Expensive.

"Could we run a check on that motor?" he asked. "It might just be stolen."

Hughes shook his head. "Forget it. It's Reilly's. Paid for in cash too." He gave a sign to the detective in the driving seat. "Let's go, Sean," he said. "We'll come back later. Maybe we'll have more luck then."

Thirty-Three

Two men had been left to guard her. Delta Five and Delta Six was how she thought of them; she deduced that they came lowest in the pecking order. Their faces were still concealed behind the black wool—and that fact came as an immense reassurance for Sweetman. It meant that she was, for the time being at least, to be kept alive. But once those balaclavas were removed . . .

The minutes passed. Sweetman heard muffled, distant voices raised at intervals—even the incongruous sound of laughter at one point. Her two captors remained mute. They may have been under orders to speak as little as possible in order to minimize the risk of their voices giving away their identities, should they be arrested at some later date. This thought reinforced Sweetman's belief that she might yet escape with her life. Delta Six was sitting in the chair recently occupied by the gang leader, a pistol lying before him on the table; though she couldn't see him from her present position, she guessed that Delta Five had taken up sentry duty by the door.

She heard the sound of the trapdoor opening and footfalls on the stairs. A car door slammed in the distance and an engine started up. Delta One had departed.

The court had been in session; the case had been placed before Sweetman's judge, jury—and possible executioner. The verdict could have gone either way. She began to sweat. Bile rose in her throat and she tasted garlic, a reminder of the dish she'd enjoyed in the Italian restaurant on Eyre Square. Spaghetti bolognese: it was not exactly what she'd have chosen for her final meal.

But Delta Two and the others re-entered the room with masked features. Sweetman heaved a sigh of relief through her nostrils. The leader noticed it.

"Good news, Orla my dear," he said. "You may collect your pension yet."

She looked at him.

"You're staying here. But don't worry; it won't be for long. A day at the most. Then we'll drop you off at the DART station or something. What do you think of that? We're not as bad as we look, eh?"

He moved behind her chair.

"Too bad about the fingers. But we had to be sure you see. A little rub with ointment and you'll be as right as rain again, believe me. No hard feelings I hope."

He came into view again.

"I'll be off now. I doubt very much if we'll meet again, so I'll wish you luck." He patted Delta Six on the shoulder. "I'm leaving this fine lad here to keep you company. You won't recognize him but he's the fella who came to your rescue in the car, God bless his kind soul. A real knight in shining armour."

Delta Six grinned.

"He has orders to feed and water you. I don't know what

we'll do about toilet arrangements but sure ye can work something out between yiz. Oh, and do yourself a favour, will you, Orla? Don't try to escape, if you can help it. If you do, he has my blessing to put one between your eyes. Okay?"

Sweetman nodded.

But Delta Two had remembered something. "I meant to ask. What happened to the petrol can?"

A companion jerked a thumb at the ceiling. "I put it under the stairs."

"A fine place for it!" said Delta Two. "We'll take it with us. Can't leave it lying there. There might be an accident, and where would that leave us?"

And then the four were gone, leaving her alone with her Sir Galahad.

Thirty-Four

Delta Six had found an old issue of *In Dublin* and was leafing through it without much interest. He didn't strike Orla as being a man who did a lot of reading.

He'd left her alone for a few minutes, to return with a pillow and a mattress that belonged to a single bed. He'd placed these next to the table. Clearly his orders were to remain in the room, day and night. The trapdoor was shut. She wondered whether the rug had been rolled back into place.

Orla had taken advantage of his temporary absence. Her left hand still hurt like the devil yet this was the hand she'd chosen to free. Men, she knew, didn't pay much attention to a woman's jewellery: an engagement ring was something a man gave to his betrothed then promptly lost any further interest in. Delta Two had completely ignored Sweetman's own ring.

He shouldn't have. She'd been flabbergasted when John had taken it from its box and placed it on her finger. It was huge, larger than any other solitaire ring she'd ever seen. Naturally she'd had it valued the following day and discovered to her amazement that it must have set John back at least £1,000. But he could afford the extravagance in those days, when he still held down his high-paying job at the printers, before the firm laid off all its compositors.

The huge diamond had a flaw, however: it had been cut well, yet polished inexpertly, so that its facets were considerably sharper than they should have been. Sweetman knew this to her cost; she'd laddered more than one pair of tights before deciding that it was always wiser to don them *before* putting on her engagement ring.

But what hitherto was a curse now became a godsend. She could revolve her left hand freely within the constraints of the cable, and was moreover able to bring her two hands together. She'd begun to saw at the loop that secured her right wrist. It was tough going; you had to concentrate on a single point. But she was succeeding, could already feel the cable loosening slightly.

Delta Six grew tired of his magazine and threw it aside. He stared at Sweetman, thinking. Then he said: "Would you fancy a cup of tea? I know *I* would."

She nodded gratefully. He went into the adjoining room.

He was gone about ten minutes, during which time Sweetman made more progress with the cable. She'd sawn through one part of the plastic casing and knew, from the more abrasive feel under the diamond, that she'd reached the meshed "screen" of the cable. The diamond cut through the wafer-thin strands of metal like a knife through butter. More plastic, then she was sawing through the copper core. She was halfway there.

Her captor returned with a tray laden with milk and sugar and two mugs of tea.

"Now, what are we going to do, Orla?" he said. "You can't drink it through your nose, now can you? But I'll tell you what: if you promise me you won't scream for help or anything I'll take that tape off. Okay?"

She nodded vigorously.

"Yeah, but you better not. 'Cos if you do, I've orders to shoot you. Do we understand each other?"

Sweetman gasped as her mouth was freed of the duct tape. Her lips felt red and raw. She gulped in great mouthfuls of air.

"I'll say this for you," said Delta Six: "you look a damn sight better without that thing." She saw his eyes appraise her from head to toe. "Matter of fact, you're not bad-lookin' at all—for a cop."

Sweetman was suddenly afraid; she felt inordinately helpless in that chair. But Delta Six was pouring milk into a mug.

"Sugar?" he asked pleasantly.

"Just the milk."

He grinned. "No sugar, eh? Bad for the figure." The appraising look again. "God, you've lovely legs, Orla. Did anybody ever tell you that?"

Humour the fecker.

"Thanks. Oh, and I'm grateful to you for putting in a good word for me back there—in the car. I didn't get a chance to tell you that."

He brought the mug of tea and held it gently against her lower lip. She bent her head and sipped. She hadn't appreciated how thirsty she was; fear made your throat dry.

"Is it all right?" he asked.

"Yes, thanks. A bit hot, but nice."

"Like meself," said Delta Six.

She laughed nervously. Change the fecking subject, Orla.

"Look, do you mind if I ask you something?"

"It depends."

"I don't know who ye fellas are—and maybe I don't *want* to know—but what have ye against my father?"

"Us? Not a thing."

"But why did ye threaten him? Why did ye kill the dog?"

He let her sip more tea. "Sure we've nothin' against your da, Orla. We're only doing a job."

"You're freelance, then?"

"You could say that. It's business, and that's all I'm goin' to say. I could get in trouble if I told you any more."

She had to know the answer to one more question.

"Just tell me this much. Why was Martin O'Neill so important? I know ye didn't kill him, but someone thought he was important enough to kill."

He shrugged. "I don't know, Orla. It's as simple as that." A pause. "Are you married?"

"Eh, yeah," she lied. "I've three kids."

"Hmm. Why are all the good birds taken?" He'd evidently forgotten what Delta Two had said about her fiancé. Again the eyes were scanning her helpless body.

Orla had sawn completely through the cable; she could move her right hand freely.

"Jayziz, but you're a fine piece altogether, do you know that?" he said in a different tone, and stammered slightly when he said it. There was palpable danger here. He moved closer, and placed a hand on her thigh. Sweetman stiffened.

"How about a kiss? Just a little one?" His mouth was almost touching hers; her lips brushed against the black wool of the balaclava. She jerked her head away.

"Ah, come on now. Sure it w-won't do any harm." The stutter again; Orla was aware that his breathing had quickened.

He grasped her hair in one hand and pulled her head forward. His other hand slid down to the hem of Sweetman's skirt, which had ridden up to mid-thigh.

"Don't . . . please."

His breathing was coming in hoarse gasps now. Sweetman suddenly recollected another incident from her childhood, when she'd been approached by a man on her way home from school. Nothing had happened, she'd been able to shake him off, yet Sweetman always remembered how his voice and breathing had sounded: excited, out of control.

"Just a little one. . . ."

Delta Six's hand slid between her thighs and began to force its way higher. She opened her mouth to protest, and found it filled with her captor's tongue, protruding from the hole in the balaclava. She shouted angrily but unintelligibly. Delta Six's tongue, wet with spittle, explored her mouth as inexpertly as a schoolboy's. The hand was pressing the Lycra of her tights against her clitoris. The man's breathing had metamorphosed into a series of bestial grunts.

Behind the chair Sweetman's hands fought to free themselves. Her attacker's hand fought with the Lycra, attempting to rend it by the pressure of his fingertips. Then he was using two hands, trying to force her legs apart. But her legs had been bound securely to the legs of the chair.

His eyes were wild as he straightened. He was moaning like a demon in distress.

Then his fingers left her private places and went to his

crotch. He unzipped his fly and fumbled feverishly with his underpants. His cock, engorged and quivering, emerged. It glistened slickly at the tip of the glans.

Orla screamed as he grasped her hair again and forced her face against his member. She blubbered as that *thing* entered her mouth.

No amount of police work could have prepared her for the sheer awfulness of the violation of her person. To be sure, she'd investigated several rape cases, had listened to sobbing victims as they recounted the assault. She'd noted down details, often horrifyingly graphic. She'd sympathized and empathized.

Yet nothing could have prepared her for the experience itself: to endure the gross indignity, the helpless anger, the sheer repulsiveness of a stranger's violent invasion of your body, wholly and completely against your will.

Sweetman was choking as Delta Six continued to thrust. Her mind screamed in protest as his—disgust heaped upon horror!—*unwashed* shaft threatened to block her windpipe. And all the while brutish sounds were issuing from his throat.

She had her right hand free.

She'd heard about it and read about it, but didn't think it was possible. Somebody-or-other in America who conducted self-defence classes for women swore by it. It was the ultimate counteraction for the rape victim. She'd no other choice than to put it to the test.

Sweetman grabbed her attacker's cock by the base of the shaft, forcing it out of her mouth. Then she gave it a hard and vicious twist, counterclockwise. She felt muscle and ligament tear beneath her fingers.

Delta Six was roaring like a wounded bull. He clutched his ruined penis with both hands, his eyes bulging from their sockets, and sank to his knees.

Shaking and sobbing, Sweetman strove to release her left hand. The cable fell away. She worked her legs out of the bonds that secured her ankles.

Free.

Delta Six was squatting on the floor, groaning and whimpering. The gun was still on the table. Sweetman picked it up with shaking hands and trained it on her attacker. She opened her mouth to speak but such was the traumatic effect of her recent ordeal that she could bring no words forth. Her hands were shaking so violently that she couldn't aim the gun.

Delta Six's face was a deathly white and he was whining pitifully. He looked as though he might faint at any moment. His eyes pleaded for mercy.

"You bastard!" Sweetman got the words out at last, "You dirty, filthy bastard! Give me just one good reason why I shouldn't put you out of your fucking misery."

"D-don't. . . ."

Sweetman cocked the gun.

"Don't. P-p-please."

She almost pulled the trigger. It was so, so tempting. But, in the end, she couldn't. Keeping the man under shot, she reached for the mug she'd drunk from and filled her mouth with tea. She rinsed as thoroughly as she could, then spat the tea angrily over Delta Six. It would be some time before she felt clean again.

Somewhat calmer now, she walked over to the stricken

man—and brought the barrel of the gun down heavily on his head. He collapsed without a sound and lay still.

Sweetman sat down at the table and laid the gun to one side. She was trembling. She stared at the phone; she could call for reinforcements. But she didn't even know where she was. Moreover she'd no great wish to make a report of her forced confinement to a member of the local gardaí; she'd suffered enough humiliation for one night.

No one need ever know.

Oh, God! She understood now. Throughout her career Sweetman had passed judgement on those rape victims who either hadn't come forward at all or, if they had, had suddenly retracted their statements or refused to give evidence that could convict their attackers. She'd considered such women cowards, even traitors to their sex. At last Sweetman understood: it wasn't quite that easy. She could imagine the innuendos of her colleagues in Harcourt Square, the whispered rumours, the talk behind her back. She'd never live it down.

Sorry, sisters, she thought, I'm just like you. I'm a coward as well. At that moment she hated herself more than she despised the unconscious man on the floor. She felt like dirt.

Gun in hand, Sweetman ascended the stair. She paused and listened. Not a sound. She pushed at the trapdoor. It lifted a fraction.

Then caught.

The door refused to budge. Sweetman's heart began to pump furiously. She tucked the gun into her waistband and pushed harder, bringing into play the heel of her damaged hand. Again the door caught.

She was sweating now, the old childhood dread returning. Trapped in a cellar. Trapped moreover with a rapist
who might regain consciousness at any moment. She pushed
again, almost weeping with frustration. Yet again the door
caught, blocked by something unyielding on the floor above.

What happened to the petrol can?

I put it under the stairs.

*A fine place for it! We'll take it with us. Can't leave it ly-
ing there. There might be an accident, and then where would
we be?*

Trapped by a door that had been left open, the door to
the utility space under the stairs. Sweetman pushed again
with all the strength she could muster. Yet she knew it was
hopeless.

She needed tools. An axe, a hammer, anything. She went
down the short flight of stairs again and looked into the
room next to that in which the unconscious man was lying.
It was a small kitchen, very untidy, and distinctly lacking in
any instrument that would suit her purpose.

She went to the room on the other side and opened the
door. It was in darkness. She found the switch.

Sweetman blinked in astonishment as the room flooded
with light. There were indeed tools here, a great many of
them. They were more than adequate to assist her in her
escape. The wooden trapdoor would be no obstacle to these
particular tools.

Some of them were designed to penetrate the metal of a
battle tank.

Thirty-Five

The street was deserted. The children were long indoors. The satellite-television dishes attached to the chimney stacks and gables watched the sky. The TV sets themselves were being watched no longer.

The same small car was parked in the yard of the end house. The house was in darkness.

"The Beamer's gone," Blade said. "But who owns the other car?"

"It's Reilly's as well," Hughes said.

"Well, he can't drive two cars at the one time."

"No, but that doesn't mean there's no one at home. Will you check that, Sean?" Hughes said to the detective.

They watched as he rang the doorbell and waited. He returned to confirm the obvious.

"What now, Blade?"

"We're going in."

"Not that it's any of my business, but you Branch men don't bother with awkward little things like warrants, I suppose. Ye just waltz into people's homes?"

"Now, now, Pat, you shouldn't believe everything you read in *The Phoenix*," Blade said. "We're really very civil and polite about these things you know. Normally what happens is: if we don't get a response at the front door then we nip round the back and knock on the door there." He winked at Hughes. "Nothing wrong with that, is there?"

They left the detective in charge of the car and made their way to the back entrance. The wall was surmounted by a cheval-de-frise of broken glass embedded in cement. Long ago somebody had spray-painted the word "NOW!" on the wall in two-metre-high letters; it was the final part of a political message that could be read from passing trains.

"Dear me," Blade said, "the back gate seems to be open, Pat. Or maybe I pushed too hard. That's the trouble, you see, when you don't know your own strength."

Hughes chuckled. "Get in there now before we're seen."

But there was no sign of life on the open, grassy expanse. Blade pushed again and the remains of the latch clattered to the ground in the yard. Hughes followed him through.

There was a small shed and next to that a coal bunker. The shed contained nothing of interest; it was used to store old cans of paint, lengths of timber and assorted junk. Blade pointed to the back door of the house.

Titch Reilly had been criminally negligent: the door handle yielded to Hughes's touch. They entered the tiny kitchen; Blade fumbled for his car keys. He depressed the button on his miniature Swiss Army pocket-knife, the one attached to his key-ring; its light threw out a weak, red beam that lit up the floor.

The kitchen light came on. Blade turned, startled, to find Hughes with his hand on the switch.

"Why not?" he said. "We didn't break in. Reilly should be grateful to us for taking care of his property in his absence."

Hughes pushed open the door to the hall. Another door,

a smaller one, blocked the way: the door to the utility space. The inspector peeked inside and wrinkled his nose.

"Petrol," he said sourly. "That's a fire hazard, so it is."

Blade threw a switch under the stairs. The space was empty save for a vacuum cleaner and a raincoat hanging from a peg.

He shut the door.

The rest of the ground floor was dirty and smelled of neglect. It was also rather bare: there was a coffee-table and two armchairs in the front room, and very little else. The other rooms were equally frugally furnished. It had all the appearance of overnight accommodation rather than somebody's home.

"So what did you expect to find, Blade?" Hughes asked.

"I don't know, I don't know. Papers maybe. Something incriminating written down."

Hughes was examining a drawerless desk in the living room.

"Assuming Reilly would be that stupid," he said.

"You never know."

There was movement in the house next door. They heard muffled voices and shortly the sound of a toilet being flushed. A door slammed.

"Jayziz, you could hear an ant fart through these walls," Hughes said. "Right, let's have a look upstairs."

There were three bedrooms, the smallest no bigger than a closet; it was in use as a storage room. Each of the others held an unmade bed. There was a chest of drawers, a chair and an ottoman in the front bedroom. Blade inspected the last without much interest.

"Are we missing something, Pat?" he said.

"Such as?"

"I mean something that should be here but isn't."

Hughes shrugged. "I could mention a lot of things: a TV, a stereo, a washing machine, books, pictures . . . "

"No, something else."

He went downstairs to the hall and stood, thinking. Hughes followed.

"You know what it is?" Blade said suddenly. "It's a phone. I haven't seen a phone."

"Maybe he hasn't got one. Maybe he uses a mobile. He probably would if he's dealing. Safer that way."

But Blade wasn't convinced. He was peering at the dust that had accumulated on a small table in the hall. A set of car keys lay on it.

"There *was* a phone here," he announced. "Look, you can see the marks. And there's the socket. So what happened to the phone? Unless . . . "

"Where are you going?"

"To the one room we haven't checked yet. The bathroom."

Evidently Titch Reilly spent a great deal of time in the bathroom. It was stocked with all manner of toiletries: after-shave, hair gels and shampoos, deodorants, soaps, shaving gel and razors. The bathtub was spotlessly clean. Next to it was a small, white, wrought-iron table. And a telephone.

"Bingo," Blade said. "Now why didn't he just use an extension? Do you understand that?"

"Yes," Hughes said, "I do. He didn't want anybody eavesdropping when he was on the phone."

Blade looked at him strangely. "Christ, Pat," he said. "I

honestly never thought of that."

"That's because your kids don't live with you."

Macken lifted the instrument and pressed a button. "Redial?"

Blade nodded, then frowned. He replaced the receiver.

"Who was that?" Hughes asked. "Anyone we know?"

"Yeah. The Guards in Drogheda."

"Drogheda? Fuck me. Now why do you suppose—"

"I don't know, Pat. Your guess is as good as mine."

The first thing Sweetman had heard was the faint ringing of the doorbell. Then the footsteps, some minutes later. They'd come from the back of the house and were unmuffled by carpeting. Next she'd heard the voices.

Her abductors had returned. A day early; there'd been a change of plan.

There were at least two men, that much she could ascertain. It was impossible to identify the voices, much less what was being said. She'd remained stock-still at the bottom of the stairs, gun at the ready. The men had paused directly overhead; she'd heard a door closing.

She'd considered the arsenal. There were assault rifles there and boxes of ammunition. Fitting a clip into one of the guns would have taken her a couple of seconds. But fear had overpowered her, paralyzing her. She remained where she was, pistol in hand, hardly daring to breathe.

The voices sounded again, once more directly overhead. Sweetman knew that when that trapdoor opened she'd have to make a stand. They'd spared her life thus far. But she'd posed little or no threat. She was in no doubt that an armed confrontation now would have a bloody outcome. But she'd make a stand. What choice did she have? Sweetman steadied the hand that held the gun and waited for the trapdoor to open.

"Admit it, Pat," Blade Macken said. "There's fuck all here. We've nothing on Reilly."

"No. It was too good to be true. To hell with it anyway."

"Don't blame yourself. He'll slip up; you mark my words. They always do. It's just that I'd have liked to be around when he did."

Blade left everything exactly as he found it. They toured the small house again but discovered nothing out of the ordinary. It was time to leave.

They found the detective on the doorstep, about to ring the bell. He was agitated.

"There's an all-points out," he told them. "It's just after coming in on the radio." He turned to Macken. "Isn't DS Sweetman working with you, sir?"

Blade had a sense of dread. "She is."

"She's gone missing, sir. In County Galway."

Sweetman heard the faint sound of the front door closing. She remained quiet, heart still pounding, and waited for some minutes more. Then she stuck the gun into her waistband and ascended the stairs again. She pushed.

She could have screamed for joy when the trapdoor opened; she hardly believed it was possible. She clambered out and stood panting. The house was dark. The throbbing pain in her fingertips, forgotten during the past minutes, returned now to torment her.

Sweetman went into the front room and gingerly pulled the curtain back a fraction. There was a car in the yard. That was an unexpected bonus. And the keys, she reasoned, must surely be to hand, perhaps on Delta Six's person.

As it turned out, they were on the hall table.

When Sweetman departed she left Delta Six, still unconscious and trussed up like a chicken with the TV cable. And before leaving she'd made sure to remove his balaclava. The face revealed was ordinary but easily committed to memory. She wondered what the others would think on finding him there, bareheaded, gagged and bound, complete with badly mangled penis and the note she'd left beside him, the one that read:

THIS IS WHAT HAPPENS TO RAPISTS
DELTA SIX

One part of her prayed they wouldn't be too hard on him. Another part hoped they'd inflict a terrible punishment for his dereliction of duty. Serve the fucker right.

Before she turned out at the gate she wound down the window and spat again.

She was somewhere on the north side of Dublin; she saw the signpost for Baldoyle and Malahide when she reached the outskirts of the housing estate.

She thought hard. But she was dog-tired, close to exhaustion; the map of the city in her mind wouldn't yield its secrets. She knew only that she was heading in the wrong direction; her apartment lay to the south. Back through the housing estate again. Then she saw the lights twinkling on the promontory of Howth and, across the water of Dublin Bay, the lights of Dún Laoghaire. She had her bearings. The coast road at Clontarf. She made a right.

The city centre was like the grave as she drove slowly over O'Connell Bridge. She'd lost track of the time and was surprised to see that the dashboard clock registered 3.10. She turned left at Trinity College and sped down Nassau Street.

Then she saw the flashing blue light in her mirror.

The Guards were the last people she wanted to see tonight. Because she no longer had her handbag, or any sort of identification. To be sure, she could tell them who she was, and a telephone call to Harcourt Square would take care of the rest. But she was in no mood for this. Her fingers were burning, her body was aching, and her mind cried out for sleep. She stopped the car.

The patrolmen were a long time in leaving their vehicle. In her mirror Sweetman saw one of them talking into his radio. She wound down her window as his colleague approached.

"Is this your vehicle, madam?"

"No, guard, it's not." Why lie?

"Could I ask to see your driving licence, madam?"

"Ehh, I haven't got it with me. Look, I'm—"

"Would you mind stepping out of the car, please?"

She did so resignedly; she could hear on the still air the voice from the police radio. So far, so routine.

Then: "Does the owner of this vehicle know you're driving it, madam?"

The spinning blue light seemed to spin faster. The face of the young Guard looked alien and threatening below the peak of his cap; she didn't understand a word of what he was saying. Sweetman opened her mouth to speak but the dizziness got the better of her. The Guard caught her as she fainted.

She came to in a strange bed in a room with pale green walls.

Sunlight was casting strong shadows. She heard the sounds and smelled the odours of a hospital. She opened her eyes.

And looked into those of Blade Macken.

Thirty-Six

"It's, ehh, this turn here," Sweetman said.

"Are you sure now?"

"Yes . . . No. Look, it was dark, Blade—and I wasn't thinking very clearly."

Inspector Hughes, sitting in the backseat, patted Sweetman's shoulder.

"It's all right, sergeant," he said kindly. "You take your time. And we've plenty of time. From what you say, that guy won't be going anywhere in a mad hurry."

They were in Kilbarrack and Sweetman was having difficulty in recognizing the place in daylight. It didn't help that all the streets were built to the same specifications; they'd already explored a half dozen but none had chimed with Sweetman's recollection.

"Maybe we should just forget it, Blade," she said.

He turned to her and studied her bandaged hand.

"That's not like you at all, Sweetman. Jesus, if they'd done that to me I'd want the fuckers banged up for a long while."

But you don't *know*, Blade, she thought. You have no idea of what they—he—did to me. He made me dirty. You think you understand a lot of things, Blade Macken, but you could never understand *that*. Not really.

Sweetman knew it was the place; she recognized the house at the end of the cul-de-sac; unlike its neighbours, it had a concrete front yard. And she wanted to be as far away as possible from the place. For the second time in twenty-four hours she was here involuntarily. It was beyond endurance.

"Now," Macken said, "is this the place or isn't it?"

"Yes."

Blade knew it was too much for coincidence. Life wasn't like that; you didn't search a house in Kilbarrack one evening, only to return to it the following morning, it having been identified as the place where your sergeant has been held against her will. He'd wanted to say: Look, Sweetman, the house at the end. That's it, isn't it? I know it is because that's Titch Reilly's place.

What the fuck, he thought, is going on? We're dealing with two investigations that have *nothing* to do with each other. Or so it had seemed. Now Reilly had suddenly become a player in both games. Baffling.

"Right," was all he said. He stopped the car outside the house.

"Blade . . ."

"Yes, Sweetman?"

"Look, would you mind if I went in alone?" She saw his quizzical look. "Just for a minute. It's a sort of, ehh . . . a catharsis. I'll call you when it's okay."

Macken looked blank. Then he caught sight of Sweetman's expression. He thought he understood.

The inside of the house was almost pleasant in daylight, if sadly in need of redecorating. Sweetman hesitated in the hall. The carpet was undisturbed, just as she'd left it. She rolled it back to expose the trapdoor.

* * *

Delta Six looked like death. His face had turned a sickly colour and there was a huge, purple swelling above his right eye. He looked to be in considerable pain. His eyes widened with fury mingled with fear on seeing Sweetman.

She ignored his glare, went to where she'd left the note, screwed it up and put it in her pocket.

Now for the most distasteful part.

Delta Six's penis had swollen to gross dimensions. The shaft hung limply at an odd angle, and was a dreadful mosaic of bruises in many hues. Sweetman almost felt remorse for the damage she'd caused. Almost, but not quite.

Delta Six screamed behind the duct tape when Sweetman took the offending object in her hand. She heard further muffled yelps and shrieks as she tucked it back into the man's trousers and rezipped the fly. She saw that beads of sweat had formed on his forehead and that he was trembling. She went into the little kitchen and washed her hands very, very thoroughly. Then she ascended the steps again and went to the front door.

"It's okay!" she called. "Ye can come in now."

Macken whistled on seeing the trapdoor. Hughes was slowly shaking his head.

They went down. Blade's eyes narrowed on seeing the bound and gagged figure. Sweetman had offered vague details of her abduction and captivity, of how she'd managed to break free of the cable and take her lone captor by surprise. He knew there'd been violence yet was not prepared for the condition in which he found Sweetman's prisoner.

"Blade." It was Hughes, in the room across the way. Macken joined him.

The room was square, lined with racks and shelves. All were filled with weaponry. There was enough firepower with which to start a revolution in a small country.

"My Christ," Blade said. "Where did this stuff come from?"

Hughes wrapped a handkerchief around his hand and picked up an assault rifle, an AK47.

"Russia," he said simply.

"All right, Sweetman, what really happened back there? You can tell Uncle Blade."

"I've told you all there is to tell. Can you drop it, Blade? Please?"

"For Christ's sake, Sweetman, the man's willy looked like a salami that'd been run over by a bus! At least, that's what the doctor said—though maybe not in so many words."

Sweetman had to smile. It was the first time she'd been able to relax since leaving Carlingford the previous morning. They sat now in the coffee lounge of a hotel in Lower Dorset Street, close to the Mater Misericordiae hospital. The place reminded Sweetman of an old-fashioned cafeteria, with fittings to match. But the tea and buttered scones were good, the service friendly.

Assistant Commissioner Duffy had called an emergency conference at eleven that morning. Sweetman had discovered she'd become something of a celebrity. Her disappearance had made the news bulletins and the morning papers; you didn't abduct a Special Branch detective sergeant with impunity. She learned that the patrolmen who'd stopped her in Nassau Street hadn't been acting routinely; there'd been a manhunt underway that encompassed five counties.

"Can I ask *you* something, Blade?"

"Hmm?"

"You recognized that house, didn't you? And don't try to deny it. I know you; I can read the signs."

He grinned. "You've a good head on your shoulders, Sweetman. I've always said it."

"So you'd been there before? And more to the point: why didn't you let on to Duffy you'd been there before?"

Blade produced a roll of mints and offered one to Sweetman. She declined.

"There's something funny going on here," he said. "I was sure in the beginning that there was no connection between the O'Neill murder and the chips heist. But—"

"Are you saying now there is?" Sweetman was peering at him intently.

"It looks that way. Or it's coincidence. But I don't believe in coincidence any more than you do."

Briefly he brought her up to date on his own investigation, omitting all but the salient facts. She was thoughtful.

"So what you're saying is that the same gang may have executed O'Neill? But that's impossible, Blade; they were looking for the killer. They were as much in the dark as we are."

"You're not paying attention, Sweetman. I didn't say that at all. What I'm saying is that we've established a link. We know that at least one of those fuckers who lifted you in County Galway was in on the van raid. You say they're freelance—and they most likely are. We'll know when Pat Hughes picks them up. But ask yourself, Sweetman: Isn't it stretching coincidence a bit far to have the same freelancers having some sort of involvement in an execution in Carlingford and a robbery at Dublin Airport? Especially since *I'm* involved with the two investigations."

"Since you put it that way: yeah, it is. But you still haven't said why you don't want Duffy to know."

Blade popped another mint in his mouth and bit through it.

"Don't get me wrong about Duffy," he said. "He's a good man. But he's a hoor for procedure and I simply can't afford that right this minute. I'm too close to nailing whoever was behind the raid, Sweetman. And whoever it was knows I'm close. He'll be extra vigilant from now on, and he'll be making damn sure there aren't leaks from his people—he'll want his minions to be on their guard."

"So what you're saying," Sweetman offered, "is that you and me are the only ones who can connect Delta Six with the robbery."

"Who?"

"Sorry, I forgot to mention it; it's what I called the bastard."

She told him of the codename her abductors used. Macken scratched his chin.

"It probably means shag all," he said. "Just a shower of lowlifes giving themselves airs. But I'll keep it in mind all the same. And yes, you're right: I doubt very much if the man I'm after knows we've made the connection—and your 'Delta Six' won't tell us very much either, if he knows what's good for him; he'd end up the same way as old Martin O'Neill. They'd get to him, no matter where we're holding him. But I'm happy with that, Sweetman. Let's keep Duffy in the dark for the time being. But as and from now, I'm treating the two investigations as one—and to hell with Duffy. He can like it or lump it."

He paused then and considered Sweetman. She looked very much the worse for wear. She'd applied a great deal of newly bought make-up to her face yet it didn't quite mask her haggard look or the dark circles under her eyes. The bandage on her left hand accentuated her frailty.

"That is," he said, "if you feel up to it. . . . "

"I do," she said tersely, and Blade wondered again about the true nature of the events that had taken place at the house in Kilbarrack.

"Okay, but there'll be no more going off on your own from now on. I'm putting my foot down about that."

"Are we going to have a row again?"

He smiled. "That's not what I meant at all, Sweetman. What I meant is that you and I are going to spend a lot of time together these next few days. First we're going shopping in Brown Thomas's. There's something I have to buy, and I want you to get yourself a new outfit." He looked at her grubby clothing. "And spare no expense. You got shop-soiled in the line of duty and I'm going to make sure the department pays for it."

"You won't hear me arguing with *that*."

"And I have to call by the bank as well. Then we're going to see a man and give him an update on his missing millions."

Thirty-Seven

Frank Naughton greeted his three visitors cordially when his secretary showed them into his office. His eye appraised the tall young brunette who accompanied Macken. Her clothes were elegant and had the crisp lines of the newly-purchased. He wondered about the sticking plasters on her fingers and the dark circles under her eyes. But the woman had only a minor part of his attention. He was drawn to the black suitcase carried by the third member of the party, a uniformed garda. The suitcase looked heavy.

At a nod from Macken, the Guard placed it squarely on Naughton's pine desk. Naughton blinked.

"You'll be pleased to know, sir," Blade said, "that we're making genuine progress in the investigation. In fact, I'd say we're pretty close to tying up the loose ends."

"That's excellent news, superintendent. I, ah, hadn't expected you'd have results so quickly. Well done."

"Thank you, sir. Oh, by the way, any further news from the raiders? Any more demands?"

Naughton shook his head. He had difficulty keeping his eyes off the suitcase.

"I didn't think there would be, sir," Blade said easily. "You see, we have a number of them in custody already."

"You h-have?"

"Yes, sir. The small fry, you understand. Now all we need

is to find two others: the man who organized the raid—and the man who hired him. But I believe we're close."

"That's, ah, excellent," Naughton said again.

"Isn't it, sir. But here's the part you'll like best of all. We've recovered your money." He patted the case.

"All of it?"

"Every last penny, sir."

He gestured to the Guard, who went to the desk and opened the suitcase. Exposed lay a tight phalanx of brown fifty-pound notes, neatly fitting the inside of the case. Naughton's mouth fell open.

"You don't seem too pleased, sir," Blade said. "God, if that was *my* money I'd be doing the polka on that desk. Probably naked as well with my face painted and a feather shoved up my bum."

The head of Mnemos sat down and spread his hands on the desk. He was breathing harshly, staring at the banknotes. It was some time before he spoke but when he did his voice was heavy with resignation and defeat.

"How did you find out? They talked, didn't they?"

"Reilly and Co? No, actually they didn't. But I'm sure they will when we pull them in."

Naughton looked puzzled. Macken removed one of the banknotes. Underneath was plain white paper. He gathered up the rest of the notes, took out his wallet and shoved them into it.

"That's my own money, Mr Naughton. Drawn from the bank an hour ago. And the suitcase will come in handy when I finally get round to taking my long-overdue holiday this month."

Macken shut the case and set it on the floor. When he straightened, something he hadn't noticed on his previous visits caught his eye. It was a tiny crucifix on the wall next to a Swiss cheese plant. It didn't fit with the Feng Shui.

"When did you suspect?" Naughton asked.

"About the money? Not for a long time as it happens. To be honest, it was only after I became convinced there was something not quite right about the emails. At first I suspected that one of your employees was behind it—exactly what you wanted us to think. But I'll come to that in a minute."

"No doubt," Naughton said drily.

"My son Peter used to do magic tricks," Blade went on. "I got him a book one Christmas. Very basic stuff of course but there was one particular trick that was very good. He used to fool the aunts and uncles when he'd do his party piece. I won't go into all the details but it involved a disappearing five-pound note. He did it very well, young Peter—had everyone fooled. He'd ask for a volunteer and he'd place a folded-up five-pound note in the volunteer's fist. And hey presto: it vanished. The secret, of course, was that there wasn't a five-pound note there to begin with, but the victim didn't know that."

"And what made you suspect that the two and a half million didn't exist?" Naughton asked. "I'm curious."

Blade looked at him askance. "Did I say it didn't? Did I, Sweetman?"

"No, sir. You did not."

"No, Mr Naughton," Blade continued, "I did not. It existed all right. We know that because I had one of our people check with your bank. There's a record of a withdrawal of that sum. And why wouldn't there be, with that amount of money involved? It was the talk of the whole bank. No, Mr Naughton, you withdrew the money and you brought it here to show me, just like Peter made a great show of demonstrating that he had a five-pound note to begin with. But the two and a half million never went into the boot of your car, did it?"

"Actually it did," Naughton said. "I took it out again before I reached the airport."

Blade looked surprised. "Hmm, I was wrong on that score so. But to return to the disappearance trick. It was very well done. Maybe a bit *too* well done. You see, all those pyrotechnics with the smoke grenades reminded me too much of a magic show. You overplayed your hand there, sir; that was the trouble. Another thing you shouldn't have done was have the raiders insist that you park the car in public view. At the airport! And directly opposite the airport police station. If you were a thief and really were going to spirit away a suitcase full of money then you wouldn't be *that* foolhardy. In short, sir, everything pointed to the possibility that, like Peter's disappearing five-pound note, the money wasn't there to begin with. It was brilliantly done, and you certainly caused a few faces to turn red—including your own; a nice piece of acting. None of us could understand how the thief managed to steal the case right from under our noses."

"My congratulations, superintendent," Naughton said. "But since no money was stolen I committed no crime. I've already returned the money to the company—though not, I need hardly add, through the same bank."

"I don't doubt that, sir. But as far as crime is concerned,

you seem to be overlooking the real crime: the raid on the van. Another fine piece of deception. And you used the same device as well. There were no Pentiums stolen that night—because there were no Pentiums in the van to begin with."

Macken's new revelation startled Naughton.

"How, you may ask, do we know? After Reilly and his boys burned the evidence? Oh, they burned it all right, but not thoroughly enough. Fire doesn't utterly destroy something. Not a petrol fire anyhow; you'd need a higher temperature to break down silicon completely. I'm surprised you didn't know that."

"I'm not a chemist, superintendent."

"Nor I, sir, but we have people who are. Now there's still the important question that remains unanswered. That question is: Why? What was it all about, this whole charade? Who benefited? You'd nothing to gain. Who had?"

"Some very important people, superintendent. That's all I'm prepared to say. Sorry."

"Being sorry isn't enough, sir. A man died that night, therefore you're an accessory to murder."

"That wasn't meant to happen! It was an accident."

"I believe you, but it doesn't alter the facts. Look, sir, you're up to your tonsils in trouble here. You can spare yourself even more by giving me names."

"I can't do that. I'd be betraying a sacred trust."

Once more Macken was drawn to the small crucifix on the wall. Naughton looked too, then looked away.

"They're not above the law, Mr Naughton," Blade said. "Whoever they are."

"No," Naughton agreed. "But there's a higher law than

the one you represent. I think you know what I'm talking about."

Macken nodded. "I think I do, sir. But tell me one thing. This is troubling me. Is Duffy one of them?"

Naughton looked blank.

"Duffy?" he asked, apparently in all innocence. "Who the hell is Duffy?"

Macken looked at Sweetman. This was the last thing he'd expected. But why was Naughton denying something that could be proven with a single phone call? He was not a stupid man.

But there would be time later for explanations. At that moment Blade wanted confirmation of his prime suspicion, the one that would link Naughton and a murder in Carlingford.

"Mr Naughton, you'll shortly be accompanying this officer to Dublin," he began, jerking a thumb at the uniformed garda, "where you'll be charged with conspiracy to murder, among other things. I want you to understand that any oaths you may have sworn to the Almighty are your affair, and I'll respect that. That's beyond my brief. There's just one final question I want to put to you. The question is: Has Sarajevo a bearing on all of this?"

Naughton looked again at the crucifix before replying. Blade saw his lips move in the same way as those of an old priest he'd observed on a wet day in Carlingford. Naughton turned.

"Yes," he said. "It has. But it's too late, superintendent. Your question is academic now."

Thirty-Eight

"How did you know, Blade?" Sweetman asked.

"How did I know what?"

"About the money."

"I didn't. I was bluffing."

"Janey!"

"That was the weakest part of the operation. See, I was pretty certain about the processors: Linda Doyle proved beyond doubt there was silicon in the burnt-out van. So I could put two and two together and decide that the raid was a sham. That led me to think that Naughton must have been in on it. If that part of the argument was true then it followed that the deal with the suitcase was a sham as well."

"So you reckoned that Naughton would break when we plonked that other suitcase on his desk."

"That's it, Sweetman. He knew we had him by the wedding tackle. I was gambling though. He could have insisted that he'd handed over the cash to persons unknown. He could have pretended that one of his people was behind it. He didn't—for the simple reason that he didn't know how much *we* knew."

Sweetman looked out of the car window as a field of incandescent yellow appeared on their right. Rape. She found herself wishing they'd given the crop another name.

"Blade, something else is bothering me. Duffy. Naughton denied knowing him but you told me that Duffy recommended you to him. You thought they were golfing pals or something."

"That bothers me too. I can't believe Duffy's mixed up in this. It isn't like him, Sweetman. He may be a bit of a bollix at times but he's straight as an arrow; I'd swear to that."

"Hmm. Speaking of swearing, what was all that about oaths?"

"I don't honestly know," Macken told her. "That was a shot in the dark as well. It seemed to hit the mark though."

"Secret societies? Blood oaths?"

"Your guess is as good as mine."

They'd reached the ring road at Dundalk. Some minutes later Blade negotiated the Ballymascanlan roundabout to the north of the town and took the road that leads to Carlingford and Omeath. He'd driven at his usual leisurely pace, and the journey from Swords had taken well over an hour.

"Okay," he said, "the way I see it, somebody—maybe Naughton, maybe not—wanted to keep both of us from looking too deep into Martin O'Neill's past. Agreed?"

"Agreed."

"So ask yourself, Sweetman: What better place to look than in O'Neill's house?"

"But Blade, we've already been over it; the Carlingford Guards have been over it. There was nothing."

Macken slowed as they came to a narrowing in the road that gave way to a sharp bend.

"Maybe you're right. But I'm willing to give it one last chance. And it's our last hope, Sweetman. The Franciscan connection isn't in place any more. When Brother Luji left for Sarajevo to see his sick sister—or his ailing hamster or whatever—that left no one that we know of who could tell us what O'Neill was up to forty or fifty years ago."

"I'm sure the old guy in Kilty—Father Boyle—could tell us a thing or two. If he wanted to."

"Forget about him," Blade said. "I know his type. You could send in the Spanish Inquisition with the red-hot pokers and thumbscrews and Father Boyle would go to the stake saying no more than his rosary. No, anything that's to be found out we have to find out ourselves. So I say we give that house in Carlingford another going over. It could be there *is* something there that'll tell us more. Something everybody overlooked. Something you wouldn't ordinarily connect to the investigation."

"If you say so."

"Let me tell you a little story, Sweetman. I'm going back a good many years now, mind you—just after I'd joined the Force. I was a sergeant then, plainclothes. Myself and a young Guard by the name of Dave Clancy were looking into a burglary. The house was stripped of everything, worth a fortune. We reckoned the burglars must have driven up in a removal van and loaded up. Well, we found evidence of a break-in all right so everything looked kosher. Only Clancy happened to be in the kitchen making a cup of tea for us, and guess what?"

"Hmm?"

"You won't believe this, Sweetman, but there was this ad

for a do-it-yourself removals firm pinned to a memo board, along with school reports, shopping lists, et cetera—you know the sort of thing. But the ad must have been at the top of the page in the local newspaper, and it gave the date. A week before the burglary. The owner had done the job himself to collect the insurance—been up to his eyes in gambling debts. But then he was stupid enough to hire the van locally—and leave the evidence for all to see. Only you'd never think of looking in the kitchen when all the valuable stuff was taken from the rest of the house."

"Janey, I'm impressed."

"Clancy insisted it was no more than a stroke of luck, and refused to take too much credit for it. 'If I hadn't a been parched then I'd never have spotted it,' he said." Blade paused then, remembering. "Those were different times, Sweetman. If I look back then, it seems to me that villains weren't half as clever in those days as they are now. You didn't need a gun either. A light tap on the head with a baton and Robert was your avuncular relation. Stop me if I'm beginning to sound like Duffy, will you?"

"I will. But I take your point, Blade. Maybe there *was* something at O'Neill's place, staring us in the face."

"Look at it this way," Blade said, "if you were to change your identity, make a clean break with the past, would you want to throw away *every*thing you ever owned? I don't think you would. Everybody has some little thing that has sentimental value for him. Worthless in itself. Me, I still have an old fountain pen my grandmother gave me when I was thirteen. It doesn't even write any more, but Nan gave it to me a month before she died and I wouldn't part with it for all the T-bone steaks in Searson's."

"I know what you mean," Sweetman agreed, thinking of her own worthless keepsakes.

"It might even be a photograph of somebody O'Neill was very attached to. Or a name in an address book. We know he had some old friends in Newry. If we could find one or two of them, they might lead us to somebody else."

The first spurs of the Cooley Mountains were appearing on their left; the jagged summit of Slieve Foye, Fire Mountain, glowed green and purple in the late-afternoon sun.

"D'you think Naughton will talk, Blade?"

He shook his head. "Not if I know my man—and I think I do. But I was thinking just now that we've at least ruled out the paramilitary angle as far as that business with you is concerned. Reilly's no more a Provo than I am. What bothers me though are those Russian guns. I can't get a handle on those."

"Are you saying that the *Russians* might be involved? In O'Neill's murder?"

"The simple answer is I haven't a bloody clue. There *seems* to be a Russian angle—along with the Croatian one. But I don't understand how Eastern Europe and Martin O'Neill go together. And my guess is that Naughton and whoever is in this with him are as much in the dark as we are about the identity of the murderer. You said yourself that Reilly didn't know. You know what I think, Sweetman? I think they're all scared shitless: everybody who's involved in this. Whoever killed Martin O'Neill stirred up a hornet's nest. And it's not over yet. Naughton said we're too late, but I didn't believe him. I was watching his face. I was watching a man who thought he had a situation under control but realized it had got out of hand. Did you see his face when I asked about Sarajevo?"

"Yeah, I did. Like someone had walked over his grave."

He suddenly slowed the car and took a sharp turn to the left.

"Where are we going?" Sweetman asked.

"To Jack's place. I just remembered he has an amazing library."

"I don't know if I follow you, Blade."

"I'm not surprised. I'm thinking about those notes you made on Croatia. The ones you left in your car."

The Galway police had recovered all her belongings from the car—everything except her mobile phone; she'd dreaded the thought of the forms she'd have to complete in order to acquire a replacement. Sweetman's bag was on its way to Dundalk, together with the jotter she'd used at the library. Blade had listened with interest when she'd given him a re-sumé of those notes.

"You only scratched the surface, Sweetman," he told her now. "About Yugoslavia. If I remember rightly, Jack has any number of books on the Balkans, past and present. I've a hunch that the recent history of Croatia is worth looking into."

"Dear me!" Jack Macken exclaimed on seeing the plasters on Sweetman's hand and her gaunt appearance. "You look as though you've been in the wars, young lady. Come in and have a brandy at once. Matter of fact, I was just about to indulge in one myself."

"Make that three brandies, Jack," Blade said. "And wars are exactly what we've come about. What have you got on Croatia? Historywise."

"More history! My goodness but we'll make a scholar of you yet, my boy." He stroked his chin. "Croatia, is it? Hmm, I've quite a bit, now that you mention it. Have a look yourself in the library while I get the drinks. You know by now where the history books are."

Blade was using the castored steps when his uncle joined them: the relevant books occupied shelves near the ceiling. Jack passed the tray to Sweetman.

"Would you do the needful, my dear?" he said. "No, Blade, come down from there. You'll find nothing of interest in that section. All propaganda; not worth the paper it's printed on."

Blade obeyed, and was startled when his uncle mounted the steps with a bound.

"Careful, Jack."

"Don't you worry, my boy. Second nature to me."

Jack plucked out volume after volume, piling them high in Blade's arms. He stopped when the count had exceeded thirty.

"That should be enough to be getting on with," he said.

It was not the most cheerful reading.

Blade laid aside *The Martyrdom of the Serbs*, a publication by the Serbian Orthodox Church in Chicago, and picked up a small book with a yellow cover. He leafed through it slowly and with mounting horror. It was entitled *Artukovitch, the Himmler of Yugoslavia* and its authors were three New Yorkers: Mssrs Gaffney, Starchevitch and McHugh.

He learned that Germany had overrun Yugoslavia in 1941 and established a puppet government under Ante Pavelić, the quisling ruler. The Croatians, who were Roman Catholics, saw their opportunity of converting the Serbs, who numbered more than two million at the time.

This they did with tremendous zeal—240,000 were forcibly converted. Moreover, 750,000 more were massacred, along with 30,000 Jews, in twenty concentration camps established for that purpose. It was, according to the authors, the most savage religio-racial crusade in history.

Blade cringed on seeing the photographs in the book. No act of barbarousness, it seemed, had been deemed too dreadful by the men who'd carried out the mass conversion. Babies had been torn from their mothers arms and decapitated; men, women and children had been burned alive in an orgy of slaughter to rival that of Rwanda or Cambodia.

"My fuck."

"Makes you think, doesn't it?" Jack said.

"It makes me want to throw up, if you must know. And I thought the Nazis were bad."

The other volume, that written by the Serbian Orthodox churchmen, pulled no punches either. Blade read how a train from Mostar and Klepca had carried six wagonloads of mothers, girls and children under the age of eight to the station of Šurmanci, where they were taken out of the wagons, herded into the hills and hurled alive, mothers and children, into deep ravines. That night the faint cries and screams of the dying could be heard echoing up from the depths until, by morning, every voice was still.

And all this, Blade read, had been done with the approbation of the Catholic clergy in Croatia. Not only had they given their blessing to the atrocities but some clerics had actually played an active part in the slaughter, while the Vatican turned a blind eye. Ante Pavelić, in their eyes, was an important bulwark against the spread of Communism.

Pavelić was a boon for the Nazis as well; he was a rampant anti-Semite. On his appointment in the spring of 1941, he immediately introduced laws that enabled him to expel both Jews and Serbian Orthodox from Zagreb, the capital of Croatia. Their property was confiscated and the death penalty imposed on anybody caught sheltering these "enemies of the State".

Sweetman munched on a cream cracker and cheese, sipped some of Jack's excellent brandy, and picked up the little yellow book that Blade had put down.

Artuković she learned, had been Minister of the Interior in the Nazi's puppet government. According to the authors, he had helped set up no fewer than twenty concentration camps for the extermination of the Serbs, Jews and other "undesirables". When the war ended, Artuković had fled to Austria, thence to Switzerland.

Sweetman stopped chewing. She'd been reading an extract from a memoir by Artuković himself. It startled her.

"Blade . . . "

"Hmm?"

She passed the book to him, held open at the correct page. "What", she said, "do you make of *this?*"

Blade read.

I stayed in Switzerland until July 1947. Then with the knowledge of the Swiss Ministry of Justice I obtained personal documents for myself and my family, which enabled us to travel to Ireland. Using the name of Anitch, we stayed there until 15th July, 1948. When our Swiss documents expired, the Irish issued new papers and under Irish papers we obtained a visa entry into the USA.

"Ireland, Blade. He was here. The bastard was *here*."

Macken nodded and turned to his uncle.

"I think," she said, "we've found the Croatian connection."

Artuković, mass murderer and war criminal, had been welcomed in the Land of Saints and Scholars. More than that: the Irish authorities had issued him with papers that had enabled him to escape to the United States. It beggared belief.

Yet the most damning indictment was that of the Franciscans. Try as she might, Sweetman simply could not reconcile the war crimes of five decades before with the gentle friars of Galway. She refused to believe this. It was propaganda. It could not be otherwise.

Or could it?

Thirty-Nine

Jim O'Neill smiled broadly on opening the door of his late father's cottage. His smile disappeared slowly, however, when he saw who his callers were.

"Hello again, sir," Blade said. "I'm sure you weren't expecting us. Sorry about the intrusion but we won't be long I hope."

"Aye, come in."

Jim O'Neill had been cooking; the living-room was laden with the smell of onions, the door to the kitchen being open. He shut it.

"Well, what can I do for you now, superintendent?"

Sweetman noticed that he left them standing; there was no offer of a seat. Macken was examining the room in a detached manner.

"If we've come at a bad time . . ." Sweetman could never get used to the man's moodiness; it was unsettling.

"No no," he said. "I've just finished my tea."

"Sir, we'd like to go through your father's things again," Blade said. "His personal effects. We want to make sure there isn't anything we overlooked."

"Fair enough. But I don't see the point to be honest. I've been through them myself again—twice. There's nothing out of the ordinary."

"Did your father fish, sir?" Blade suddenly asked. He was looking at the display of tied flies. "I do a bit of fly-fishing myself. Matter of fact, my son and I had been planning a bit of fishing in Wicklow before all this came up. Some nice ones here."

"Aye, my father used to. He'd do a lot of salmon fishing in the Blackwater. He claimed it was the best river in the world for it."

"That's what I heard too." Blade was moving slowly about the little room, picking up objects and setting them down again in the manner of someone browsing in a bric-a-brac shop. His actions seemed to irritate O'Neill.

"Look, superintendent," he said, "I've tidied up the bedroom and put his stuff into a couple of boxes. Maybe you'd like to go through those again?"

He nodded. O'Neill left and returned with two large cardboard boxes, which he placed in the middle of the floor.

"I think you'll be wasting your time," he said, "but work away. Can I leave you to it? I'm just going to wash up."

"Thank you, sir. You're most helpful."

The boxes contained items already familiar to them both: Martin O'Neill's shoes and clothing and a number of toiletries. Blade examined them without much interest.

"It makes you think, doesn't it, Sweetman? Eighty-five years on the planet and this is all he had to show for it." He shook his head sadly.

"Don't bother going through the pockets," she said. "They were all empty. Funny, that. You'd think you'd have found loose change or something but there wasn't a thing."

"My dad was like that. Never carried anything in his

pockets if he could help it. Said it ruined the cut of his suits."
He looked around the room. "What about papers? Letters?"

Sweetman shook her head. "The lads down at the station have a boxful of papers. I've been through it—thoroughly. Nothing of interest. If Martin O'Neill received any letters at all then he must have thrown them away."

"There were none at all?"

"No. You think that's out of the ordinary?"

"Yeah, I do." He scanned the walls of the room. "And what about photographs, Sweetman? We've only the one of O'Neill himself. But why aren't there photographs of anyone else? That's what I'd like to know. Everybody has photos of some kind. Family, friends, holiday snaps. But we didn't find a single one. There's that old sixties' song that goes, 'People take pictures of each other, just to show that they really existed.' Well, except for that old black-and-white one, Martin O'Neill might never have existed."

Sweetman returned the items to the boxes, stood up and smoothed her skirt.

"I know what you're saying, Blade. It *is* odd."

Jim O'Neill came through from the kitchen, wiping his hands on a tea towel.

"Any luck?"

Sweetman shook her head.

"Can I get you a coffee?" Doing the washing-up seemed to have improved his mood.

"That'd be very nice, sir," Blade said. "Milk and three sugars for me."

He was standing by the low bookshelf, head tilted, reading the titles on the spines; he didn't turn round. Sweetman saw Jim O'Neill frown again, then leave again for the kitchen.

"Ah!" Blade cried abruptly, plucking a book from the shelf.

Sweetman's heart leaped; she joined him.

"*Shōgun*," he said, flipping through the thick, dog-eared paperback. "A great read altogether. Did you ever—"

"No, I didn't," she said with irritation. "For God's sake, Blade; I thought you found something."

He returned the book, squatted, and began scrutinizing the others, taking out a volume now and then and glancing at its cover. Some were school textbooks.

"He was obviously an avid reader, the late Mr O'Neill."

"Most teachers are, Blade."

Sounds of crockery reached them from the kitchen.

"Hmm, *Hamlet* and *The Merchant of Venice*; we had them at school."

"Really? So did we."

"He'd a lot of dictionaries as well," Blade remarked. "English, Irish, Italian, French. . . ." He ran a hand along the books. One tattered volume was missing its spine. He pulled it out and studied the title. It was Langenscheidt's *German-English / English-German Dictionary*.

"Ah, yes," he said. "I used to have this one myself." He thumbed the pages. "When I was in the army."

Something fell out and fluttered to the floor, just as Jim O'Neill entered the room again. It was a snapshot. He went over and picked it up.

"Anyone we know?" Sweetman asked, looking over his shoulder.

The photograph showed a couple dressed in summer wear. They were perhaps in their late sixties, and seated at a table in what looked like an outdoor restaurant. On closer inspection Sweetman saw it was the yard of PJ's pub in Carlingford; the naive map of the town was visible in the background. But the detail wasn't good because the photographer had contrived to point the camera into the sun.

"No, I can't say I know them," O'Neill said. "It could be anybody."

"They look foreign, sir," Blade observed. "German or Scandinavian."

The snapshot had been taken by a camera that registered the date and time in the bottom right-hand corner. It read: *13.08.99 : 15:42:07.*

"That's this time last year," Blade said.

"What's that sticking out of her bag?" Sweetman asked. "Is it a newspaper or a magazine?"

O'Neill peered more closely at he photograph. "Looks like a newspaper to me."

"It's hard to make out," Sweetman said. "Maybe we can have it enlarged."

"That won't do you much good," O'Neill said. "You'd only be enlarging the grain—what's already there. You'd need the negative." He saw her look. "I dabble a bit in amateur photography," he explained. "I wouldn't be very good though."

Then a thought seemed to hit him.

"Of course! Dad's eyesight was very poor. He had a pair of reading glasses but they weren't much good to him. He preferred to use a magnifying glass." He looked about the living-room. "I'm sure it's here somewhere."

He found the glass in a desk drawer and returned to the photograph, holding it close to the window.

"It's a tabloid," he said. "Have a look."

O'Neill had been correct: enlarging did nothing to render the photograph clearer. It did, however, brighten the image somewhat. Sweetman turned to Macken.

"It's not an Irish paper," she said, "or an English one. It's got a blue square with white lettering but I don't recognize it."

"I do," Jim O'Neill said. "It's the *Bild*. *Bild Zeitung*. German. It's the most popular rag in Germany—their equivalent of *The Sun*. I know; I went with my fourth-years on a trip to Heidelberg last summer."

Sweetman considered this. "So they're a German couple —or maybe Austrian."

"No, I wouldn't think so," O'Neill said with conviction. "Nobody reads the *Bild* except the Germans. It's just a gossip and scandal sheet. No self-respecting Austrian would touch it with a bargepole. They'd buy the *Frankfurt Algemeiner* or the *Süddeutscher Zeitung* instead. You can get them in newsagents in Belfast and elsewhere—or on the plane coming over."

Blade had taken the magnifying glass and was studying sections of the snapshot. He paused over the face of the man.

"That's strange," he said.

"What?"

"It might be the light, or a fault in the printing." He passed the glass to Sweetman. "Have a look at the eyes."

Sweetman did.

"I see what you mean. Funny I didn't notice that before. They seem to be different colours."

"Red-eye," O'Neill offered. "It's hard to avoid when you're using a flash. The light bounces off the back of the retina, which is red."

"No, sir," Blade said, "it was taken outside. They weren't using a flash." He held the print closer to the window. "The eyes don't match. One of them's brown and the other's blue. Very unusual."

So unusual, in fact, that such an abnormality sticks in the memory. Sweetman recollected another man with mismatched eyes, another German. She'd seen him only days before, in the yard of PJ's pub.

Blade had been right when they'd spoken in the hotel in Dorset Street, Dublin: she didn't believe in coincidence any more than he. It went far and away beyond coincidence that two Germans, one young, one elderly—two men who shared a most uncommon ophthalmic defect—should also have shared, on separate occasions but within a twelve-month period, the hospitality of a Carlingford public house.

"May I hold onto this, sir?" Macken asked.

"Aye, certainly. If you think it's important."

"It might just be," Blade told him.

Forty

"Did you stop to wonder, Sweetman," Blade Macken said, "why this was in the dictionary?"

He propped the photograph against the telephone on the table in Carlingford garda station.

Sweetman put her pen down. She'd been making notes, adding to the strands of information she had, trying to find links between them. She was making little headway. It was like watching television with your nose up against the screen: a nonsense of flickering coloured dots until you stepped back from it.

She'd divided her notes in three. Part One dealt with Martin O'Neill's past. There were so few facts, and those were outweighed heavily by Blade's conjectures. His theory of O'Neill's having been a "sleeper" for the IRA, though promising at first, was looking progressively weaker. Yet she was still intrigued by those words of Serbo-Croatian that Jim O'Neill had fished out of his suppressed childhood memories.

Pasce malo. They must, she assured herself, mean *something* to the investigation.

Part Two dealt with paramilitary involvement in O'Neill's murder. She could discount a Loyalist execution—nobody had taken that too seriously anyway. Now it was looking extremely unlikely that Republican terrorists were responsible;

Titch Reilly had been as much in the dark as she. And mystery still surrounded the reasons for the threats to her father and her own abduction. Who had given the orders? Frank Naughton? Blade was convinced it went higher than that.

Part Three had certain elements in common with the other two. Sweetman was convinced now that something nasty had reached out of O'Neill's past, something he'd thought he'd buried a long time ago. She'd written and underlined the name Pavelić, together with the year 1947. In some way, Croatia was involved, Germany too. And the only Germans to figure in the equation so far shared a curious mismatch in eye colour.

Sweetman looked from one set of notes to another, trying to decipher the unifying pattern, the hidden code.

She pondered Macken's question.

"Why the photo was in the dictionary?" she said. "I'd say the old guy was using it as a bookmark."

"That's what I thought as well. But why that particular dictionary?"

"What's this, Blade?" she said with a grin. "Your Inspector Morse impersonation? Next you'll be calling me Lewis."

"Be serious now for a minute will you? All right, here goes: It's my guess that Martin O'Neill was using the dictionary to translate a letter. In German."

"Hmm. I never thought of that." She frowned. "Are you saying that this couple"—she picked up the photograph—"were writing to O'Neill in German? But why would they do that? Jim said his father didn't speak any foreign languages."

"Maybe Jim was wrong, Sweetman. They weren't all that

close, remember. And for a man who didn't speak any foreign languages he certainly owned an awful lot of dictionaries."

"Right, I'll go along with that. Only, if Martin O'Neill *did* speak German why did he need a dictionary?"

Blade smiled. "Let me ask you this: how many foreign languages do you speak?"

"Ehh, none."

"That's what I thought. I only speak the one myself: German. And very badly too. But I used to be pretty good at it, when I was stationed in Stuttgart. I made a lot of friends there, Sweetman, and I kept in touch for a few years after I left. I still do, even if it's only a card at Christmas. But the point I'm making is that some of them would write to me in German. No big words or anything but I'd still have a dictionary beside me to check something I didn't quite understand."

"And you think that was the case with Martin O'Neill?"

"I do." He pointed to the photograph. "I think O'Neill must have got chatting to this pair in PJ's last summer. His best friend Donegan said he was friendly and talkative, and he may have said something to them in German. You know how it goes with tourists: they get chatting to some local and the next thing you know they're posing for a snap." He tapped the photograph. "And there it is. It's my guess the couple sent him that print, as a memento."

"And a letter in German, which O'Neill translated, using the dictionary we found it in."

Garda O'Donnell came into the room, excused himself and went to a filing cabinet.

"Exactly, Sweetman," Blade said. "It's also my guess that he spoke very good German too. Did you see how well-used that dictionary was? It was practically falling to bits. And look at the age of those two. I think they must have been delighted to meet somebody here who could chat to them in their own language. Most young Germans speak very good English, but the older ones don't."

"Like the ones we saw that day in PJ's yard."

"Yes. You're quite sure about the eyes, are you? I couldn't see them from where I was sitting."

"Quite sure. One brown, one blue."

O'Donnell turned.

"Sorry to interrupt, sir," he said, "I couldn't help over-hearing. You wouldn't be talking about those four Germans, would you? The ones hanging around PJ's?"

"Maybe," Macken said. "What about them?"

O'Donnell shut the drawer of the filing cabinet.

"I was wondering about them myself, sir. They're still here you know. They've two campers parked down beside the sailing club. Been there over three weeks now."

"So what's wrong with that?"

"Nothing I suppose; they're entitled to park there as long as they want. They're not breaking any by-laws or anything. It's just that they seem to have come equipped for some serious sport but spend all their time sitting around drinking."

"Are you sure about that?" Sweetman asked.

"I am, sarge. We've been keeping an extra eye on things since the murder. As I say, they've all sorts of gear with them: bikes, waterskis, surfboards, the works. But nobody's ever seen them actually *doing* anything."

"Strange," Macken said.

"Ah sure maybe it's this place, sir." O'Donnell said. "We're such an easygoing lot around here you can forgive somebody for not wanting to do anything strenuous when they can just sit around and enjoy the *craic*. That's my idea of a holiday too. Me and the wife go to Spain every year and just hang around the beach and the pool doing feck all. We've enough to do the rest of the year; that's the way we look at it."

"Where did you say the campers were parked?" Macken asked.

"At the harbour. Not the castle end, the other side—just outside the sailing club." He frowned. "Is there something we should know about these Germans, sir? Have they been up to something or what?"

Sweetman was looking at her notes. The flickering, random dots were beginning to coalesce into a pattern.

"No," Blade said, "not that I know of. I'm simply ruling out possibilities."

They took the car, turned left into the narrow street that led down to the coast road; Carlingford Harbour lay beyond. With King John's Castle behind them they followed the road to the edge of town and turned left again. A sign pointed to a guesthouse with the incongruous name Shalom. There was a small car park opposite, and the entrance to a boatyard.

The two campers were identical in make and model. They stood nose to tail on the tarmacadam. There was no sign of occupancy. The curtains of both vehicles were pulled back, inviting inspection of the interiors. Macken quickly scanned the vicinity and peered into the leading camper.

There was nothing unusual. A small table sat between two couches that did double-duty as bunk beds. There were maps on the table, sun-block cream, a bottle of Power's whiskey and four glass tumblers. The rest of the interior was as tidy and orderly as you'd expect from a camper whose owners were German. There was a stove, a tiny fridge, and what appeared to be a chemical toilet. A harpoon gun sat in a rack affixed to the wall above a cupboard.

The other camper was even tidier; it looked as though it was used less frequently than the first.

"Take a look at that lot, Sweetman," Blade said.

Sweetman took a look. Gary O'Donnell had been correct about the sports equipment. There were two touring bikes secured to the rear of each camper. All were expensive, eighteen-speed models. A thief would have had no difficulty in making off with them but this, she mused, was Carlingford, one of the few remaining places in the world where theft was virtually a stranger. Front doors were still left open all day in the town.

O'Donnell had also mentioned the surfboards and waterskis. Four of the former and two of the latter were secured to the roofs of the campers. All looked brand new and unused. Like the bikes, they exuded quality and expense.

"This stuff must have cost an arm and a leg," Blade said. "And it's sitting here, just gathering dust. What do you make of that?"

"Maybe nothing, Blade. I've a friend who had her own mini-gym installed at home. The whole shebang: weights, treadmill, computerized rowing machine, the lot. She used it for a week or so and then got bored."

But Blade wasn't listening. He was inspecting the small, low trailer attached to the rear camper. It contained a tent, a very ordinary though capacious tent, folded neatly and tucked and secured.

So far, so innocuous. Or was it?

"Tell me, Sweetman," he said, "what's wrong with this picture."

She shrugged.

"The tent, Sweetman. The tent doesn't add up."

"You'll have to explain that."

"I will. Take a look at the campers, the bikes, the water gear. That's all top-range stuff. Do you honestly believe that people who can afford that sort of sports gear would be the type of people to cart along a tent in an open trailer exposed to the elements? I don't. I think they'd have the sort of tent that fits in a *covered* trailer. And look at this trailer. The shape's wrong. It's too long and it's too shallow for a tent."

Sweetman was squatting beside the trailer. Carefully she lifted an edge of the folded tent.

"You know what, Blade? I don't believe this *is* a tent."

"What?"

"It's a tarpaulin."

Macken joined her and helped unfold more of the material. It was indeed a tarpaulin he saw now. The folded canvas had been used to cover something the trailer had once carried, and carried no longer.

Something the size of a small dinghy.

Forty-One

The bishop saw the house in daylight. Its Palladian grandeur and size, seen on this beautiful August afternoon, would have delighted a man with more leisurely business to attend to. Its parks and gardens spread far, their flowers alive with bees, the trees a choir gallery of songbirds.

The bishop noticed none of this. He sat in the back of the Daimler and stared straight ahead. He didn't acknowledge the chauffeur who presently opened the door, and he looked past the young man in the grey suit who enquired after the quality and comfort of his journey here from County Galway.

The men had come at short notice; they seldom, if ever, met on Wednesdays. But the summons had been urgent and none had questioned the importance of the meeting.

There were no handmaidens present, and the dining-table was bare. Once seated, the bishop immediately got down to business.

"I am shocked," he said. "I am shocked and sickened beyond measure. This was not part of the design. Not part of it at all."

The man facing him at the far end of the table looked sheepish. "I share your distaste, your grace," he said. "But we had no choice. All other means had failed and we felt that drastic measures were called for." There was a murmur of assent from the others present.

The bishop steepled his fingers. He sighed heavily.

"What am I to do with ye at all?" he asked. "I ask ye to find a solution to a problem and ye go and create an even bigger one. Murder. Abduction. Torture—and the Lord only knows what else. What possessed ye at all?"

"The driver's death was an accident, your grace," another said, "and one which all of us here profoundly regret. And as for the police sergeant: we meant her no harm either. Things simply got rather out of hand. The gentlemen we engaged for the assignment—"

"'Gentlemen'!" the bishop exploded. "Is that what you call them—these . . . these . . . cut-throats and criminals?"

"We didn't engage them direct, your grace. We weren't to know. And I humbly and sincerely apologize on behalf of the society."

The old cleric rose, bony hands spread wide on the table. His face was flushed.

"Apologies aren't enough! The damage is done, the flood-gates are open. Don't you understand? You have just placed the Church in an untenable position. My God, if I *think* about what they did to that poor girl. It should never have happened. Never."

He sat down again, his wrath spent. He eyed the assembled men one by one.

"The question now is: What's to be done about it? You call yourselves the lay-soldiers of Christ, so *ye* tell *me*. To use the military parlance, what do ye propose doing about damage limitation?"

There was silence, broken only by the light coughing of an elderly man seated to the right of the bishop.

"The one thing that should be uppermost in our minds," the bishop said, "is that our Holy Mother Church should not be harmed in any way. Are we clear about that? Not one whiff of church involvement. If there's any danger at all of leaks then I want each and every one of ye to use your financial resources to staunch those leaks. I want silence bought—at any price."

"I think we can take care of that, your grace."

"I *know* you can." He cast his eye about the table. "You can start with the riff-raff responsible for this outrage. Your dogs of war. I want them called off at once."

"Er, that could be difficult, your grace."

"What!"

"The, er, line of communication seems to be broken, your grace. Our liaison is unable to contact them. They've gone to ground as it were."

"Well, find them, man! Use any means at your disposal. But make sure this thing ends here. Understood?"

Heads nodded.

"Good. Well. Having got that much off my chest, I'd just like to say that whoever it was who handled that business with the Franciscans in Galway did very well. That, at least, is one problem safely out of the way and, please God, will trouble us no more."

"Amen to that," said one of the gathering.

"Now," said the bishop, rising and reaching into a pocket, "let us all join in a decade of the rosary. Our prayers, I fear, are sorely needed."

Forty-Two

Sweetman was waiting in the lobby of the Village Hotel, Carlingford, leafing through a brochure outlining the attractions of the Táin Village holiday centre, when Macken showed up. He was dressed in black: jeans, light sweater, a canvas hunting jacket and black Reeboks. Twilight was descending on the town and the first of the evening's revellers were already in the adjoining bar. She returned the folder to a stand on the reception desk.

"Well?"

"They're there," he assured her. "And by the look of them they'll be there till closing time." He noted her expression. "What's the matter, Sweetman?"

"Ehh, I've been thinking it over. I'd rather *you* did this, Blade. You know I don't like pubs. I've—"

"No, Sweetman, no. I'm not having you break into that camper. I'm in charge, not you. If we're found out and there's trouble—which there will be—then it's *my* arse they'll want. And don't argue with me; my mind's made up. You can like it or lump it."

"There's still time to apply for a search warrant. . . . "

"There you go: arguing with me."

Sweetman spread her hands. "But why not? Look, they're foreigners, Blade. If you and me were in Germany and the

Polizei wanted to search *our* van, they wouldn't have any bother getting a search warrant."

Blade shook his head. "I'd never get a warrant. There isn't a shred of evidence against them."

"There's the dinghy. . . . "

"What dinghy? Use your head, Sweetman. Have we evidence that there'd ever been one on that trailer? No, and you can be damn sure they'd have wiped it clean of fingerprints before putting it in the water."

She was unfazed. "What about the blood on the shell suit, and the hair fibres? You said the blood had been DNA tested."

"Yeah, but the Germans haven't been. And we can't simply ask them politely if they'd care to have a swab taken down at the station. They'd be on to their embassy like a shot. Sorry, Sweetman, but we've nothing other than our own suspicions. No judge would go along with that. It has to be this way."

She nodded glumly, and he could tell she was anticipating her role with disdain. Presently he said: "You only have to keep an eye on them in the pub. Order a coke or something. Oh, and I wouldn't wear any make-up either if I were you."

"What's that supposed to mean?"

He reddened a bit. "Jesus, Sweetman, do I have to spell it out? You're a good-looking girl and—"

"Woman."

"Whatever you're having yourself. What I'm saying is that we don't want some leery-eyed local setting his cap at you, do we? 'Cap' being the operative word."

"Okay, point taken." The prospect Blade had conjured up

urged her into giving it one more try. "Look, are you *sure* we can't change places? No offence meant, Blade, but I'm younger than you, and more agile. I could—"

"Sweetman, I'm not going to be climbing in through the window. The thing has a door you know." He looked at his watch; it was nearly nine-thirty. "You'll be officially off duty in half an hour. Now, I want you to behave just like any other visitor. There's plenty of tourists there so you won't be drawing too much attention to yourself."

She shrugged resignedly. "What about radios?"

Blade didn't reply but reached into the breast pocket of his hunting jacket for his own unit. He then set both his radio and Sweetman's to back-to-back mode. There would be a two-way link between them without extraneous communications from the police frequency. He returned her set.

"Keep it switched off. You'll be the one alerting *me* if they move, not the other way round. I'll be wearing an earpiece but you obviously won't."

"Got it."

"Have you a gun?"

She tapped her bag.

"Good. I doubt if it'll be necessary anyway. My guess is that they dumped their own firearms in the Lough. That's what *I'd* do. But you never know."

He stood up. "I'll be taking the car down to the harbour. If the coast is clear I'll make my move at ten-thirty precisely."

"What if you can't get the lock open?"

"Then I'll just have to break a window after all, won't I?"

She smiled. "One more thing, Blade. Codes."

"Yes, I was getting to that. I'm Alpha One, you're Alpha

Two. The suspect is Bowie."

Raised eyebrows.

"David Bowie. One brown eye, one blue."

"Hmm, nice one, Blade! Bowie it is."

Macken waited in the car, parked at the same spot he'd chosen earlier that day. He was facing north, could see on the far side of the Lough the lights of Rostrevor and the more distant Warrenpoint twinkling in the haze raised by the water that had been warmed all day by the sun's rays. The Mourne Mountains were a high, black wall against the darkening sky. Above the leading lights that marked the mouth of the estuary the full moon was rising, appulsing the lesser radiance of the planet Venus.

He sat in the passenger seat, a surveillance trick he'd learned many years before. A young couple strolled past, so lost in each other's company they barely noticed him. The clock on the dashboard read 10.28.

Blade opened the door and shut it gently behind him. He checked his radio and adjusted the earpiece for comfort.

The campers were as he'd last seen them, still with undrawn curtains. He went to the leading one and peered in at the window.

Nothing had changed: the maps, whiskey bottle, tumblers and sun-block cream had remained undisturbed. Blade had no wish to explore both vehicles. He'd a shrewd idea that the leading camper was used as headquarters, hence the four tumblers. It followed then that clues—if any—would have to be there.

He went to the side that faced the yard of the sailing club.

He'd considered this carefully: there was a slight risk of traffic or pedestrians on the road, whereas the likelihood of his being spotted from the club was small. In any case the camper door was on that side.

The only difficulty was that lights were burning in the clubhouse. There were windows open and Blade heard talk and laughter. He surmised that a party of sorts was in progress. He hadn't made allowance for that, hadn't considered it at all.

It came as no surprise that the camper door was locked; Carlingford might be relatively crime-free yet no sane visitor would leave an unattended camper unlocked. The lock, however, was of a type unfamiliar to him; Blade decided that it wouldn't yield easily to picking. He fumed. He'd suggested to Sweetman that he'd break a window but that had been a half-serious remark. The night was still and the noise might carry far.

But luck was with him. Somebody had left a small window at the rear slightly open. Blade remembered the layout of the camper; it was the toilet window.

It was tiny. Sweetman, he decided, would have little difficulty in getting through it. But Sweetman was in the bar and it was too late now to change the plan. Moreover he'd no way of knowing how long more the Germans were planning on staying in Carlingford; tonight might well be their last night of carousing.

It was then that Blade remembered the maps on the table. Their presence was a pointer. The Germans had stayed put for three weeks, according to Guard O'Donnell—and therefore had no need of a map.

You consulted maps when you were planning a journey.

He'd just have to continue. He placed a foot on the tow-bar of the camper and hoisted himself, using as handholds the bicycles lashed to the rear of the vehicle.

The bar-latch was designed to prevent the window being opened fully and Blade cursed. He stepped down from the towbar and considered the situation. Tools were needed. There were some in the boot of his car. He hurried back to it.

It was 10.47.

Sweetman had been in the pub since a little after ten o'clock. It was crowded now. There were two entrances: one from the street, the other from the yard. She'd managed to find herself a position at the counter, whence she could monitor those entering and leaving the lounge.

A man with a guitar had seated himself beside a small glass cabinet. Local lore insisted that the cabinet contained the bones and clothing of an ill-starred leprechaun who'd been struck by lightning in the Cooley Mountains some years before. The guitarist was giving of his best with a mixture of Irish ballads and country songs. Sweetman thought the man had a good voice but only the tourists were listening; the local people talked among themselves above the music as though the entertainer didn't exist.

The four Germans were at a table in a far corner; she'd recognized the prime suspect even at that distance; the mismatchment of the eyes was clearly visible by the garish light on the wall a little above the table; he sat facing Sweetman.

The air in the lounge, despite the open door and windows, was already muggy with cigarette smoke; she felt a headache coming on. Most of the patrons, with the exception of a few local men, were in shirtsleeves or thin tops; it was an unusually warm evening. The television set to Sweetman's left was tuned to BBC2. Jeremy Paxman was soundlessly introducing his second victim of the evening: the Member of Parliament who continued to deny a liaison with a rent boy.

Sweetman feigned interest. Her wearing of a short-sleeved blouse enabled her to check the time on her wristwatch with no more than a quick glance. It was 10.55. Thirty-five minutes to closing time, and she had it on good authority that PJ's shut punctually. She hoped that Blade was experiencing no difficulties.

Forty-Three

Blade was sweating. He'd cursed again when checking the contents of the toolkit; it was singularly lacking in instruments that would lend themselves to his needs. What he required was a hammer, or a tool that could act as one. There was only a lug wrench, an unwieldy item at the best of times, made as it was for one purpose only. He'd also taken a large, rubber-handled screwdriver that could do duty as a demolition tool.

Now he stood balanced on one foot atop the towbar, leaning against the back of the camper. He'd opened the lavatory window as far as its latch would allow. With his left hand he held the tip of the screwdriver against the underside of the latch, having positioned it at what he'd concluded to be the latch's weakest point. He'd tried using the lug wrench as a crude crowbar in an attempt to force the window. That had failed, so now he swung the wrench awkwardly, striking blow after blow against the handgrip of the screwdriver. The bicycles that had hitherto helped him maintain his balance hindered him now; their frames pressed painfully against his ribs. Twice so far he'd almost toppled from his perch. At the ninth or tenth blow he felt the bar of the latch give slightly.

Car lights. Blade jumped down off the towbar. His cuff snagged on a bicycle handlebar and he lost his grip on the screwdriver. There was the clatter of steel against steel. He ducked out of sight of the road. The car passed his own and was gone.

It was 11.09.

By the light of the moon Blade located the fallen screwdriver and clambered up on the towbar again.

He succeeded at the fourth blow; the latch broke. He dropped his tools and clung to the window frame, breathing hard. But the work was only beginning; getting through that small aperture was going to be an undertaking in itself. Poised there on one foot, sweating like a gourmand chef, he considered calling the whole thing off.

What had he *really* got to go on? The flimsiest evidence. A group of young foreign tourists who lugged about with them top-of-the-line sports gear yet spent most of their time doing next to nothing. A young man who shared an eye defect with an older man in a holiday snap. A trailer built to carry a dinghy but being used to transport a tarpaulin. It was preposterous. If his reasoning were proven wrong and he was caught in the act of burglary then he'd have more than egg on his face; Duffy would have him up before a disciplinary board.

It was that last thought that drove him onward—and upward. Blade took a tiny pencil flashlight from a pocket of his hunting jacket, switched it on and clamped it between his teeth. Then he raised the little window, returned both hands to the sill and hauled with all his strength. As he felt his arm muscles protesting he cursed his years of smoking, drinking, and lack of exercise.

Yet he was pleased to see he'd calculated correctly; with a

bit of effort he could just about fit through the opening.

His flashlight revealed a room with all the generous dimensions of a laundry chute. It was just as empty too, save for the chemical toilet whose cover, Blade noted with relief, was firmly in place. There was nothing else for it but to drop head first and hope for the best.

With hands outstretched to break his fall, he launched himself through the window.

But he'd been careless. His mind had been focused on gaining access to the exclusion of all else. He'd secured his radio to his waist, threading its strap through a loop on the back of his jeans. The radio was caught by the base of the window frame. The loop snapped; radio and earpiece parted company. Unheard and unnoticed by its owner, the set fell on the tarmac between the campers. Its rubber case saved it from destruction.

The time was 11.15.

The guitar player was doing a request for two Canadian girls at a table near Sweetman. It was "The Mountains of Mourne", Percy French's paean to the locality. One of the girls appeared to know the lyrics and was supplying a passable harmony.

The four Germans were enjoying themselves. The men were drinking beer, the woman what could have been rum and cola. Their conversation was growing more animated with each passing minute.

Sweetman considered her own glass. She'd been nursing the sparkling water, making it last, and now the bartender was giving her disapproving looks. She finished it, ordered another. When she turned round again to face the room, the man with the mismatched eyes was heading in her direction, elbowing his way through the throng.

The German passed her without a glance and made for the door to the yard. Sweetman paid for her drink, picked it up and made to follow. A young man, handsome in a rough sort of way, blocked her path. He was holding a pint of stout and his eyes were bright, his face flushed. Yes, Blade had cautioned her about unwelcome attention, and here it was—though he'd been wrong about its wearing a cap.

"You're not from around here, am I right?" the young man said.

"No," Sweetman replied curtly, "I'm not."

She tried to elbow past the man but he positioned himself firmly between her and the door. She was becoming flustered; for all she knew the German was on his way back to the camper.

"Excuse me," she said with firmness.

"Why?" leered her persecutor. "What have you done?" A man leaning against the counter laughed.

"Look, will you please let me past? I need some air."

"Air? Yeah, I fancy a bit meself. What say we have a bit together?" Another coarse laugh from the man at the counter.

Sweetman felt frustration and anger rising. She was sorely tempted to reach for her ID and wave it in the man's face, but couldn't risk it. The clock was ticking and the German had still not returned.

"Leave that girl be!"

Sweetman turned at the sound of the raised voice; so did

others. She looked into a familiar face: that of old Liam Donegan, Martin O'Neill's best friend.

"Sure I'm doin' nothin', Liam," the young man protested. "Or have you your eye on her as well?"

"I'll have you know", Donegan said in a loud voice—and Sweetman suddenly remembered his deafness—"that this young lady is with the Guards."

For feck's sake, Sweetman thought anxiously, keep your bloody voice down.

But there was no stopping the old man. His strident voice vied with that of the guitar player. "If you're not careful, young Sean Regan," he said, "she'll have you behind bars for molestation."

"It's all *right*, Mr Donegan," Sweetman protested. Please, please, don't let the German come back now—not right this minute. "Now, if you'll excuse me," she said to Regan.

This time he allowed her to pass, while appraising her breasts and throwing a wink to his friend at the bar. Sweetman pushed through the open door, into the fresh, night air. She gulped in mouthfuls greedily. Her eyes stung.

But she saw now the reason for the German's absence: the lavatories were outside and, at that very moment, he emerged from the gents. There were other people in the yard and he paid no mind to Sweetman. She looked at her watch: 11.20.

She hoped to heaven that Blade had completed his illicit work by now and was on his way back to the hotel.

Blade nursed a bruised forearm as he shut the toilet door behind him. Yet his tumble had been less of an ordeal than he'd feared. He took the flashlight from between his teeth and let its thin beam play around the floor of the camper. He drew the curtains.

The interior was spotless. There was no trace of occupancy apart from the items on the table .

He went to it. The maps were of France and the Benelux countries. I was right, Blade thought: they're making travel plans. There was also a guidebook. Someone had written something hastily on the cover. It read: EI 363, 15.35, DON.

EI. Blade recognized the designation; EI 363 was an Aer Lingus flight. And somebody called Don. Yet another player in the game? He committed the short message to memory.

He opened a cupboard at eye level. It contained crockery, canned goods, tea and coffee. Nothing suspect.

A drawer below the cooking hob held cutlery, another toiletries and make-up. There were also a number of documents, some bearing the names of the camper's owners, a married couple: Georg and Ursula Godenrath. There was an international driving licence in Georg's name, with a passport-sized colour photograph affixed. The eyes didn't match in colour.

So "Bowie's" name was Georg Godenrath. Thoughtful, Blade continued to search among the papers. There was nothing else of interest—or, if there was, then its import lay beyond the scope of his deficient German. He replaced everything exactly as he'd found it and shut the drawer.

There was a closet opposite; Blade pulled it open and shone the light inside. Clothing was hung neatly. A shelf held a camera and a camcorder, a personal stereo and other, innocuous, items. He was about to shut the closet door when his eye was drawn to something stuck to the inside. He trained the beam on it.

The colour photograph resembled the one he'd found in Martin O'Neill's dictionary. It had been taken at the same table in PJ's yard; he saw that the date printed in a corner matched that of the first snapshot; there was only a few minutes' time difference. But the person who'd taken this one had posed the sitters so that the sun shone full on their faces. There sat the man from the first photograph, smiling into the camera, the colours of his eyes clearly captured on the emulsion. Somebody else sat now in the chair hitherto occupied by the woman.

That somebody was Martin O'Neill.

Blade's mouth was dry as he stood contemplating the picture. The sole photograph the Carlingford gardaí had of the murdered man was in black and white; seen now in a full-colour image, O'Neill looked rather different, though it was clearly the same man; the mismatched eyes attested to that.

Blade had committed the black-and-white portrait to memory; now he saw that he'd have to revise that image. He saw now that the two men in the colour photograph bore more than a passing resemblance to each other.

They might have been father and son.

The entertainer at PJ's had timed his repertoire to end five minutes before closing time. He stood up now and introduced in a clear, loud voice his closing number: the national anthem. Those seated got up as he struck the opening bars. Through the smoke haze Sweetman saw the German woman giggle as she turned in her direction. The amorous Sean

Regan had lost interest in Sweetman; he was chatting up one of the Canadian girls.

Sweetman left her drink unfinished on the counter and slipped out the door, ignoring the frowns of several men who sang along to the national anthem. Out in the yard, she strode briskly past the tables and potted palms, and moved into the shadows by the gate. She activated her radio.

"Alpha Two to Alpha One. Over."

She waited. No response.

"Alpha Two to Alpha One. Come in, Alpha One. Over."

Sweetman started to worry. She looked at her watch. Eleven thirty.

"The Soldier's Song" had ended and already several patrons were leaving the pub. She didn't spot the Germans among them but hadn't expected to; she'd noted that the men had had almost-full pints in front of them.

She tried Blade again, and yet again. Still no reply. She wondered if he'd switched his set off. But that was unlikely; he was too much of a professional to make that sort of slip-up.

Sweetman decided to return to the pub. She'd have to watch both exits. Before doing so, she made yet another attempt at contact.

Macken's radio squawked, unheard by its owner, in the shadow at the rear of the camper. Its message was too faint to be heard through the closed windows.

Besides, Macken was preoccupied; he hadn't even noticed that the radio was missing, nor was he keeping track of the time. His adrenaline was pumping as he opened drawer after drawer, cupboard after cupboard, searching for that vital piece of evidence that would link Georg Godenrath and his companions to the O'Neill slaying.

He needed that evidence; the photograph was not enough. Blade was convinced that the young German was related to the older man. Father and son? Uncle and nephew? But such a tie, if genuine, still didn't implicate either man. That each had visited Carlingford meant nothing either. He sketched the scenario: Parents enjoy a holiday in Ireland: parents recommend the locality to son and daughter-in-law: young couple travel to Carlingford with friends. The most natural—and most innocent—thing in the world.

And the photographs? Parents write to friendly, German-speaking local they've met, enclosing a snapshot. Perhaps there's a correspondence. "Be sure to tell young Georg to look me up if he's in these parts," writes friendly local. "I'd love to meet him and his wife." And young Georg promises to look up friendly local, even takes along a photograph so that he'll have no difficulty recognizing him. Innocence itself.

Yet Blade remained unconvinced; an inner voice was telling him that certain things didn't add up. There was, for example, the fact that the young Germans had remained in Carlingford in the wake of O'Neill's murder. Nor did the murder seem to have affected them as much as it should have, had the dead man been a holiday friend of Georg's parents. And there was still the matter of the dinghy that should have been there but wasn't.

Thinking back on the events of that night, Blade was unable to say why he chose to look in the fridge. To be sure, it was the sole remaining part of the camper that he hadn't searched. He'd found nothing besides the photograph, and it simply wasn't enough. There *had* to be more. . . .

The little unit was stocked with cartons of milk, cheese and other dairy products. There were two six-packs of beer and a litre of tonic water. He was surprised to find four rolls of unused colour film in one of the diminutive compartments, then recalled that a friend of his had the same habit; he maintained that refrigeration prevented his films "from going off".

Blade pulled down the flap of the freeze compartment. He saw a plastic container. Ice cream? The container bore no wrapper. Blade trained his torch on it. Outside, on the tarmac behind the camper, his radio squawked again; an agitated voice issued from the little speaker.

Blade drew the container from the freezer and placed it on the floor. The light-blue plastic betrayed nothing of the contents. He stuck the flashlight between his teeth again, and prised open the lid.

There was ice, a great deal of it; ice that had been broken into pieces, as a fishmonger does to preserve his wares. Blade carefully pushed aside some of the frozen packing.

And nearly dropped the torch in consternation.

There were two milk-white orbs resting in the ice. They were veined with red. The ice in their immediate vicinity had been stained the same colour. Two irises stared sightlessly up at him.

One was blue, the other brown.

Forty-Four

Sweetman tried to keep to the shadows as she walked slow-ly down the narrow street that leads from PJ's pub. Cars passed her, their headlights illuminating the backs of the four people who sauntered up ahead, one of the men with an arm about the shoulders of his female companion. She heard the four talking loudly and good-humouredly in their foreign tongue, and their frequent laughter. The men's gaits were unsteady at times. It was 11.40; most of the bar's pa-trons had left the premises.

The end of the street gives on to a large, open area. There is grass in the middle and two roads fringe it. The four turned left, in the direction of the harbour.

Sweetman ducked into the shadow of a wall and thumbed her radio.

"Alpha Two to Alpha One. If you're not out of there yet, get out now! Repeat: Get out now! Over."

Still no reply, as Sweetman had feared. What in God's name was Blade doing? What had gone wrong?

The four had crossed the busy main road, dodging cars that drove at excessive speeds. Sweetman gave the Germans a one-minute start, then set out after them, not hurrying. There were a number of people strolling along the pavement overlooking the harbour and she merged with them.

Where the harbour wall ends there's a signpost for the Shalom guesthouse. The four turned left there and were temporarily lost to sight.

Sweetman activated her radio again.

For three minutes or longer Macken had remained rooted to the spot, staring at the dreadful trophies in their cold bedding of ice.

He had no doubt they were trophies. *They must have gouged out his eyes before they shot him.* Guard Donnelly's words. *Now why do you suppose anybody would want to do a thing like that? And to a nice oul' fella like Martin?*

"But what did *you* do, Martin?" Blade softly enquired of the dead eyes. "That's the question, isn't it? That's what we should be asking. What did you do to deserve this?"

"My father was a sadist," Jim O'Neill had said. That may be, Blade thought, but Martin O'Neill had been guilty of cruelty in the home, had abused his wife and son. A serious matter in itself, yet it hardly justified a stranger travelling here from Germany with the express purpose of killing him in a most horrific way. It made no sense at all.

Blade rearranged the ice, covering up the eyes again, and pressed the lid back on the container. He had the evidence he needed. It was time to go. Explanations would come later.

The two white campers stood out starkly in the light of the full moon, now almost directly overhead. Sweetman and the four people she tailed were the only visible sign of life in this part of Carlingford. Faint laughter carried from the clubhouse. She remained under the trees flanking the car park.

They'd arrived at the campers, were standing outside the farther vehicle, at the side overlooking the yard of the sailing club. Sweetman was disturbed to see Blade's car parked on the grass verge opposite the guesthouse. She bit her lip. Surely to God he wasn't still in there?

Then she heard the German woman cry out in surprise.

"*Aber die Vorhänge sind zugemacht,*" she said. "*Wer hat das getan?*"

"*Ich nicht,*" a voice answered.

"*Ich auch nicht,*" said another.

"*Verdammt!*" said the man at the woman's side.

Sweetman spoke into his radio, urgently.

"Alpha Two to Alpha One. Bowie's here. Get out now!"

She saw one of the four duck low, searching for something at his feet.

"Alpha One, get out of there!"

The man looked around him, then made for the rear of the leading camper. Sweetman saw him bend down, then straighten again. He was holding something in his hand.

"For feck's sake, Alpha One, if you're in Bowie's place, then get the hell out!"

Sweetman's radio crackled. Jesus, at last! But the voice that came from it was an unexpected one. It spoke with a heavy, mid-European accent.

"Hallo," it said. "Such terrible language you are using, for a lady, whoever you are. Not nice at all."

The voices had stopped Macken in his tracks, just as he was preparing to leave the camper—this time by the door—the container with its ghastly contents tucked under his arm.

They'd come back. He was trapped—and Sweetman hadn't warned him. He patted his pockets. It was only at that moment he discovered that his radio was missing. It had been the least of his concerns, determined as he'd been that he'd have completed his clandestine operation long before the camper's owners returned. He'd no idea where the radio had got to, but now was not the time to speculate.

Blade retreated from the door and looked around. He'd explored every cubic inch of the inside of the vehicle and knew there was no hiding-place. None, that is, except the lavatory. He made for it, and had shut himself in, at the same moment he heard a key rattling in the lock of the camper door.

There came the sound of nervous, angry voices, and footfalls in the enclosed space.

"*Niemand hier*," a voice said.

Blade understood: There's nobody here.

"*Und die Vorhänge dann?*" somebody else asked.

Vorhänge, Vorhänge . . . What the fuck did that mean? He trawled deep in his memory, willing those words and phrases of German he'd picked up in Stuttgart to rise again to the surface. He remembered: they were talking about *curtains*. Blade had drawn them, and somebody had noticed.

He heard footsteps approaching. He stiffened, held his breath, and dipped into a pocket of his jacket for his pistol.

But the footsteps stopped before they reached his hiding place. He heard the sound of a door swinging open. The fridge door.

"*Scheiße! Es ist weg!*"

They were missing something, Blade deduced—and by

the blue Jayziz he knew what that something was.

"*Bist du davon überzeugt?*"

"*Natürlich bin ich davon überzeugt!*"

"*Scheiße.*"

There was a long pause, then the first speaker said: "*Wir müssen unbedingt weg. Jetzt. Hier bleiben ist viel zu gefährlich.*"

"*Glaubst du das es die Polizei war, Georg?*"

It was going much too quickly for Blade to follow to the letter. But he caught the gist of it: Georg was advising them to go and somebody else was talking about the police.

"*Die Polizei? Weiß ich nicht, kerl. Joachim, mach deiner Wagen fertig—und etwas plötzlich, ja? Ushi, steig im Kabine.*"

No doubt about it: they were preparing to leave. Blade heard the door opening again and feet hurrying. The door was slammed shut. Moments later he heard the engine starting. Behind him, the other camper was revving up. Lights shone on the toilet window.

He was trapped; he couldn't leave without being spotted in the headlights of the other vehicle. And he held in his hand the sole piece of evidence that could connect these people to Martin O'Neill's murder.

Sweetman, lurking behind the trees, saw two men race to the rear vehicle. Both engines started up almost as one.

She felt powerless. She had not an inkling of what had happened when the Germans entered the first camper. As far as she was concerned no crime had been committed. It would be the height of foolishness to spring from her place of concealment, gun in hand, and order the drivers and passengers to come out with their hands up.

Where in the name of God, she asked herself, was Blade? Had they discovered him in the leading camper, the one with the drawn curtains, and overpowered him? She'd heard no gunfire or sounds of a struggle. But if he wasn't in one of those vehicles then where could he have got to? The car was still there so he hadn't returned to the hotel.

This was Blade's operation; he'd ordered her not to show her hand without his permission. But Sweetman couldn't stand around and do nothing if Blade was in danger.

Backup? No, she couldn't risk it. One of the Germans had Blade's radio. If he knew how to use it then he could easily find the police frequency and intercept Sweetman's request for reinforcements. It might even blow Blade's plan— whatever harebrained plan he had up his sleeve.

But she had to think fast. The leading camper was already moving off.

Sweetman scurried, head low, to the other vehicle, and saw the trailer, the one that held the tarpaulin. She fumbled with the nylon rope that secured it. It was more by sheer luck than design that she managed to loosen it in time. She raised a fold of the canvas and slid under it, just as the camper pulling the trailer moved off with a jerk.

The vehicles turned out of the car park, shortly joined the main road, and roared away in the direction of Dundalk.

Forty-Five

It was now or never; Macken had waited long enough. He thought his situation ludicrous: sitting in the dark on a toilet in a tiny cubicle with a pair of dead eyes in a Tupperware container for company.

He judged by the rate the camper was travelling (easily read by the closing speed of oncoming traffic), that they'd covered at least thirty miles since leaving Carlingford. The luminous hands of his watch read 12.45, so they must be more than halfway between Dundalk and Drogheda.

Blade was in no doubt that Georg Godenrath was heading south. The airport lay in that direction, and he felt sure that a rendezvous was planned with whoever was arriving—or departing—on Aer Lingus flight EI 363. With "Don". He'd had ample time to consider this. The time noted down— twenty-five to four—was not for another fifteen hours, and he wondered how his "hosts" planned on passing those hours. This was assuming the rendezvous was indeed sched- uled for later today; the message might well be an old one.

They would have to lie low, knowing the police were in- volved now. He was almost certain they knew: he'd heard the woman referring to *die Polizei*. Blade asked himself what he'd do, were he in their position. Jettison the campers, most definitely; they were too conspicuous. But it appeared as though they wanted to put as much distance between themselves and Carlingford before daybreak.

Blade made his mind up. He eased the door open. All clear—he'd expected nothing less. The interior of the camper was exactly as he'd found it, with the exception of the table, now bare.

A door with a window at eye level separated the driver's cabin from the rest of the vehicle. Through the glass Blade saw the heads of Georg Godenrath and his wife, outlined by the lights of oncoming traffic. There was no rear-view mirror; there was no risk of his being seen.

He reached for his pistol, and began making his way slowly and carefully through the swaying camper.

Sweetman was thanking her gods that the night was warm. None the less her teeth chattered. The wind of the camper's slipstream whistled past her, causing the canvas that concealed her to buck and toss with every flurry. There seemed no end to the journey. For the second time in less than forty-eight hours her hands were numb. But the numbness was a blessing: she felt no more pain in her scorched fingertips.

The camper had stopped twice at traffic lights on the ring road in Dundalk. Now Dundalk was many miles behind, and the next set of lights was at Drogheda.

What in the name of God, she thought, am I doing here? She'd asked herself this several times since her impulsive move. She felt ridiculous, lying in concealment in a trailer belonging to a couple of tourists. Sweetman had shared Blade's conviction that they were behind the O'Neill murder but, the longer she thought about it, the more she was troubled by doubts. She'd look a right eejit should Blade be proven wrong.

She made up her mind, as her legs began to show signs of numbness as well. When the camper stopped at the next set of traffic lights, Orla Sweetman was *out* of there.

Blade gripped the door and wrenched it open in almost a single motion. Two heads turned as one. Shock and disbelief.

"Keep your hands on the wheel and your eyes on the road!" he ordered.

The German was reluctant to take his gaze off Blade's pointing pistol, but obeyed. The woman in the passenger seat continued to stare in bewilderment.

"Who the hell are you?" she said.

"Police. Just keep driving in a straight line, Georg. I wouldn't want this gun to go off by accident."

"I would not too," Georg assured him. "What are you doing here?"

"Making an arrest."

Georg turned round again. "You cannot be serious. We have done nothing wrong."

At that moment a radio squawked and Blade squinted to see where the sound was coming from. He saw his missing radio on the dashboard. It was tuned to the garda frequency. Evidently Georg Godenrath had used a two-way radio before.

He knows what he's doing too, Blade thought. Had Sweetman put out an alert then it would be broadcast. The fact that they were still on the road meant that the hunt had not yet begun.

Sweetman. Would she still have her own radio back-to-back, on his preset frequency? There was that chance. There was also a greater chance that Sweetman was long out of range.

"The radio," he said to the woman. "Give it to me."

Ushi Godenrath obliged. Macken leaned against the door frame, still holding Georg under shot, and thumbed the dial.

"This is Alpha One calling Alpha Two. Alpha Two, do you read me? Over."

Sweetman couldn't believe her ears when the message came over on her radio. When last she'd seen the other set it had been in the hands of a German tourist. Now this.

"Alpha Two responding. Blade, where in the name of all that's holy *are* you? Over."

"I might ask you the same."

"Well, I'm only freezing my behind off in someone's fecking trailer. Doing about sixty, I reckon, halfway between Dundalk and Drogheda."

There was a pause while her disclosure sank in.

"Oh, my fuck. What happened, Sweetman? What went wrong? No, don't answer that—I *know* what went wrong. Jesus, I'm really sorry."

"That's okay, Blade. Now I've told you where I am. What about yourself? Over."

Blade told her.

"I'm going to have this character pull in just up ahead, Sweetman. You sit tight until we all stop, okay. Then arrest those other two. I'm calling in for backup now."

"Roger, Alpha One. Over and out."

"So," Blade said, when he'd made the call to Drogheda garda station, "you be a nice boy, Georg, and pull in to the side. Just up here on the hard shoulder."

"And what if I do not?" he said without looking round.

Blade hesitated. There was a strong smell of alcohol in the driver's cabin. Georg and his pals had been drinking heavily, and now Georg was showing the reckless bravado of a man who was far from sober.

"Then I may have to shoot you," Blade said. "And I'll translate that, just so we understand each other. *Dann muß ich du schießen*."

The German laughed.

"Then we will all die. Have you thought of this, Mr Policeman? And I should tell you that your German is fucking terrible."

Ushi looked at Blade and grinned.

Blade had had enough. There were, in his experience, two sorts of young German. You had, on the one hand, the easygoing type, the type you find on every old hippie trail from Morocco to Malaysia. On the other hand, you had people like Georg and Ushi, people whose arrogance and one-upmanship gave their nation a bad name. He was growing very, very angry.

"Don't play fucking games with me!" he shouted. "Stop this van at once."

And he put the gun to Georg's temple.

The events of the next few seconds occurred so fast that Blade was to recall them as a blur.

Ushi lunged, catching his gun hand and throwing it back.

The gun went off and the bullet ricocheted off the metal ceiling of the driver's cabin. He heard Georg cry out in pain. Then Blade, under the momentum of Ushi's attack, lost his balance, fell, and slid down the aisle of the camper, striking his ribs against the rear wall.

And suddenly the camper, out of control, was careering into the path of oncoming traffic.

Blade heard Ushi screech. There was a crash like thunder, lights invading the camper. Blade was thrown back the way he'd come.

Dazed, he heard an engine whine wildly and tyres screeching behind the vehicle—and another roar and a rending and screaming of metal. Blade was tossed about yet again like a rag doll.

Then there was a silence. And Blade found that silence the worst part of all.

Shocked, dazed and bleeding, he managed to find the door. He half-walked, half-fell through it.

And hit the roadway at the feet of Orla Sweetman.

Forty-Six

The gardaí had cordoned off a stretch of the NI some twelve miles north of Drogheda. The carnage was great, though not as fatally disastrous as it might have been.

"You were *damned* lucky, sir," Inspector Walsh said, as he sat briefly with Macken and Sweetman in one of the ambulances before it bore them to Drogheda. "Both of you. By rights you should be dead."

Macken inspected his bandaged arm. He had indeed been lucky; he'd come free with no more than a few bruised ribs and some minor cuts and grazes. Sweetman seemed to have escaped serious injury as well.

"I still don't really know what happened," he said. "It all seemed to go so fast—as these things do."

"From what we can make out, sir," Walsh said, "the leading vehicle—the one you were travelling in—went over to the wrong side of the road, right into the path of an oncoming car. The driver of the car was lucky too. He sustained a broken arm and chest injuries but he should be grateful to be alive at all. We think the camper must have caught the car a glancing blow."

"What about the Germans?" Blade asked.

"The two behind are badly hurt," Walsh said. "Crashed into the side of the first camper. But it wasn't as bad as it could have been. They'd braked; there's tyre marks on the road." He looked at Sweetman. "You were in *that* vehicle, weren't you, sergeant?"

"Yes sir, in the trailer, under a load of canvas."

The inspector pulled a face. He didn't know quite what to make of all this. He wanted to speak his mind but dared not—not when a superior officer was involved, and certainly not when that officer was Detective Superintendent Macken of Harcourt Square. He knew Blade's reputation.

"And the other two?" Blade said. "The ones in the leading camper?"

"The girl's dead, I'm afraid, sir," Walsh told him. "Died on impact I'd say. She must have been on the passenger side; it's a left-hand-drive job. The man is critical. He sustained massive injuries—including a gunshot wound."

"It went off by accident," Blade said laconically.

Inspector Walsh made no comment. He nodded, and left the ambulance. He was met by two uniformed Guards, who were anxious for news.

"It *is* Blade Macken, isn't it, sir?" one said.

"It is. And all I can say is that it's the quarest business I've seen in a long while. A long while."

He went to a squad car, shaking his head and muttering.

They were offered cups of strong, hot coffee at the garda station in Drogheda. Sweetman requested tea instead. Her body and mind cried out for sleep. She'd reached that stage in sleep deprivation—compounded by post-traumatic stress—when sounds are amplified and distorted, colours are overbright and dazzling, and the nerve ends lie exposed.

She hadn't expected it to end this way. It was so sloppy.

She'd hoped that this investigation might resolve itself in satisfying fashion. Not a casebook study perhaps, but one none the less wherein the disparate strands would somehow have met, to be tied and sealed and delivered to Harcourt Square.

Instead, the body of evidence comprised a pair of discarnate, ill-matched eyes that resided temporarily in a freezer in Drogheda; a dinghy and a blood-soaked shell suit in Phoenix Park garda depot that may or may not have belonged to one of four suspects of foreign origin; the corpse of a pretty, young woman in a hospital morgue, her husband on life-support, their pals seriously injured.

A door slammed close by and Sweetman was startled. It was Blade Macken, emerging from the men's room. He smiled at her weakly. The strip lighting was hurting her eyes. She rubbed them.

"Are you all right, Sweetman?"

"A brain transplant might help." She nursed her bruised arms, her sore fingers. "A new body mightn't be such a bad idea either."

Blade slurped when drinking from his coffee mug. The sound jarred.

The door of the incident room opened again. Inspector Walsh came in, clutching a fax.

"You'll be pleased to know, sir," he said, "that that flight number checks out. It's an Aer Lingus flight from Frankfurt. Twice weekly; lands at three thirty-five."

Blade brightened. "Someone was expected on that flight. Someone called Don."

Walsh smiled. "That's what I thought too, sir. But luckily one of the lads has a bit of German. That flight is every

Monday and Thursday. And Thursday in German is *Donnerstag—Don* for short."

"Shite," Blade said. "I knew that myself. I forgot."

But it was an insignificant detail; the important thing was that the inquiry wasn't over yet. Some loose ends at least might still be tidied up before their return to Harcourt Square.

Walsh passed him the fax.

"That's a list of the passengers who'll be arriving tomorrow. Is there anybody you might recognize, sir?"

The name was near the top. Blade's eyes widened slightly and his pulse quickened.

Godenrath, Markus A.

The door opened once again at that moment. A garda in uniform entered; he was carrying two steaming mugs.

"More sustenance for the walking wounded," he called out brightly.

His jaw went slack. Coffee and tea slopped out onto the floor.

"Jayziz. Orla! And Superintendent Macken. They didn't tell me it was *ye*. Be the holy!"

Mick Strong, Orla thought. The bould Mick Strong. That's all we need now.

But . . . he isn't pleased to see me. No, he isn't pleased at all. I shouldn't even *be* here.

I should be in a cellar in Kilbarrack.

Her lack of sleep had had its deleterious effects. It had also sharpened her hearing, as the ears of the vixen, exhausted by the hunt, will hear the baying of her approaching pursuers. She recalled a voice heard through an intervening door.

Sweetman launched herself from her chair. It fell back with a crash. Mick Strong went white; he didn't feel the hot liquid that splashed from the mugs and scalded his hands.

What he did feel was Sweetman's right fist as it smashed into his nose.

He staggered back against the wall. The mugs rolled across the floor.

"Bastard!" she screamed.

"Sergeant *Sweet*man!" Blade roared. His hands pinioned her arms. She was shaking with rage. Strong was holding his broken, bloodied nose with both hands.

"W-who knew that B-Blade Macken and me were going to Dundalk on the seventh of August, inspector?" she asked. "The day after the O'Neill murder. "*Who?*"

Walsh looked baffled. "Er, nobody. I didn't even know myself."

"I didn't think so," Sweetman, a little calmer now, said. "Superintendent Macken was surprised that somebody in Drogheda knew about it. And I think you'll find that Garda Michael Strong has been in touch once too often with Harcourt Square the last few days—early on Monday evening in particular."

Strong was starting to protest. Walsh silenced him.

"I also think you'll find," she continued, "that Garda Michael Strong has been away from the station a lot the past few days—maybe swapping shifts with other Guards."

"*That* I can confirm," Walsh said. "How *is* your mother now, Mick? Any better?"

"Blade," Sweetman said coldly, "meet Delta fucking One."

Forty-Seven

The monitor at the terminal gate announced that the flight from Frankfurt, due to touch down at Dublin Airport at 15.35, had undergone a ten-minute delay before take-off. Blade didn't mind. He'd arranged to meet the interpreter here at the desk at half past three and there was still no sign of him.

He'd managed to catch some sorely needed sleep at the station in Drogheda. The bunk had been far from comfortable but Blade had dropped off almost as soon as his head touched the pillow. He was feeling better now.

Sweetman said something and pointed. One of the airport police was coming their way, a thin, balding man in tow. He carried an attaché case, and a mackintosh across one arm.

"I think that's our man now," Sweetman said.

Joe Cunningham had been able to find Fergal Merry at very short notice. The interpreter was due to join a European Parliamentary delegation in Strasbourg that evening but had promised to make his services available to the gardaí for at least a couple of hours. Macken had assured Cunningham that two hours would suffice.

Merry's demeanour belied his surname. He introduced himself to Macken and Sweetman with a dour expression and a limp handshake.

"I understand that you'll be interviewing a German gentleman, superintendent. Do you know what part of the country he's from?"

"Does that matter?"

"No no, not unless he's from Lower Bavaria. Sometimes that particular dialect can be troublesome."

"You're telling me," Blade said. "No, we have reason to believe he's from Mannheim or the surrounding area."

"Fine. That'll be no bother at all then." Merry consulted his watch.

"The flight was delayed," Blade said. "But it landed a minute or two ago. We should be seeing the first passengers soon."

Merry nodded.

"Sweetman," Blade said, "why don't you take Mr Merry to the interview-room. We don't need a whole reception committee for our friend."

He watched them go, the tall policewoman escorting the saturnine little man with the briefcase. He didn't like to dismiss Sweetman like that, yet he wanted to be the first to see Godenrath senior. He wanted to be the first to see, face to face, the sort of man who was capable of masterminding the plot to torture and kill Martin O'Neill, the sort of man who was capable of dispatching his own son and daughter-in-law to do his bidding.

He'd seen his photograph—was holding it in his hand at that very moment—and the man looked not at all as a monster should. He looked plain and downright ordinary.

The first of the passengers were approaching the gate; men and women with hand baggage, business people returning from an overnight stay in the Federal Republic. Blade craned to view the faces. He in turn was subjected to bemused looks as the passengers filed past him. Blade ran a hand through his hair. He'd forgotten his dishevelled appearance.

And then he was there. He looked smaller than the man in the photograph, and older. Could a year make so much difference?

Blade put his age at between sixty-five and seventy. He was dressed for a holiday: khaki slacks and a dark blue, short-sleeved shirt. A suntan accentuated the whites of his eyes—and their mismatched pupils. Blade signalled to the two airport police officers. An unnecessary gesture; they'd spotted the suspect at the same moment as he.

"Markus Godenrath?" he heard the sergeant say.

"Y-yes." The voice was soft and gentle.

"Will you come this way, sir?"

They escorted the flustered man to the interview-room with Macken bringing up the rear. Godenrath's nervousness increased when he saw another Guard there, and Sweetman, the plasters on her left hand and across her right cheek, and the multitude of bruises.

"I do not understand," the elderly German said. "What is the problem, please?"

"Please sit down, Herr Godenrath," Blade said, and the man noticed him for the first time. I suppose I must look like a fugitive from a war zone as well, Blade thought. His black clothes were dirty and torn, and plasters hid his own cuts and bruises. The German sat down at the place reserved for him.

"I'm Detective Superintendent Macken of the Dublin

Special Branch and I'd like to ask you some questions." He nodded to Mr Merry, who rattled off a translation.

Blade produced the photograph and slid it across the table. He saw Godenrath's eyes open slightly, then return to normal.

"Do you recognize the man with you, sir?"

He shrugged. Cool bastard, thought Blade.

"The picture was taken only a year ago. And you don't recognize the man?"

"*Nein.*"

"No," said Merry, rather needlessly. Or were there nuances in the pronunciation of the word *nein?* News to Blade.

He made a curt gesture to one of the airport police. The officer understood and ducked into an anteroom, to return carrying the type of box employed by hospitals to transport freshly harvested organs to be used as transplants.

"Perhaps you'll recognize these," Blade said grimly. The coolness of the man was infuriating him.

He opened the box and removed the plastic container within. He prised off the lid, scooped out a handful of ice and threw it into the freeze box. He saw Sweetman shudder when he'd exposed the gruesome trophies; she turned her head away. Without another word Blade pushed the container across to Godenrath.

His face was unreadable. Blade had expected the normal, human, reaction. Horror. Shock. Even guilt? But there was nothing; the face was an expressionless mask.

To hell with you, Markus Godenrath, he thought. If that's the way you want to play it then I can play hard too.

"It's a shame that they mean nothing to you, sir," he

said quietly, "because your daughter-in-law Ursula died last night because of those eyes. And Georg is in intensive care."

He waited for the interpreter to finish his rapid, almost synchronous, translation. You needed more words in German. He saw Godenrath's eyes widen.

"*Die kleine Ushi? Tot? Nein doch. Und das liebes Georgchen. . . .*"

"Little Ushi? Dead? Surely not. And dear Georgie. . . ." said Merry, deadpan as ever.

"I'm afraid so, sir. There was a traffic accident. Georg's two friends were hospitalized as well, but they're out of danger." He leaned across the table. "Would you like a lawyer? You're entitled to have one."

"*Nein.*" He was staring at the dead eyes.

Sweetman cautioned him. He nodded numbly.

"The first question I wish to ask," Blade said, "concerns the deceased, the man with you in the picture. We knew him as Martin O'Neill. I'd like you to tell us who he really was."

Godenrath picked up the photograph. Gone was the cool demeanour. He trembled. Macken saw that his eyes were moist.

"His name was Andrija Princip. He was my uncle."

Forty-Eight

"I was born Anjo Princip," Godenrath said, "in the town of Samobor, Croatia. It is close to Zagreb. I am a Serb, as was my father, Milos Princip."

Macken was glad he'd requested a stenographer. The foreign names, he knew, were going to pose difficulties. But their phonetic equivalents, taken down in shorthand, could be converted at a later stage; what he dearly wanted now were the facts. As Godenrath spoke, he appreciated how close they'd been to uncovering them.

None the less, the revelation of O'Neill's true identity had startled him considerably.

"I was nine years of age when the war reached us and my country was overrun by the Nazis. I did not know my uncle then; he had lived abroad for many years and had lost touch with the family. He did not even know of my existence. He returned to Croatia, you see, when many of the Serbs had already been rounded up; few were left in Samobor."

"This was in the spring of nineteen forty-one?" Blade asked.

"Yes. You are very knowledgeable, superintendent."

"I've been doing some reading. I know about the mass conversions—and the slaughter."

"Such terrible, terrible times. If there is a God, then he

must surely have despaired of the human race during the last century. Or was Carlyle correct when he said: 'Is there no God then but at best an absentee God, sitting idle ever since the first sabbath on the outside of his universe?'"

Macken glanced at Sweetman. Mr Merry's time was not unlimited and Blade was in no mood for philosophical digression.

"Tell me about your uncle, sir."

Godenrath looked at the photograph again and sighed.

"Andrija Princip—the man whom you call Martin O'Neill —was one of the first Orthodox Serbs to convert to Roman Catholicism when the Germans came. He was a graduate of the University of Zagreb and had worked for a time as a schoolmaster. He went to America before the war to seek his fortune. He was not successful in this, therefore he returned. Pavelić . . . You have heard of Pavelić?"

"Yes, the quisling ruler of Croatia."

"That is correct. Pavelić saw much in my Uncle Andrija and when Andrija joined the Ustashe military police—which was no better than Hitler's SS—Pavelić ensured that he gained promotion quickly. He and my uncle were of like mind, you see. They were opportunists of the worst sort."

"Would you like a glass of water, sir?" Blade asked.

"No, thank you. I was about to say that my uncle very soon obtained a much sought-after appointment, as camp commander of Jasenovac."

"The death camp."

Godenrath nodded and pointed to the photograph.

"It is scarcely possible to believe now," he said, "but that man was responsible for the extermination of more than one hundred thousand people, most of them Serbs, but many Jews and Gypsies as well. Oh, and Andrija enjoyed it. He enjoyed every moment of it, especially the cruelty. And the blood. He seemed to delight in the blood. Lord God in heaven, there were moments when we thought that the Devil himself had come to Jasenovac!" A long pause, a reflection. "You see, superintendent, Andrija had been given a hard time of it when he was a schoolboy. He had been cursed with the genetic disorder that is common to the Princip family. *This.*"

Godenrath was pointing to his own mismatched eyes.

"I wouldn't have thought," Blade said, "that it would have made that much difference."

"Wouldn't you? Then you would be wrong. In my part of the world we are intensely proud of our race. Some of us can trace our ancestry back to Attila the Hun. We are careful too about whom we marry, which families we marry into. Our blood ties are very important to us. And that is why those of my family unlucky enough to be born with eyes like these can expect no mercy from their neighbours. We were mocked and taunted as children, called 'mongrel', 'half-breed', and other names too coarse to repeat. My father, when a boy, did his best to ignore the taunts; Andrija did not. Is it not inexplicable how pain endured in childhood can affect a man so deeply that his hurt carries on into adulthood?"

"Yes, it is," Blade agreed.

"Andrija behaved like a devil in Jasenovac. It was as though every Serb put to death had been one of those who had made fun of him as a child. He took great pleasure in overseeing each mass execution personally. Then the doctors arrived."

"The doctors?"

"Yes, and I think I will have that water now, thank you very much."

One of the airport policemen went to fetch a glass. Blade saw that Godenrath was trembling slightly. He didn't know precisely when the transformation had taken place: the moment when he'd no longer regarded Markus Godenrath as a murder suspect but as a victim. Perhaps it was when Godenrath heard of the death of his daughter-in-law.

Then Blade learned about the surgeons of Jasenovac. In the manner in which Josef Mengele had used Auschwitz as his private laboratory, the Croat surgeons had regarded the Serb prisoners as human guinea pigs. He saw even the unflappable Mr Merry pale as Godenrath gave his account of the frightful deeds perpetrated in the name of science.

Their aims were similar to Mengele's. Eugenics was the god at whose altar they worshipped; racial impurities and congenital defects were the enemies that had to be eradicated.

And Andrija Princip, camp commandant, saw his opportunity of becoming one with the Aryan race that had seized power in his country. He would no longer be a half-breed or mongrel: Princip would become a true, blue-eyed conqueror, the scourge of the people who had despised him as a boy.

"He was always present", Godenrath said, "whenever experiments of an ophthalmic nature were conducted. No outrage was too gross, or unthinkable, for this monster. Children were torn from their mother's arms and subjected to unimaginable suffering in Andrija's quest for the means by which an eye could be transplanted from one socket to another. It was hopeless, of course; such things were impossible in nineteen forty-one." He spread his hands. "Now, at the start of a new millennium, "we can do as much—and a great deal more besides. How I wish that we could not!"

The past days had given Sweetman a taste of pain that was barely tolerable. She tried to imagine the suffering undergone by the victims of the demon surgeons of Jasenovac. She could not.

"And your father?" Blade asked softly.

Godenrath nodded. "Milos Princip, my father, had the misfortune to be sent to the camp. He was as a lamb to the slaughter. Andrija could not believe his luck; here was a man who shared the same gene pool as he. His own brother! Could anything be better? Milos was a hated Orthodox Serb; Andrija was a Catholic Croat. You see, superintendent, my uncle—God damn his soul! and I say this without remorse—and my father had always been rivals. Milos had the brains, you see; Andrija had the ambition. But what is ambition without the intelligence to channel it? Milos was the one who excelled in everything. *Everything*. Andrija was the brother who *wanted* everything. He hated Milos. I do not believe that he himself appreciated the extent of his hatred; not, at any rate, when they were growing up together."

"So he found out that Milos was his prisoner," Macken prompted.

Godenrath sipped some water. He seemed to have aged within the span of several minutes. Then his face flushed; his eyes were wild.

"His prisoner. Yes! To do with as he chose. And, by the living God, he did just that, superintendent. I wasn't there but the reports reached me. Do you know what Andrija had those demons do? They removed his eyes—both of them—*without an anaesthetic.* Can you imagine that? Can you imagine the torture my father must have suffered?"

Blade thought he could. Barely.

"I have this on good authority," Godenrath said. "The testimony of somebody who was present when this unspeakable act of barbarousness was committed."

"I believe you."

"He died that evening. My father. A combination of shock and blood poisoning. He died in the arms of a man who conveyed the news to my mother."

The same policeman who'd brought Godenrath his water came to replenish the glass.

"So you wished to avenge his death, sir." Blade felt as though another person was speaking.

"And can you blame me, superintendent!" He lowered his voice. "They got off scot-free, the perpetrators of genocide in Croatia. Did you know that? All of them: Pavelić, Artuković and the rest of those vermin."

Blade was alert. He'd hoped to place the foreign names in the trusty hands of the stenographer. Yet he'd just heard one name spoken, not read, for the first time. He remembered: Artuković, alias Anitch, the war criminal who'd found sanctuary in Ireland in 1947.

"Tell me about Artuković, Herr Godenrath."

He seemed happy to unburden himself. Blade learned how the genocidal Pavelić—together with his army and his equally genocidal minister—was forced to retreat before the Allied forces. The State documents had been stored in Pavelić's palace; the dictator felt certain that the Allies would attack Russia and he could return to Zagreb; later those documents would be used against him.

There was gold as well. Masses of it. In the manner of Himmler's death camps, Jasenovac and the other Croatian killing centres had accumulated the gold fillings, rings and watches of their victims. The gold was taken to the Franciscan abbey at Zagreb and hidden beneath a confession box by the friars.

Blade stopped Mr Merry at this point.

"Did you say 'Franciscans'?" he asked in astonishment.

"Yes."

He looked at Sweetman; she too had not remained unmoved by this extraordinary revelation.

"Please go on, Herr Godenrath," Blade said.

But the elderly man had taken the cue.

"Yes, superintendent, that is how the Croatian butcher, Artuković, escaped from my country. The Church of Rome helped him. Then it helped him again when he was living with his wife and daughter in Switzerland. Through the Franciscans at Fribourg they managed to obtain documents which allowed them to travel to Ireland. They remained here a year then left for the United States. For years my countrymen attempted to have Artuković extradited. They finally succeeded in nineteen eighty-six but he died before he could stand trial."

"And your uncle? Andrija Princip. Where does he figure in all of this?"

Godenrath took another sip of water. He looked extremely tired. Not physically; he had the look of a man who has grown weary of the injustices of the world.

"I do not know," he told Macken. "It was rumoured that Andrija and Artuković fled Croatia together, that they journeyed together to this country. It would make sense; they were very close. But those were simply rumours, as I have said, and I discounted them at the time."

"But last August you found out that the rumours were true after all."

"I did, superintendent, and it was no more than a quirk of fate that led me to him. I had discarded the notion a long time ago of ever finding my father's murderer. So many of the evil men who slaughtered hundreds of thousands of my people have never been brought to account; I had resigned myself to the fact that Andrija Princip would never stand trial for his crimes."

And you made *certain* he never would, Blade thought; you made certain in the most effective way possible.

"My wife and I were touring Ireland last summer. It was odd, because Carlingford was to be our final stop; we had planned on boarding the commercial ferry at Warrenpoint and leaving for Stranraer in Scotland, to travel down to the south of England at our leisure. Who could have known what I was to find in that little bar in Carlingford? At first I could not believe my eyes; I thought I must be going mad! I thought that all those years of lusting after vengeance had taken their toll, causing me to see things which were not there. But I knew immediately that it was he. His was a face I could never forget."

Blade stopped Mr Merry again.

"Just a minute," he said. "I wasn't aware that Andrija

and Herr Godenrath had met in the camp. Did I miss something?"

"No, we had not," Godenrath said. "I saw him, but I do not believe that he ever truly saw me. I saw him from behind barbed wire, as he strutted about the compound. I watched his dreadful cruelty. He did not notice me because, on the advice of the man who was looking after me, I took to wearing a bandage over one eye, as though I was permanently wounded. Many men and boys were bandaged therefore it did not look at all out of place. So I was able to study the face of the monster. I burned it into my memory, and knew that I should never forget it."

"I see," Blade said. "I understand now." He paused. "What I don't quite follow is your name: Godenrath. I can see why Andrija changed his, but why you?"

He smiled thinly. "For a number of reasons, superintendent. But principally for my own safety. You have no conception of what it was like in those times! All around us people were being slaughtered like beasts, whole villages wiped out. No one was spared, not even the children. In the extermination camp called Jasenovac the policy was to put to death a prisoner who had been there longer than three months. I was fortunate. A relative of mine had some influence and through his intercession I was released and handed into the safekeeping of a young German couple named Marco and Alicia Godenrath. They took me to Hamburg and raised me as their own child. I shall never forget their kindness, and the risks they ran on my behalf. And so it was, superintendent, that I grew up in Germany as Markus Godenrath, my adopted name."

"So Andrija never suspected you were anything but German."

"Not for a moment. He was pleased to be able to practise the little bit of German he had, conversing with a man whom he took to be a native of Germany. He joked about how alike we were in appearance, this man calling himself Martin O'Neill. I went along with it, pretending to share the joke. That was when I suggested the photograph. I said I wished to show my friends in Germany the uncanny resemblance I bore to a retired schoolteacher in Ireland. Andrija thought it was a capital idea."

Blade excused himself, stood up and went to the stenographer. Sweetman saw him whispering something to the young woman, who nodded, gathered up her things and left the room. Hmm, Sweetman thought, the rest is off the record.

Blade returned to the table.

"To get back to the photograph, Herr Godenrath," he said. "It was for another purpose entirely, am I correct? You needed it so that his killers could identify him. Or had you thought of murder then?" He looked across at Sweetman. "I'm asking you this for your own protection, sir."

Godenrath smiled then, taking Macken aback. He found himself wishing that he hadn't dismissed the stenographer. Hadn't Eichmann smiled in the dock in 1946?

But the smile was gone as quickly as it had come and Blade knew it for what it really was: the *rictus sardonicum* of the man who suddenly appreciates the full extent of the crime he's been recounting with apparent dispassion.

"The killing was Georg's idea," he said. "Please do not misunderstand me, superintendent; I have no wish to place blame on my son in order to evade justice myself. It is too late for that now. What I am saying is that Georg elected to take my place, as it were, to fight his father's fight, and I am proud of him because of that. Ushi too—may God have mercy on her soul!"

And on yours too, Blade thought. He could not condone the act the son had perpetrated, yet found it hard to sit in judgement on a man who'd set out to slay a monster.

"Georg worked out the plan with his friends: Joachim Neubauer and Hans Ströbel."

"The two men in the other camper?"

"Yes. You must understand a thing about the young Germans of Georg's generation, superintendent: they feel—the majority of them—a deep sense of shame regarding their country's past. They will not allow the Hitler period to be forgotten. And who can blame them? To forget the past is to deny that it ever existed. And once you deny the past then you run the risk of history repeating itself."

"So how did Georg and his friends prepare?"

"They had all three been in the army; all young men must do military service in Germany, as you doubtless know. All three had done theirs at a camp near Göttingen, and were quite familiar with its layout. Therefore they travelled to Göttingen and took lodgings in the city at the beginning of May. In the evenings they would frequent the bars where the national servicemen came to drink, and made friends with several of them. One night they plied two soldiers with schnapps and returned with them to the hotel where Georg was staying, there to continue drinking. Soon the soldiers had drunk so much that they passed out and, while they slept in a stupor, Georg and Hans borrowed their uniforms and identity cards. You have seen Georg, superintendent; you will know that he looks younger than he is, especially when the light is poor. And so it was that they were able to enter the army compound unchallenged. They remembered where the armoury was and broke into it, stealing handguns and other equipment.”

So now we know, Blade thought, where the murder weapon originated. We can rule out Russia.

“They planned Andrija Princip’s execution as one would plan a military operation,” Godenrath said. “Georg and Ushi took my camper; Hans and Joachim purchased an identical vehicle. They set off together in July, when they journeyed first to the south of Portugal.”

“To buy the dinghy.”

Godenrath raised his eyebrows. “You know about that?”

“These things can be traced, sir.”

“I see. Extraordinary. However, from Portugal they journeyed to France and took the ferry to Ireland. Georg was taking a great risk of course yet he felt certain that nobody would examine the campers at borders. With Ushi and he in the lead camper and his two friends behind they looked just like any other group of young people on summer vacation.”

Godenrath paused for a long time. He drank some more water before continuing. Contrary to Blade’s expectations, Mr Merry was showing no signs of impatience, even though he soon had a plane to catch. He was clearly caught up in this remarkable account. Would it, Blade wondered somewhat cynically, be retold in Strasbourg tonight as an interesting after-dinner story?

"You will no doubt be aware of the rest," Godenrath said. "Georg never seriously believed that the police would mistake the killing for a terrorist execution. He thought the slogan on the wall was, to use his own words, 'a nice touch'. You see, it is close to the Serbo-Croatian *Jebo okupatora!* and this was the very battle-cry of my people when the Nazis invaded us."

"And the eyes, Herr Godenrath? Was removing the eyes Georg's idea?"

"Is that important?"

"Yes."

"Very well. If you must know, it was *my* wish. When Georg had made up his mind that Andrija Princip must die, I requested that he remove those eyes that had been the cause of so much suffering and grief. Georg was to do the killing and bring the eyes to me. Instead he chose to stay on in Carlingford. The hubris of the young, superintendent. He wished to see how the Irish police go about solving an insoluble crime." He shook his head. "I repeat: the hubris of the young."

Blade sat in silence for more than a minute. Mr Merry still showed no pressing urge to leave just yet. But as far as Blade was concerned the interview was at an end. Certainly he had more questions, but didn't think Markus Godenrath was in a position to supply answers. They concerned the role of the Franciscan friars in all this—how a mass murderer could have sought and obtained the help of a soft-spoken friar called Luji, alias Benedict, from Galway. He had a feeling that much of the secret life of Martin O'Neill would remain elusive.

"I have just one last question, Herr Godenrath," he said.

"Yes?" The man looked exhausted.

"Did you request Georg to remove the eyes *before* he killed your uncle?"

"No, superintendent," he answered slowly and painfully. "No, I did not. There is, I am certain, a touch of the monster in all of us—even in one's own children."

"Are we arresting him, Blade?" Sweetman asked when they were alone.

Mr Merry was en route to Strasbourg; Godenrath was being treated to tea and a light snack in an adjoining room. The extraordinary interview had gone on for two and a half hours.

"On what charge, Sweetman? For incitement to murder? For aiding and abetting a criminal? I don't know; maybe you can advise me. What would *you* do in my place?"

"As a police officer or as a Christian?"

He smiled. "Can't you be both?"

"I like to think I *am*. You want to let him go, don't you?"

He nodded.

"Then I say let him go. Look at the poor old fella. What age is he? Seventy? He looks about eighty. Think of what he's been through, Blade. You don't survive all of that without going a bit loopy." She showed her palms. "Okay, so he spent most of his life thinking about revenge—but I would too if they'd done a thing like that to *my* father. 'An eye for an eye.' Isn't that what it says in the Bible?"

"Hmm, I was wondering when someone would quote that."

"But," Sweetman went on, "that's the *Old* Testament. And not even the Jews live by that rule any more. Look at Simon Wiesenthal, the Nazi hunter. He was through much worse than Godenrath, but vengeance was never his motive. He always insisted that his purpose was to have the war criminals *admit* what they'd done. That was enough for him."

"And you think that should be enough for us as well?"

"Yeah, I do. It's not our fight, Blade. Janey, look what happened in Bosnia in the nineties. The Serbs got their own back. Maybe if the world had heard Godenrath's story then that might never have happened. But the Croats always denied what they'd done, and they suffered the consequences."

He looked at her queerly, this attractive young woman with a rich lode of intelligence and human insight.

"Why *did* you become a Guard, Sweetman? No, don't answer that—I believe I know." He glanced at the door to the adjacent room. "Now: I suppose I'll have to break the good news to him before we have another corpse on our hands. Then it's Carlingford."

"Carlingford? I don't understand."

"I know you don't, Sweetman. How's the hand? Can you drive? I want to be there in a hurry."

"You're not making sense. I thought we'd this all wrapped up."

"Wrapped up? Far from it, Sweetman. We've still a long way to go, and Carlingford's our next stop. I'll explain on the way."

Forty-Nine

Jim O'Neill answered the door in his dressing-gown. He was unshaven. It was close to eight in the evening. He looked nervously from Macken to Sweetman to Guard Gary O'Donnell. They hadn't come on foot this time: a squad car stood parked in front of the cottage. O'Neill admitted them.

Macken came straight to the point.

"Why did you lie to us, sir?"

"I d-don't understand."

"No? Well, let's start with Dr Brophy, shall we? You remember: your shrink. The man who 'brought you back' to your childhood, the character who unlocked all those suppressed memories. *That* Dr Brophy, sir."

O'Neill bit his lip.

"He doesn't exist, does he, sir? You won't find him in the book. And it's not that he's ex-directory. He's ex-*every*thing. The BMA never heard of him; nor did any other medical association; nor did the RUC."

Blade motioned to O'Neill to sit.

"That's usually the trouble when people make things up, sir," he continued. "They want to be so convincing that they go into far too much detail. But innocent people aren't like that; they're usually very vague about dates, names and things. But you thought that by giving us the name of your fictitious psychoanalyst your story would be more plausible. You shouldn't have done that, sir. Because we're the Guards. We don't take things on trust; we check and double-check."

O'Neill was silent, looking at his slippers.

"However," Blade continued, "I wouldn't have checked your story in this case. Why? I don't know. Maybe I felt sorry for you—you having lost your father in such a brutal way. Or maybe because you played your part so bloody well. Innocence itself. You're Oscar material.

"But I checked for a different reason you see. I wanted to know whether those Serbo-Croatian words were correct. I only had your pronunciation, and that was phonetic. My contact at the university needed more than that for confirmation. I tried to call you on Sunday night, to get Dr Brophy's address and phone number, but you were out. You see, I happen to know that shrinks record their sessions, so those words in Serbo-Croatian would have been on tape, exactly the way you pronounced them. But they weren't, were they, sir? Because there was no Dr Brophy, and therefore no tape."

"No."

"No. You described that session so *well* too. How many times did you rehearse it in your mind? Or maybe in front of the bathroom mirror? No, don't answer; it doesn't matter. But once again you supplied a detail that you needn't have bothered with: a phrase in Serbo-Croatian. Oh, I know why you did it: you wanted to feed us a clue. And you succeeded in that. You knew—you *thought*—we'd never make the Croatian connection alone and unaided. It was way too outlandish for simple plods like us. And you were the clever-clever one. There was no reason in the world why you

should have given us those words, but it suited your purposes—and your vanity. You wanted us to believe that we'd
made the connection ourselves, even though we'd misinter-
preted the clue in the beginning. How you kept a straight
face last Saturday morning is beyond me, when I was telling
you my theory about your father being a member of the IRA
who spoke Serbo-Croatian. God, you were brilliant; you
were even *contradicting* me, telling me it was all a load of
crap. Talk about double bluff—I don't know if there's even
a name for it. Triple bluff maybe."

O'Neill patted the pockets of his dressing-gown, took out
a packet of cigarettes and lit one.

"It worked though, didn't it?" he said.

"Oh certainly it worked. Like a dream. You wanted us
to dig up the dirt on your father. You wanted the world to
know what a monster we'd been harbouring all these years.
And you wanted to expose those responsible for helping him.
Only you had to do it without us knowing of your involvement."

"How did you find out? I'm intrigued."

"About your lie? Through my contact at the university.
Oh, you were thorough, sir. You got the words right: they
do mean 'dirty little dog'. Except the pronunciation of the
word for 'dog' was completely off. At first I thought this was
just a lapse in memory on your part—I mean, it was a long
time ago. But Serbo-Croatian is a funny language, as I've
been told. It's a bit like Irish: it's almost impossible to pro-
nounce right unless you've heard it spoken. But you hadn't,
had you, sir? You *read* it. And never having heard it spoken
you thought that word was pronounced 'pasce'. In actual

fact it's very, very close to 'pasha', which is a word you'd know and be far more likely to use. But it didn't look like 'pasha' when you read it—in one of your father's books." He jerked a thumb at the bookcase. "One of the books you got rid of, when you didn't need it any more."

O'Neill drew deeply on his cigarette and studied the bookcase.

"Once again," Blade said, "you got caught up in the details. You could easily have taken the books out and dumped them and no one would have been the wiser. But no, you had to go one step further: you had to replace the books with others. So what did you do? You substituted them with some of your own, to fill the empty spaces. But here's where you slipped up on that score." He looked at Sweetman. "Had it not been for Sergeant Sweetman then I wouldn't have noticed. But she commented on the fact that we both did the same Shakespeare plays at school: *Hamlet* and *The Merchant of Venice*."

"So?"

"We did them in *secondary* school, sir. I checked with the education board in Northern Ireland and they told me it's the same there: Shakespeare isn't on the primary-school curriculum. And your father was a primary-school teacher. So what was he doing with the school versions of those plays?"

"You're working on conjecture now," O'Neill said sourly. Guard O'Donnell was standing between him and the door, arms folded.

"I agree, sir," Blade said. "Your father could have bought those plays anywhere, but I didn't think he did. But now we come to the matter of the photographs. You and I agreed that it was highly unusual that there was only one picture of your father in existence. And a black-and-white one at that. So we'd no way of knowing that your father had eyes that didn't match. If we *had* known then we might have taken the inquiry off in a completely different direction. And you couldn't risk that. So you got rid of all the pictures of your father, leaving us only the one. Which you yourself took. Did you print it as well?"

O'Neill nodded.

"I was sure you did. Because you let slip that you dabbled in photography. But even in black and white I might have noticed that the eyes didn't match, so during the printing you made sure they did. Am I right, sir?"

"Aye."

"You certainly had me fooled. Full marks. I was puzzled, you know, why nobody in Carlingford mentioned Martin O'Neill's unmatched eyes. I suppose it was just one of those things. Everybody who knew him probably took it for granted that we'd have known as well. But somebody actually *did* tell us: his best friend, old Liam Donegan. 'Them quare eyes of his' was how he put it, only I didn't make the connection at the time."

O'Neill sat down on the settee and rubbed the stubble on his cheeks.

"Are you finished?" he asked.

"Not quite, sir. There's still a few blanks I want filled in. I have my theories all right; I just want to hear it from you. How did you manage to find the Godenrath family?"

A direct hit amidships. Jim O'Neill looked startled. He reached for another cigarette. His hands trembled slightly.

"Take your time," Blade said. "We have all night if needs be."

"I placed an ad in some German papers."

"The ones you mentioned that day? Too much detail again, sir. Most people in this country would never have heard of those newspapers but you seemed to know more about them than a casual visitor to—where was it? Heidelberg—would. What did the ad say?"

"That I was a history professor, looking for survivors of the concentration camps in Croatia."

"I see. But why Germany? Why not run the ad in Croatia itself?"

"I did. In fact I placed ads in most European papers. I've a file *this* big in Kilkeel. All letters from former camp inmates. It's harrowing stuff. God almighty, what that man was responsible for!"

"And you knew all along, sir."

"Of course I did, superintendent. You said yourself that nobody makes a clean break with his past. Dad kept diaries, wrote to old friends in Croatia and elsewhere. The fucker was actually *proud* of what he'd done. Mam and me weren't supposed to know—but there are things you can't keep secret from a kid with an inquiring mind."

Blade was thinking back to the conversation he'd had with Liam Donegan, and of Martin O'Neill's mysterious visitor. Old friends in Croatia and elsewhere. Another "Irishman" who was not what he appeared to be? *Let the younger men carry on the struggle now.*

"So Markus Godenrath told you his story," Blade said.

"In graphic detail. It was the eyes that did it, that led me to put two and two together. All the dates corresponded. Dad's sudden appearance as a Galwayman in nineteen forty-eight; the missing past."

"So you checked up as well, sir? You said you'd been to Knocklone."

"Knocklone and the Franciscan abbey in Galway. I spoke to Brother Louis, you know."

"Luji. The friar from Sarajevo."

"Yes. A truly holy man, superintendent. He remembered me when I was a wain, the time he'd visited Dad. I simply couldn't reconcile the saintliness of that man with the stories I had on file, the stories of the survivors. How in God's name can men of the cloth behave that way? It defies belief."

"Perhaps", Blade said quietly, "belief played a big part in it. They believed they were saving the world from evil. From Communism."

"Aye."

"Then you went to Heidelberg last year. To see Markus Godenrath. It had nothing to do with your school."

"To Mannheim, actually—not that it matters. Last summer."

"Hmm. And that's where you devised the plan. You, Godenrath and his son Georg."

O'Neill nodded. "Georg was brilliant. The 'military operation' was his idea you know. And Ushi insisted on coming along as well. Did you know she's half Serbian too?"

"No, I didn't." Blade was loath to inform O'Neill that *kleine Ushi* now lay dead in a morgue in Drogheda.

"But Markus Godenrath had to be sure we had the right man; he didn't want any mistakes, innocent blood on his hands. We hit on the idea of him going to Carlingford with his wife, as tourists. I suppose you thought it was coincidence that they met there."

"No, sir, I didn't." *I don't believe in coincidence any more than you do, Sweetman.*

So Godenrath had been protecting Jim O'Neill. The father-slayer.

"Who pulled the trigger, Mr O'Neill?"

"I think you know that, superintendent."

"Yes, I believe I do. We found hair fibres on the shell suit. The DNA didn't match your father's, but it was extremely close. Like a father's and son's would be. I just wanted to hear it from you."

O'Neill rubbed his cheeks again and shut his eyes.

"The fucker killed my mother. Did you know *that?* Oh, she drowned all right. But he drove her to it; he made her life a hell on earth. And he fucked up *my* life too. May he rot in hell!"

It was over. Or very nearly. Blade had one final question. He needed the answer to something that had perplexed him from the start. He had his vanity too.

"The shell suit, sir. How did it figure in your gambit? Why did you leave it behind in the dinghy for us to find?"

Jim O'Neill startled them. He threw back his head and laughed. He laughed so loud and long that tears came to his eyes.

"What a neat little world you inhabit, superintendent," he said at last. "The puzzles have to fit into place, don't they? Everything has to have a reason, everything has to make sense, the ends have to be tied up. But I've news for you: life isn't quite that simple. Why, you ask, did I leave the shell suit behind? Well, here's the answer: I honestly don't know why." He smiled. "And you can dwell on the question for the rest of your days, you can concoct all the theories you want—you're so bloody good at theories. But I doubt if you'll ever discover the answer. You wanted a neat ending? Sorry to have to disappoint you. There *are* no neat endings in real life. Martin O'Neill, I think, is proof of that."

They stared at each other hard and long, both unblinking. The hunter and the hunted. The strategists.

There was no more to say. Blade nodded to Gary O'Donnell. O'Neill looked up as he approached.

"We have to take you down to the station, sir," O'Donnell said.

He nodded.

"I suppose there's no point in cautioning you now," Blade said. "You've told us enough."

"No, there isn't." He rose from the settee, and looked down at his dressing-gown and slippers. "Give me a wee minute to change, will you?"

"Of course, sir."

The bedroom door shut. Blade heard a key turn. He was on his feet at once.

"Shite! He's locked it."

He pounded on the timber.

"Mr O'Neill, I'll have to ask you to unlock this door."

"With respect, superintendent: fuck off."

"Come on, sir, open it now."

Silence.

"Is there a way out through there?" Blade asked O'Donnell.

"Only through the window, sir."

"Right."

Blade took three paces back and charged. His shoulder connected with the door—and his arm connected with his bruised ribs. He yelped with pain.

"Merciful fuck!"

"Are you all right, Blade?" Sweetman asked.

"Never better." There were tears of pain in his eyes.

"Allow me, sir," Guard O'Donnell said. He drew back his booted foot and aimed for the lock. It shattered on impact and the door flew open—in the same split second that the gunshot sounded.

Blade was the first to enter; Sweetman found him staring grim-faced at the corpse on the bed, and the heavy-calibre handgun in the lifeless fingers.

"I believe," he said, "we've located the murder weapon."

Fifty

Assistant Commissioner Duffy was in shirt-sleeves again, both windows in his office open. The temperature was rising fast on this late-August morning. He gestured to two chairs in front of his desk. Macken and Sweetman remained standing. Duffy frowned.

"Something the matter, Blade?"

"You could say that, sir."

"Well, spit it out, man. It's too hot for games. And I've neither the time nor the inclination. This place is like a madhouse this morning."

"I'll be brief so," Blade said. "I understand we picked up Titch Reilly and clubmates."

"We did. We were saving him for you. I know you've a lot of questions you'd like to put to him. Well done, by the way, Blade. Two murder inquiries sorted the same week. That has to be some sort of record. My congratulations to you as well, Sweetman."

But Sweetman was looking at the floor. She sensed Blade's fury, knew the storm was about to break. Duffy felt it too.

"Let's leave Reilly to one side for now," Blade said. "He's small fry. I'm more interested in Frank Naughton."

"Hmm. The chip merchant. . . . "

"Yes, the fucking chip merchant!"

"I don't like your tone, Macken."

Macken placed both hands on the desk and glowered. Sweetman glanced up and saw a vein in his temple throbbing.

"Frankly, I don't give a monkey's toss *what* you like, sir," he snarled. "The way I see it, there's been some dirty work in the Naughton affair, and I want the answers to some straightforward questions."

"Get off your high horse, Blade," Duffy warned. "Whatever it is that's eating you, you won't get far with that attitude."

"All right," Blade said. "I'll come straight to the point, so. Why was I taken off the O'Neill murder just when I was starting to get results? Answer me that."

Duffy shook his head. "Is that what's bothering you? For God's sake, I thought I'd explained all that. There was nobody else at the time; you were the best man for the job."

"And it was no more than coincidence that you and Naughton were cronies? Is that it?"

"What are you talking about? I didn't know the man from Adam."

"*What!*"

"Sit down, Blade, sit down. You'd give anyone a stroke just looking at you." Blade hesitated. "Come on now. You're acting like a miffed prima donna. It isn't like you."

Macken sat; Sweetman too.

"That's better," Duffy said. "Right, I repeat: I didn't know Naughton. Okay, I heard his name mentioned on a few occasions but that's as far as it went. What makes you think we're 'cronies' as you put it?"

"Because he told me so himself." *Your reputation precedes you, you see. Plus the fact that your commissioner and I know each other very well. He agreed at once.*

"Did he now? Well, he's a lying bastard—as you proved."

"Are you saying you didn't commend me to Naughton?"

"Yes, Blade. I didn't. The commissioner did."

Shite.

The penny dropped.

Duffy was the assistant commissioner, his official rank. Yet to all at Harcourt Square he was more than an 'assistant'. In everyday parlance he was the commissioner, the Commish.

"Maybe you need that holiday more than I thought, Blade," Duffy said gently. "You look a bit off-colour."

Blade shook his thoughts free. He was himself again. He stood up.

"I'm okay, sir," he said. "Matter of fact, I'm fighting fit. Where did you say we're holding Reilly? I hope his cell is soundproof."

The garda commissioner looked up in annoyance as Macken, unannounced and unexpected, strode into his office at the garda depot in Phoenix Park. His eyes followed every movement as Blade drew a pistol from inside his jacket and dropped it on the desk. The barrel made an ugly dent in the polished mahogany.

"What's this, Blade?" the commissioner said. "The service revolver? I've a bottle of Scotch in the drinks cupboard there. What do you want me to do? Lock the door from the inside after you're gone?"

Blade was in no mood for levity, and this attempt at humour couldn't have been more inappropriate. Just hours before, the previous night, a man had locked a door from the inside and blown his brains out with a gun. Blade's friends thought that such sights were grist to his mill, that Blade had long ago inured himself to them. His friends were mistaken.

"No, sir," he said coldly. "It's *my* service revolver. As of now I'm resigning from the Force."

The commissioner frowned.

"And I don't have to call you 'sir' any more either. I just did it there from force of habit. No, commissioner, from now on I think I'll call you by a more appropriate name. 'Cunt'."

"I *beg* your pardon."

"A man died last night because of you. Maybe not directly, but if you hadn't tried to keep me off the investigation then I might have got to him before he had the chance to decorate his duvet with his own brains."

"I don't know what you're talking about, Macken."

But Blade knew he did: the commissioner's eyes spoke chapters, if not volumes.

"Don't you, cunt?" He smiled darkly. "See? I'm getting used to it already. Well, here's something else that's going to come out in the trial. You not only have Jim O'Neill's blood on your hands but the blood of a young German woman who died the night before last. That could have been averted as well."

"You're talking crap."

"Am I? And while we're about it, cunt, we can throw in Sweetman's abduction and torture for good measure—plus any number of obstruction-of-justice charges."

He leaned across the desk. The commissioner met his stare without blinking.

"Did I mention a trial, cunt? I believe I did. That's exactly what it's going to be: a civil trial in the Central Criminal Court. And that's the reason I've resigned. There'll be no garda inquiry you see, so there'll be no hiding behind special commissions and tribunals. No, this'll be an action taken by a civilian against the Guards, one in which you'll be named as an accessory to murder and fuck-knows-what-else."

The commissioner shook his head with vehemence.

"Blade, I understand your anger. But the truth is, I didn't know. You'll have to believe that. I didn't know."

"*Das habe ich nicht gewüßt. . . .* "

"What?"

Blade smiled. "That's what the Nazi foot soldiers said when they were put on trial—the ones who held open the doors of the gas chambers. *Das habe ich nicht gewüßt.* I didn't know. And it's very apt, in the circumstances, after what I heard yesterday."

He paused then, glancing around the office at the commissioner's collection of photographs. The commissioner with four Irish Presidents, and with visiting foreign heads of state. The commissioner inspecting his "troops". The commissioner in an old-fashioned garda uniform sometime in the fifties.

"By the way," Blade said, "what did *you* do in the war, Daddy? Did your kids ever ask you that? No, you're too young. You wouldn't have been a Guard when Artuković and Princip came to Ireland in forty-seven. But *somebody* on the Force helped them, I'm nearly certain of that—and I've a sneaking suspicion you know who that somebody was."

The commissioner leaned back in his chair.

"Frank Naughton is a friend," he said. "*Was*, I should say. I acted in good faith when he asked me to put my best man on the investigation. And you still are the best we have, so you can stick that gun back under your armpit. I acted in good faith, Blade, and you'd have done the same, given that those chips are worth what they are. I'd no reason to suspect that the robbery was anything other than what it appeared to be."

"So Naughton was behind the whole thing? That business with Sweetman as well."

"It's beginning to look that way, yes. We'll know more when all the statements are taken: Guard Strong's and the others'."

Blade was thoughtful.

"What about the Catholic Church?"

"What about it?"

"They're involved as well."

"You have proof of that?"

"Er, no sir."

The commissioner paused and fixed Macken with a shrewd look.

"Are you a Catholic yourself, Blade?"

"No, sir."

"I didn't think so. Well, we Catholics, as I'm sure you know, place great stock in confession. Non-Catholics have a tendency to scoff at it, to look on it as a kind of cop-out. But it's not; it's a very valuable instrument."

"I don't know why you're telling me this, sir."

"Bear with me. Confession is good for the soul, particularly if you're a clergyman. In fact, it's invaluable if you're a priest or a bishop. You won't receive forgiveness through confession unless you're truly repentant—and you can't receive the Eucharist unless you're in what we call the state of grace."

"And this 'state of grace' can only be achieved through confession, is that it?"

"That's it. So what I'm saying, Blade, is this: If members of the Church were involved in this in any way, then in order to continue being clergymen they'll have to go to a confessor and say: 'Bless me, Father, for I have sinned.' And they really *will* be sorry; they have to be. Do you see the point I'm making?"

"I believe I do, sir."

"But I know what you're thinking. You're thinking that they're getting off scot-free. And they are, for the moment. But that's only because you'd be hard put to find evidence against them. Frank Naughton will go to his grave denying their involvement, and he's our only link to them. But Blade, don't worry. They'll have to answer to a higher power, and they know it. Which is why I very much doubt that they'll ever dare involve themselves in such things again."

Blade considered this. Before today his meetings with the commissioner had been brief and superficial: an underling reporting to his superior. Now he was beginning to see the man in a new light.

"I'm truly sorry I called you a cunt, sir," he said. "I truly am. I was completely out of order."

"Ah, I've been called worse, Blade." He chuckled. "Well, perhaps not, come to think of it. But I'll forgive you this time. Here, have a cigar. You look to me like a man who could do with one right now."

He passed a humidor across the desk. Blade hesitated—but not for long.

"Don't mind if I do, sir," he said, reaching for a long, green-leafed Havana. "You can't beat a decent smoke. It seems like years, so it does."

The commissioner's office faced west. As Macken drew leisurely on the fine cigar, a ray of light from the window to the man's right fell upon his silver-grey hair. The sunlight also illuminated a photograph on the wall. It showed the commissioner in the company of the Catholic Primate of All Ireland. And an elderly bishop whose eyebrows were white and thick. Directly beneath the photograph was an object whose twin Blade had seen some days before, in another office.

It was a small, silver crucifix.

In County Galway, a farmer named Sweetman picked up his phone on the third ring.

"Yes?"

"It's John, Matt. From the bank. Are you sitting down?"

"What the hell do *you* want?"

"You know that loan you have with us?"

"Of course I know that feckin' loan!"

"Don't have a heart attack now, Matt. Thing is, you don't have it any more."

"Eh?"

"You're gone. Wiped from our files, as if you never existed. They had a computer crash in head office, you see. We haven't a single record of you taking out a loan with us. Would you credit it?"

Matt Sweetman decided it was better to sit down after all.

"I hope," he said, "this isn't another of your gombeen tricks, John. What about that contract we signed five years ago? The one in your filing cabinet."

"Contract? What contract? What filing cabinet?"

A slow smile of understanding spread across Farmer Sweetman's face.

"Jayziz, you're all right, Doherty."

"You're not so bad yourself, Sweetman. And doesn't the Lord move in mysterious ways his wonders to perform?"

"He does indeed. Alone and unaided."

Author's Historical Note

In 1991 Antony Farrell of The Lilliput Press, Dublin, introduced me to the work of the man I consider to be Ireland's greatest ever essayist: Hubert Butler (1900-1991).

I avidly read a fine collection of his work, *Escape from the Anthill*, paying particular attention to an essay entitled "The Artukovitch File".

The remarkable events it recounts resonated very much with me, I having grown up close to where the fleeing mass murderer sought (and found) sanctuary in 1948, a year before my birth.

I am grateful to the late Mr Butler for having shed light on a shameful episode in recent Irish history, and it is my hope that *Eyeless in Cooley* may lead to a re-examination of those dark times.

David M. Kiely, born in Dublin in 1949, has published 14 books, both fiction and non-fiction.

He left Ireland in 1974 and travelled extensively for two decades. He lives in Newry, County Down, with his wife, the bestselling author Christina McKenna. Her novels include *The Misremembered Man* and *The Godforsaken Daughter,* the latter published in 2015.

He is indebted to Vere Lenox Conyngham, owner of Anaverna House, Ravensdale, where he taught creative writing. This lovely house inspired that of Jack Macken.

www.ingramcontent.com/pod-product-compliance
Lightning Source LLC
Chambersburg PA
CBHW060934120726

47910CB00002B/327